FROZEN WITH HORROR

On one corner of a butcher's table, a big cellophane bag lay unraveled, unzipped, and waiting for her. She felt weightless as he lifted her onto the table and into the clear polyethylene bag.

When he finished sealing her in, he locked the hasp at the top.

Overhead was a thick cable with a pulley on a universal joint. Sitting her upright, he connected bag and hook. Then he pressed a lever and she was lifted and moved off. When it came to an abrupt stop, the whine of the mechanism suddenly silent, she was hanging between an enormous slab of bacon on one side and a beef carcass on the other.

Inside the bag, her terror jolted her into keen awareness of her situation. She had no doubt any longer: the nightmare was real.

But her scream could not be heard beyond the freezer . . .

PINNACLE'S HORROR SHOW

BLOOD BEAST (17-096, $3.95)
by Don D'Ammassa

No one knew anymore where the gargoyle had come from. It was just an ugly stone creature high up on the walls of the old Sheffield Library. Little Jimmy Nicholson liked to go and stare at the gargoyle. It seemed to look straight at him, as if it knew his most secret desires. And he knew that it would give him everything he'd ever wanted. But first he had to do its bidding, no matter how evil.

LIFEBLOOD (17-110, $3.95)
by Lee Duigon

Millboro, New Jersey was just the kind of place Dr. Winslow Emerson had in mind. A small township of Yuppie couples who spent little time at home. Children shuttled between an overburdened school system and every kind of after-school activity. A town ripe for the kind of evil Dr. Emerson specialized in. For Emerson was no ordinary doctor, and no ordinary mortal. He was a creature of ancient legend of mankind's darkest nightmare. And for the citizens of Millboro, he had arrived where they least expected it: in their own backyards.

DARK ADVENT (17-088, $3.95)
by Brian Hodge

A plague of unknown origin swept through modern civilization almost overnight, destroying good and evil alike. Leaving only a handful of survivors to make their way through an empty landscape, and face the unknown horrors that lay hidden in a savage new world. In a deserted midwestern department store, a few people banded together for survival. Beyond their temporary haven, an evil was stirring. Soon all that would stand between the world and a reign of insanity was this unlikely fortress of humanity, armed with what could be found on a department store shelf and what courage they could muster to battle a monstrous, merciless scourge.

Available wherever paperbacks are sold, or order direct from the Publisher. Send cover price plus 50¢ per copy for mailing and handling to Pinnacle Books, Dept.17-261 475 Park Avenue South, New York, N.Y. 10016. Residents of New York, New Jersey and Pennsylvania must include sales tax. DO NOT SEND CASH.

DYING BREATH

Robert W. Walker

PINNACLE BOOKS
WINDSOR PUBLISHING CORP.

PINNACLE BOOKS

are published by

Windsor Publishing Corp.
475 Park Avenue South
New York, NY 10016

First printing: September 1989

Printed in the United States of America

Till my dying breath, and beyond,
I'll love my sister,
Sybil,
to whom this book is dedicated.

Prologue

Grinning insanely, greedily, he was, and had been, ravenous for reason to smile this way; he was not given to outbursts of joy. Instead, he was a typically grim killer who felt a sudden high of giddiness just staring at his creation, born of a nice night's work. He liked what he saw, and what he smelled. Staring back at him through the clear vinyl body-length bag, were two white pupils, the eyes having rolled back in their sockets, the anguished cry left on the lips, and the rubber-chicken posture. The backbone had gone slack, as if the universal joint's hook were jabbed into it instead of the sack tie. The head had tilted like that of a broken doll. Only her hair—although damp and plastered to the head—looked alive in there. But then, hair and nails grew even in the grave—the last to know.

He'd opened the big sack several times before, prolonging the death like a kind of slow, langorous lovemaking. He'd inhale much of the victim's carbon dioxide as it escaped the bag, getting high on it, hallucinating and thereby getting in touch with his inner self and his own demons, the demons that motivated him. He opened the bag again to take in great whiffs of death, perspiration, CO_2, and musk: intermingling odors that soaked in a marinade of fear. You tie someone, they begin to sweat and sweat and a kind of animal odor overcomes them. You cut off their oxygen in degrees, deprive their senses, you get an even more pungent odor than mere musk.

Life reduced down to so little, really, a mix of just the right balance of chemicals. Always most fascinating to see *it* expire, and to mark down the all important details in his ledger. One day his extensive notes would be revered and debated, questioned and studied, admired and accepted. For he was a scientist foremost, involved in scientific methodology and research, the study of the respiratory functions in particular being of great importance. No great mind in all the modern world, or in the history of the world, had ever explained how a man could, for instance, blow hot air or cold air at will. And no one had sufficiently explained the connection between breath and the life of the soul.

There were so many unanswered questions. Questions other great minds had called unanswerable. Unsolvable, hell! He was nearing an answer any day now . . . any day. Until that time, the work came first. Someone had to solve the unsolvable. Time was running out for mankind. Time was evaporating along with the protective layers of ozone above the immediate heavens. He meant to save man from himself, or die trying to salvage at least one man's soul—his own, Solomon's soul. He'd seen the reports on the nightly news; he had seen the statistics with his own eyes. It was an overwhelming task, and a dirty job, but somebody had to do it. And you couldn't wait for City Hall or the Red Cross or NASA or ocean explorers. You do and you're as bad as the rest. You had to damned well do it yourself, if you wanted it done right, if you wanted it done at all.

He had to do it.

If he didn't do it, who would?

He was doing the city, the people, and even his victims a great favor; everyone benefited from his scavenging the streets . . . in the long run. And those who nobly gave of themselves to the experiments, they might be remembered in time, too, for he kept a ledger of names. Names that were as shining and as important as the names on any war memorial or list of astronauts dead in the line of duty; for these warriors and astronauts were the first to explore in Solomon's domain. The end result to the body might be asphyxiation, but their essence inhaled by him went on astral journey to meet with and be with Solomon, the keeper of their killer's soul. There was poetry and art and science in all of it.

There were other reasons, even more pressing and immediate; and, when he was honest with himself, even more rewarding. He stole their breath away. He inhaled the CO_2-filled bag and from it gathered in his mystic power and spoke directly to his own soul, a soul with a name, a king's name: Solomon. A soul meant for great things, great discoveries, wonders the world had presently no notion of.

After the breath of life—or soul—left the body, he would reverently untie the top knot, or in some cases

9

the zipper, to inhale with all his might for that indescribable, unimaginable CO_2 high. It almost always put him in touch with his higher self, which was in touch with a higher being, a being that directed his movements. A being without name or face, horns or scepter, but a force so powerful he gave himself over to it each time. He'd read about the force in books on ancient Eastern religious sects. He had studied methods of reaching the force, and he had discovered that the quick route to Solomon was exactly this way: deny another human breath and inhalation, take the resultant "holy air" of the dead, and steal it.

He hefted the industrial strength, heavy-duty, see-through bag off its universal pulley and hook. The body inside was small and curled and shriveled, looking like a child in the womb, quite at peace with its surroundings now. The scrap heap of bone and flesh must be discarded now. He took firm hold of the body, holding it gently, the stiff, cold plastic rustling like leather in the silent walk-in cooler. He'd been so high on his work that he had paid no attention to the fact that his own skin had turned blue. Out the door and he lay his transformed, unhappy burden on the linoleum floor. Taking a jacket to cover the face inside the bag, a wellspring of bitterness erupted deep within. He hated this part, the cleanup and cover-up, so many mechanical motions he must go through robotlike, so many decisions that led to the same problem—a place to dump the remains. With the first several, he'd taken great pains, driving great distances, after having spent days scouting locations like a filmmaker's flunky. He'd located silent and lonely knolls, lakes, and rivers. When he had lived in

Blue River, Oregon, this was a simple matter. When he'd lived in Los Angeles, there was the desert. In Chicago, you had to drive literally fifty miles in any given direction to find the smallest space. It had gotten so bad, he had taken to using city dumpsters, seldom-visited viaducts, train passes, sewers, and culverts, and one had gone into Lake Michigan.

Hefting the bag out to his van, he could see the beads of perspiration on the woman's boyish face. She had been a homeless tramp and hooker; now she was a true free spirit. At least free to be with and please Solomon, to feed his spirit many times over, perhaps through eternity. The eyes were two dilated, milk-white orbs, the mouth slack, the panting tongue drooped, bone-dry, over her lips and jaw, distended, already bloating with gases that seeped into cell walls.

He stood staring at the silent figure. He preferred seeing it alive, seeing it struggle. Its suffering gave him peace and a strange sense of power like nothing he'd ever felt before. A power indescribable, a godlike power. He enjoyed control and power over other living things, but until now he had no idea who, or what, had put that odd lust into his mind.

With Solomon's spiritual help, he located a viable dumping ground for what he considered trash. It was forty minutes and eighteen miles from where he had stolen the spirit of his victim. It was a dumpster caravan behind a series of closed department stores and businesses. He drove into the alley, casing the area for cops or anyone else standing about. He saw no one. His work was nearly done for tonight. He wished to keep the bag, as they were damned expensive and difficult to get, especially the zipper bags. He now hefted the body from the rear of the van and tore at the zipper, opening the top of the bag. He then hefted her, bag and all, over the lip of the dumpster and watched the weight of the body slide down and away with a bit of urging on. It was like a burial at sea. Except that this sea was made up of plasterboard, two-by-four discards, broken panes, bottles, and debris. He looked down from the top as he rumpled the large vinyl bag into a ball. Her body lay akimbo, like a mannequin in disassembled parts amid the rubbish. The jostling had rolled her eyes back and her pupils stared up at him, the only witnesses to his secret.

His part in the work, he told himself again—while all important—should remain anonymous.

He carried the large and cumbersome bag back to the van. His arms ached painfully from deep within; his legs, too. Stress, he supposed. It was as if something vile was this minute moving fluidly through his bloodstream to every artery, sending out a message of poison and weakness to every muscle. It was understandable, seeing as how it was almost dawn, and in a few hours he'd have to open the shop and spend hours upon hours of unimportant, useless, mindless work, and put off Solomon's work.

Sweat trickled down from his brow, under his arms, and along his thighs from the crotch. It was tough work for a tough man, removing unwanted and useless people in the name of science and spiritual research, in Solomon's name.

He came down from the empty crate he'd placed

alongside the dumpster, so he could look in over the top for a final glance at the job he had done. His whole life had been preparation for this. The important experiments. Now he was in earnest; now he had a purpose that anyone could understand, that even *he* could understand, finally. Finally, he had gotten the message.

Where am I, he wondered when he came out of a semiconscious state, glancing about. He saw the body again. A car whizzed past at the end of the alley, followed by another and another and a police patrol car. He oriented himself, thought about which way he'd come, where he'd entered, and how best to leave unnoticed. Go home for what remained of the night.

He got down from the dumpster and started away, taking in a great whiff of the warm, smelly air of the black alley. A series of stores lined the alley, each with a dumpster or two of its own. He'd chosen poorly, he realized, seeing that next door to the hardware store was a liquor store. Cops routinely cruised liquor stores, front and back. He hurried away, taking himself several doors down before cutting through a T-section of alleyway that went in an entirely different direction. He relocated his delivery truck and started away in it.

He drove out at a glaring neon sign proclaiming an all-night grocery store, and a man with an apron on and a cigarette in his mouth got a fleeting glimpse of him. He turned his face away, and silently cruised off.

He wondered, as he made his way toward home, if he had or had not lowered the lid of the dumpster. No matter, he reasoned. No one would disturb the dead.

The kid had appeared to be perhaps seventeen, eighteen tops. She had gone to a better world, a world where nothing could ever hurt her again, a place of no sensation, and a place where she didn't require oxygen.

In a few minutes he was well clear of the incident and climbing onto the Kennedy Expressway, blaring at someone who refused him easy entry. Then he snapped on his Mendelssohn tape, feeling the great man's music and a sublime euphoria overtake his brain like a rising flood of warmth and incredible power. Once more he had done it. Once more he had saved another soul from the debauchery of this hell called Earth. And he had tasted of the passing of that soul through his own nostrils and lungs. A sense of accomplishment filled him with pride. A sense of mission filled him with the desire to go on, to fulfill himself again, now that he understood what Solomon had been trying for years to tell him.

After all these years, he told himself in the cab as sound poured from his tape, "After all these years, my invisible Solomon begging me to see and understand, and finally, finally I do."

At last, he heard his inner soul tell him, *at last you are feeding me.*

One

"You want the watered-down version, or do you want it straight?" Grant asked Chief Inspector Kelso over the phone. It was a cheap, even crude joke under the circumstances, but Kelso always appreciated crudity in the face of death. Dean Grant was referring to the father suspected of the murders of a family of four. The uniform cops in Hammond, where it happened, had told every plumber's joke and sewer and rat hole story they'd ever heard in painful effort to show themselves strong enough to deal with this ugliest of jokes perpetrated on three girls and a woman. Dean had spent much of the day wading through water in an otherwise spotless and familiar suburban basement.

Dr. Dean Grant, Chief Medical Examiner for the City of Chicago, had only come in on the case at the request of the Hammond authorities, including the coroner here. Hammond was a noisy, dirty, bustling, medium-sized city undergoing a lot of development and growth. Situated at Chicago's toenail, this meant more than a lot of asphalt dust, detours, and irritation. It also meant there was a burgeoning transient population. Fly-by-night businesses and quite a few quacks and charlatans worked the Hammond streets and byways, along with the prostitutes and drug dealers. But this was not a street crime: this was the kind of Middle-America crime that seemed doubly tragic against the background of suburbia, where tract houses built to specs should have been dwellings for normal, even happy families.

Dean's official jurisdiction ended some six miles away, but he had been called in at the express request of Hammond's Dr. Samuel Carol, despite Dean's fee. Dr. Carol was a fine forensics man himself, and had once in fact been Dean's mentor at New York University. He was pushing seventy and had "retired" from the M.E.'s office in Detroit a few years before. Dean respected the old man immeasurably.

Dean Grant was up to his hip boots in putrid water and blood. What had begun as a plumbing problem in the house next door, had, for an entire block, become a back up of horrendous proportion. A man named McGuri had telephoned for a plumber a month before, as he was experiencing a sluggishness in his toilet's draining. Before the plumber had gotten round to McGuri's, other plumbers were called by other neighbors. Some complaining of terrible odors emanating from their pipes. Then one of the handymen of the neighborhood, going to work on McGuri's pipes, found some small bones, scraps of cloth, and pieces of flesh. He'd first taken this for sewer slush and declared that somehow the sewage system was backing up into the pipes. When McGuri examined the bones plucked from his pipes, his heart shuddered. He'd been in combat. He knew what human finger bones looked like. There was no mistaking the bones clogging his pipes.

The authorities were called in. The builders and developers of the subdivision were called in. Maps of underwater pipes and connections were examined. All of the houses in a given row shared the same drainage system. It became clear to Hammond authorities that one of the houses on the block very likely held the key to the ghastly mystery. Human finger bones causing toilet problems in McGuri's house were most likely the tip of the iceberg.

And they were.

The mystery had quickly escalated into a plumber's worst nightmare. Clogging the drains, toilets and sewers of this small subdivision called Sleepy Hollow, were the remains of at least three people. Or at least parts of three separate people. Putting any indentity to them would be a true forensic puzzle. There remained the fear that Emil Schletter, the owner of the house—a mild-mannered, soft-spoken middle-aged man with thinning hair and horn-rimmed glasses—had murdered his entire family, three girls and his wife, diced them into chunks, and ran them through the disposal. Which, by the way, was backed up and broken down, the motor burned out. Schletter himself had disappeared. An APB of twenty-four hours had not located him.

Of course, he, too, might well be somewhere in the sewer lines, in which case an all points bulletin had been futile from the beginning. No one, at least not the coroners, had ruled out the possibility that Schletter, heavily into some dastardly business, had been the first to go down the drain, followed by his family when the killer had finished with them. But the interior of the house did not look like the scene of a massacre. The killer/butcher was practiced at washing away bodily fluids and blood. And Schletter was an undertaker.

Other than what bubbled about in the backed up lines throughout the house, the place was immaculate and ornately decorated, as neat as a pin. Everything meticulously and scrupulously in place. The hatchet work had been done in the basement in one location, near the utility sink, washer and dryer, and laundry slide. It'd been determined that heavy objects—bodies—had come careening down this laundry shute. There were dents and a recently broken hinge. But again, no bloodstains, which meant the victims had not been bludgeoned or stabbed. Dean imagined they'd either been drugged or suffocated, placed in the shute one at a time, and mutilated one at a time. The work of a tidy madman.

He told Kelso all this, until Kelso groaned. "I am in kind of a rush, Dino," he said into the phone, back at Police Precinct One, downtown Chicago. "You're right, just give me the bare bones report."

Dean tore off the gloves he'd been wearing, allowing his skin to breathe. "Evidence unfolding as slowly as a dripping faucet—"

"Enough. Jeeze, Dean, you're the only man I know who can upset my stomach long distance."

Dean explained to Kelso the condition of Schletter's basement on his arrival. The floor and washtubs

18

where the dismemberments had occurred had been scrubbed with soap and brush; blood remained in the fibers of the brush.

"Doesn't sound like a hit man, or random violence typical of a jealous neighbor, or an outraged business partner."

Dean agreed. If some intruder had gotten into the house, even a hired assassin, there'd be blood everywhere. Killers for hire weren't too subtle about their jobs. Even less subtle were people who suddenly burst out in a murderous rage.

"Not a lot of blood for sampling. There was none. And no way to reconstruct the crime in the Schletter house from marks on walls, floors, or carpeting."

"The whole story's in lead pipe and water," Kelso said, shaking his head.

"Teflon."

"What?"

"They use plastic pipes now."

"Oh, yeah, right."

"Rather thin diameter at one and a quarter inch, cost savings to the builder. If it were a more expensive house, with full two-inch pipes, maybe he'd have gotten away with the brutal murders."

"We got the picture Hammond faxed over. Every cop in the city's on the look out for Schletter. Every train, plane and—"

"Anyway, we're slowly amassing enough at this end to begin to make some general IDs. Positive IDs will have to wait for dental forensics."

"Any truth to the stories we're hearing on police band?"

"More than on NBC."

19

"Really?"

"Bank on it. So far we *know* two females are in there, and we suspect the other two are as well. Real hard to put it together with so little, but it's a given that no male bones have as yet turned up. First parts found are most certainly from a girl in her preteens, and we've found the knuckle bone of an adult female, along with a piece from her femur. Found these at a neighbor's house, causing back up at that location."

"I thought that was impossible when I heard it."

"Ever hear of the guy who's pet python got loose and crawled down his toilet, and promptly slithered up his neighbor's toilet?"

"No, can't say that I have."

Dean was talking on a porta-phone, standing in the basement of the death house, water covering his feet. He stared across a large table that was now strewn with pieces of bone and jelly matter that looked like frozen fish filets that had defrosted badly. Dean had a friend who was an archeologist at the University of Chicago. He'd visited him in his dingy little lab, and on his work tables were the takings from a dig, most items rusted, molded over, bent and ugly and misshapen, mere pieces of metal and strips of leather. It looked like a collection of junkyard pickings, stuff that ought to have remained in the tailings at the site of the dig. But each minute glass fragment, boot heel, or razor strap told a story.

Dean's table held scraps of cloth, flesh, and hair, with bones as shattered and minced as ground glass. Each formed a part of the whole grisly, grotesque puzzle, the jagged edges of which fit into one another only fitfully, or not at all to the untrained eye. It was

20

indeed a macabre archeology, this business of medico-legal examination, his microscopic search of the dead. A coroner worked for the "Crown" in times past, during dire emergency and suspicious death; his sole purpose was to determine if the death were suspicious enough to seize a suspect, and to be damned sure no one profited by cheating the king out of monies and land that would then revert to the state. Today, the men who performed such functions were doctors instead of butchers or barbers or undertakers. Today, they had to have a superlative education, and they must not, Dean felt strongly, answer to any one man, but rather to society as a whole. A bit more of polish and purpose, he believed. He no longer was going about seizing land or gold the murderer had pocketed; his job was no longer for the Crown but for the people, just as a district attorney's was.

"We're going to need another table set up down here," Dean shouted to one of the uniformed policemen who were going in and out, helping with whatever they were called on to do.

Just then a man in a Roto-Rooter jumpsuit came stumbling in, his arms up in the air.

"What the hell's going on here? What's happening here?" he was shouting.

"Hey, I got to go, Kelso. Don't expect me for a few days."

"But we can't spare—"

He hung up on Kelso and went to the dumbstruck Roto-Rooter man. "Somebody call you?"

"Why'daya think I'm here, for *lunch?* Jesus, Mary and God, what is that stuff? Smells to high heaven, and I'm used to stink, but this ain't human."

"Afraid it is human. Who telephoned for you?"

"Schletter."

The room fell silent and all eyes were riveted on the heavy-set Roto-Rooter man.

The cops surrounded the man, immediately drilling him with questions, pinning him in a corner of the room, standing in the little lake of the basement. Overhead, to the left of his ear, was an embroidered and framed: Bless this House, Oh, Lord We Pray.

"Where did he call you from, did he say where?"

"No! I mean, yes . . . he was here."

"Here?"

"So, shoot me. I assumed he was."

"You're sure he didn't say where he was calling from?"

"Back off, back off! Jesus Christ," he threw up his hands. "Schletter's on contract with us. Has been for years. Guy was just a schmoe, he didn't look like he could hurt a fly."

"Never mind what he looked like!" shouted the cop.

"I didn't talk to him. He called and left word his pipes needed a thorough going over with the heavy-duty stuff. I swear—"

"When, dammit? How long ago?"

"Two weeks. We don't guarantee service overnight you know."

The police, circling the man and intimidating him completely, asked if calls were fielded by any individual, if calls were accepted by machine, if Schletter might have been taped?

"Yeah, yeah, yeah," the Roto-Rooter man replied, nodding.

They hustled the man out, telling him they wanted him to take them directly to his offices. This done, Dean, Dr. Carol, and the Hammond city sewer guys went back to the work they'd been so glad to get a respite from, even if it was for only a few minutes.

Dean wasn't a heavy drinker, but he felt he could certainly use a shot glass of whiskey at the moment. He heard and partially saw Lieutenant Pleasance on the stairs. He'd remained behind to oversee the investigation from here. Pleasance had been the man who had opened this ungodly can of worms, having gotten the warrant to rip away Schletter's lock and enter the premises. Terry Pleasance was that sort of rumpled cop who cared nothing for fashion, or even that a shoelace might be untied. He was overweight, but carried it well. His red nose and red-splotched cheeks marked him as a drinker, the color rivaling that of his hair. Dean's own red hair was thin and brown by comparison to the fire crop that Pleasance sported.

"Tell me how you found the place when you first entered, about the first few hours here," Dean asked him.

"What for, Doc? You got all you need right in front of you on that filthy table."

"Call me thorough. Humor me."

Pleasance, a third-grade lieutenant detective, was bored. He'd told the story so many times already, and he was sick to death of this basement. "Let's go up."

They did so, and Pleasance dug into the refriger-

23

ator for a beer, "Miller time. You want one?"

Dean took it for the purpose of getting Pleasance to accept him as a partner in all this hellish mess.

Pleasance made a show of opening his beer and downing it halfway before coming up for air. "I never stepped into anything like this before . . . made me lose my lunch. We found both the toilets overflowing, water and . . . and stuff floating everywhere. The basement was full of water. I had Artie Lobach climb into the crawl space to take off the main house trap, free it up, you know."

"No water come out," said Artie Lobach, the head of the city inspector group the cops had called in. He stood just in the doorway, eyeing the beer. Pleasance pointed to the fridge and told him there was more. He joined them at the kitchen table, swinging about in the cushioned swivel. "Nice chairs, huh? Well, anyway, I reached in deeper and snapped off the inside cap. Jesus that damned thing was clogged tighter'n a thirteen-year-old . . . oh, sorry . . ."

One of the dead girls was thirteen.

"Anyway, I flash the light up in there and I swear I started tearing stuff away with my nails, except I decided, even with the gloves on, I really didn't want to touch this stuff. It wasn't ordinary hair and grease and food, more like some live animal had gotten stuck down there. Completely blocking the water, and what remained in the disposal."

"When Artie come out of there, he pulled a bunch of the sludge with him. Felt real sinister to me right away."

"Yeah," agreed Artie, a jocular, heavy man with bushy eyebrows and a large face, made the larger by a sweeping mustache that was showing gray amid the black. "You said right away it wasn't right."

Pleasance continued. "I found some tin foil, wrapped the stuff, and took it down to Dr. Carol." Carol was downstairs yet, an old man but a bull for the work. "He's the closest thing Hammond's got to an M.E., he's our coroner, and does good work. He got right over here after he telephoned you."

"Dr. Carol was a professor of mine some years back," Dean told them. "I agree, a fine man and a good coroner."

"After that Artie and his guys started work on opening the other sewer lines," said Pleasance.

"We got more identifiable pieces of flesh and bone," said Artie with relish, enamored of the horror house by now. "We got all that stuff you've been putting on the table."

Dean had seen pieces of cloth and female undergarments amid the flesh and bone, including a brassiere and a girdle. He knew the search of the drainage system, here and in neighboring houses, could go on well into the following day and night.

Dean thanked the men for their frankness and returned to Dr. Carol. Carol employed a simple mental trick: he did not consider the dead remains to be people. He thus had a kind of shield around him that to the laymen present made him seem made of iron, or rather, without a heart. He also had a booming voice, which didn't help matters.

"See what we have here, Dean?" He held up parts of a lower and upper jaw with a few teeth still embedded in the jawbone. "It's a set from a teen. Here, you can see the molar. The dental records will

25

confirm it, but it will take weeks, perhaps months to confirm all we suspect here."

"But you already know what will be confirmed, Doctor, don't you?"

"Not altogether, Doctor, but perhaps you do, now that you're so famous? Catching that pyromaniac in the manner that you did and—"

"Ken Kelso did all the hard work on that one."

"And those scalpers down in Florida?"

"Blown way out of proportion, at least my part in—"

"And what about that caseload involving the floaters, so many people drowned by that horrid killer? I knew I must call you in the moment I learned of this matter."

"I appreciate that, Dr. Carol, really."

"Then, tell me, what kind of cold-blooded man is this Schletter?"

"I think he's a man who has gone stark, raving mad. What triggered it, we may never know, unless he tells us."

Carol dropped his gaze and nodded. He lifted in his gloved hands a miniature deformed foot that looked like a tadpole or an opposum fetus, just a thumbnail of flesh with the minutest toe impressions. Dean gasped and felt himself quake.

"She was pregnant?"

"About five months along. But who was pregnant, Dean? Mother or daughter?"

Two

The cops typically believed it common sense to call it murder when they discovered a body trashed or dumped, and this one was dumped in a trash can. Murder had appeared obvious from the outset. Few people died of natural causes in such a place, perhaps a derelict or street person of some age; sometimes a kid who'd overdosed on heroin or crack. But no clean and sober person, even dying of disease, normally sought out such a place to die. So far as the cops saw it, killers who particularly hated their victims dumped them ungraciously in such heaps, sometimes at a landfill, a junkyard, auto graveyard, or in a sewer. In fact, lately a number of such unhappy places had given up bodies.

What troubled Sybil Shanley, M.E. with the Chicago Office of the Coroner, was the fact that some of these unfortunates, despite sex, age, and circumstance, had died from asphyxiation. Not violent strangulation, or a sudden loss of oxygen, but slow and methodical asphyxiation with hardly a bruise on

27

them. What bruises she had been able to determine had come as a result of jostling and carrying and pitching *after death*. In some cases she'd even seen the so-called undertaker's fracture, which caused a black bruise at the back of the neck where the head had been allowed to snap off the support of the backbone. It occurred whenever a body was mishandled.

A trained eye told her it was so, but a trained eye— even hers—wouldn't impress Inspector Kenneth Kelso, or even Dean much, not without methodical documentation, careful recording of what she found in the sections she cut and studied and labeled.

Murder looked the best bet, and yet, it was a strange murder indeed. No broken neck or bones, no skull injuries, not a trace of blood except in the nasal passages and all about the retinas and covering areas of the epidermal layer of skin, where blood vessels had burst. Her autopsy of this latest victim left no doubt in her mind—and despite what important sojourn Dean felt he was on in Hammond, and despite the feelings of some old teacher of his out that way—he had a rising epidemic on his hands here. People were dying of asphyxiation, relatively healthy people with no internal or external cause of death beyond their somehow being cut off from life-giving air.

She'd tried to tell Dean once before, but it was as if he remained too drained by the recent pyromaniac case to deal with even the thought of yet another lethal idiot stalking human prey on the streets of Chicago. It looked as if she herself must make a case for the possibility, and if it was so, to prove it in no uncertain terms. To her way of thinking, knowing

28

what she knew to be the truth about medical practice, there was no telling just how many such victims had gone unreported, a death certificate signed, and the John Doe, Jane Doe—or in some cases, Little Doe—was entered at cost to the city and forgotten. It shouldn't happen. Each was supposed to be reported to the M.E. if it were at all a "suspicious death," but doctors, among others, disregarded that law all the time. Legally, they had no right to sign such a death certificate. Any sudden, unexpected death of someone not under a doctor's care ought to be reported to Dean Grant's office.

One of these cases she just happened to question while going through the death certificates, all of which must be rubber-stamped by the coroner's office. It was a young man or boy, late teens, needle tracks on his arm, an assumed overdose victim, yet no drugs were found in his blood, and therefore the physician signing the death certificate made the cause of death "occlusive coronary artery disease."

She had gotten in touch with the doctor who signed the certificate, and he grudgingly gave her several weak-kneed reasons for heart blockage as the cause of death. "There were no external signs of violence, no drugs or poisons."

"Where was the body found?" she'd asked.

"On our doorstep. He struggled to get to the hospital and almost made it, but his heart gave out."

"Please, send me a record of every moment," she told him, and received his report days later, a kind of slap from the doctor who could easily have gotten it to her the next day. From what she could gather, neither the hospital nor the doctor in question had

29

done anything grossly wrong because the patient was dead on arrival. There wasn't much they could do to him. But there wasn't anything they had done for him either to explain his condition. An autopsy found fatty deposits about the left ventricle of the heart and some constriction in the main artery leading to the heart, but at his age this seemed highly improbable as the cause of death. Other notations on the condition of the dead boy led her to wondering about the possibility of poisoning, and some words of description regarding the corpse—long since in a potter's field—forced the question of suffocation. Distended eyes pocked with red flecks, for instance, the body sweat-soaked from a fever of some intensity just before the onset of death. One of the attending physicians had wondered about the possibility of an exotic disease, malarial in nature. Nothing of the kind was found in the blood, nor were any poisons. Nothing of the kind was found in liver sections or sections scalpeled from other organs. The mystery ended with Dr. Mortimer Fowler's occlusive coronary artery disease. Fanciful talk for a blockage or closure in the arteries. So satisfied and smug was Dr. Fowler with his pathological report, that the man had not even bothered to retain blood, urine, and stomach contents for future analysis. And this really pissed her off.

Dr. Sybil Shanley was no longer just an autopsy assistant to the medical examiner, Dean Grant; she was now an associate with the rank and title of Deputy Chief Medical Examiner, and figured to take over for Dean one day as Chief Medical Examiner for the City of Chicago. No one—especially not her last boyfriend who'd finally given into the fact that she was a career woman and not a baby-maker or male-ego masseuse—could ever accuse Sybil of being too humble or without ambition. What steamed her in this male-dominated world was the distinction that made a proud female doctor *arrogant,* and an ambitious female doctor *greedy,* when such characteristics in men were highly prized. Thank God Dean didn't look at her with blinders on. Thank God he'd seen her potential and had given her the respect and admiration that she had worked so hard and so long to earn. She was now an associate whom Dean treated as an equal, a partner, and a sounding board that talked back. She'd proven herself capable both at his side and on her own. She was an excellent microscopist and an expert on trace elements. Her paperwork was first-rate and she never balked at anything Dean Grant had asked her to do, before now. He'd left for Hammond rather abruptly and urgently, and the news coming from that quarter was ghastly and disturbing. He had left her with an admonishment: "Go lightly where Dr. Fowler is concerned. He could very well be mistaken in his diagnosis, but he has a lot of powerful and well-placed friends who could make your life miserable." And Dean's, she assumed.

Regardless, she had put in an order for exhumation of one John Doe, #129865 in the City of Chicago's Potter's Field number 269. She had to have that body on her table. It cried out for her as if from the grave, pleading. She felt drawn to it, to explain Fowler's stupid mistake perhaps. But also because she sensed some thin connection between #129865 and the other victims of asphyxiation; some tenuous thread perhaps between the causes maybe. Hard to pinpoint.

Poison. There had to be some sort of poison involved. Her mind played over the word, poison. Sybil Shanley had been involved intimately with what at first appeared to be Dean's obsessive preoccupation with floater cases coming into the office the year before. She'd given him the benefit of doubt, even kept her deepest concerns to herself— that Dean was headed for a crack-up. She had performed autopsies on floater victims, searching for trace elements that could conceivably link people of all ages and condition, by the presence of a single fiber type or thread of hair belonging to the killer. She had come through for Dean at that time, as she had on other occasions, performing her part to unmask murderers, rapists, child molesters, and armed robbers.

She had been with Dean a long time now and she'd adopted his oft repeated rule of thumb, along with a great many other Grant prescriptions, tendencies, and predilictions. Dean always said, "Suspect the worst, prove the facts." It was the first part, the suspicion of the worst-case scenario that gave even coroners nightmares. She was suspecting some sickening truth at this very moment, and had been for a number of days, ever since the discovery of a Jane Doe, found in a trash dumpster on the sixteenth, who lay at rest now in the freezer compartment. Her death certificate currently read: "Death by asphyxiation, cause unknown." If she was honest with herself, she had no more answer for the condition than Dr.

Fowler had had for the boy. Her mind flashed back to her first meeting with the dead girl.

She had been doing a workup for a case involving a rape victim, working on the DNA code of the man suspected of the rape, when word came in that a body had been found in a dumpster near Lincoln and Belmont. Would she go or should they send a medical assistant to the scene?

In all suspected homicides someone from the M.E.'s Office, or linked via a network of medical assistants and non-medical men who were merely evidence technicians, was sent in. This in addition to "tour" doctors scheduled for duty at all hours of the day and night. But the medical examiners were the only ones skilled in forensics and pathology. The Office preferred, whenever possible on what appeared an obvious homicide, to send in the true death investigator, the M.E. Sybil recalled an earlier dumpster death that had gotten her curious about asphyxiation causes, so much so that she went back to a textbook on the subject written by the esteemed Gonzalez.

She asked only one question of the dispatcher who'd made the call. "Any outward signs of violence on the body?"

"None."

It was all she needed to hear and she was off.

"Pick up will be in the lot in two minutes, Dr. Shanley," said the dispatcher voice.

She was delivered to the scene by a police squad car. It was dusk and growing darker by the minute, and when she got to the scene several roof flashers had been rigged to shine down into the dumpster where the white body lay like discarded meat, flies making a breeding ground of her, especially about the eyes which Sybil knew she must preserve as best she could. For the eyes would go a long way to prove asphyxiation as the cause of death, if that was indeed the cause here. No one had touched the body to turn it. She might be lying atop her own blood from a wound in the back. If the flies were not so heavy, the dead eyes would be staring right at Sybil. Sybil, to the amazement of Chicago's finest, climbed over the edge of the dumpster and shouted for her medical bag to be handed down. For a good hour, deep inside the coffin, she performed the necessary work on the victim, determining early on that here, too, was a victim of a crime that left no violent marks, and she dared guess the blood would tell her nothing as well. But the skin tone, with its patches of blue, spoke of bleeding under the skin, and the eyes also said asphyxiation. She was willing to bet her career on the truth of it.

The police photographic squad had gotten in behind her, asking Dr. Shanley to back against the wall of the dumpster so they might take their shots of the victim. They remained above, using a zoom. A colleague and friend from the police forensic lab showed up. Donald Carr, by name, she knew him to be an excellent forensics man in his own right. He asked if she'd concluded her tests yet, and she told him she could use his help. He climbed in and shared the macabre setting with her, dusting flies away, pulling out a can of spray that neither the flies nor Sybil could stand. Sybil dug out her scalpel from her pocket where she preferred to carry it at all times.

They worked closely within the confines of the dumpster, Don sometimes stumbling about, losing his glasses at one point. It was difficult, close, and grotesque, as if working inside a metal crypt. They could have had the cops overturn the dumpster and do the sample-takings and examination in better air, with more space to breathe, on the outside, but Dean would do it this way, and she'd be damned if she'd do it any other way. Besides, she knew deep down that Don had only climbed into the death trap because she was a woman and he was a man and couldn't very well stand about waiting outside or above the dumpster with all those macho cops looking on. He'd never live it down. Still, before it was over, part of her had wished that Don, or some inexperienced, overanxious cop had gotten on the scene first and had done just that, turned the body out. If the cause of death was as she suspected, it mattered little if the body was disturbed. But it was the medical examiner's job to see that nothing was removed from the scene, and to carefully study the general position and condition of the body, and the ground around it—whatever that ground may consist of. Here it was partially soup, rotten vegetables, planks, and discarded pipe, a floor bed that shifted with any movement. The harsh lights didn't keep her from cutting herself on a piece of glass, nor did they leave anything to the imagination.

"Any notion on time of death?" someone above her asked.

She looked up to see Inspector Ken Kelso staring down at the body, past her and Don. "Well?"

"Good to see you, too, Inspector," she replied.

"You know Dr. Carr."

"Don," he said, giving a nod to Carr. "Any notions how long she's been here?"

"Time of death's difficult to determine. Body's warm, but then today's July sun has been baking down on this metal," said Don, noncommittally.

"Deeper tissues are quite cool, though," said Sybil. "I'd say sometime last night. Muscles are rigid due to rigor which normally doesn't take place for six hours or so—"

"Though time for this varies, you understand," said Don. "Body seems too warm for this length of time to have elapsed, but then what Dr. Shanley says about rigor . . . and it *was* a hot day, and the signs of insect attack . . ."

"No external signs of injury," said Sybil.

Kelso brushed flies away from himself. "Sexual attack?"

"No external evidence of it," said Don.

"Everything points to some type of asphyxiation," she said.

"But we're not prepared to make that judgment yet," countered Don Carr. "We need autopsy time, and I'd like to assist Dr. Shanley."

"We've got a lot of other cases hanging fire, Don. Take an unidentified victim—a streetwalker from the look of her—how you going to justify that?"

"Smooth justice, Inspector Kelso," said Sybil.

"Dr. Shanley's asked for my assistance," lied Carr.

Kelso's large face showed a half frown of thoughtfulness which only served to infuriate Sybil, but she managed to keep her thoughts to herself. He finally said, "All right, Dr. Carr, be my guest," replied

Kelso. "Kill two birds with one stone. We need a police officer present at the autopsy anyways . . . may as well be a useful cop, huh, Sybil?"

It infuriated her that Kelso could not bring himself to call her Dr. Shanley. It further infuriated her that, implied deeply within the gentlemen's bargain they had struck, Carr would be watching over *the woman* so no mistake would be made. Or was it the insinuation that Carr wanted some time alone with her? Or was she just getting bitter and paranoid where men were concerned? Or all of the above? They'd never been close friends, she and Kelso, but there'd always been a strange friction and attraction between them. But he'd seen her enter the M.E.'s Office as a novice, and go through stages of development. He was like an uncle or a stepfather, a bit too familiar with her, and it likely never occurred to him to call her anything but Sybil.

"Well, get us something to go on, you two. So far, around here, nobody's seen or heard a thing. Later."

He was gone and Sybil's blood pressure lowered. Don was staring at her, and then he said, "Sorry, I didn't mean to sound like a toad, but when that man's around, I don't know, I get the shakes. I don't know why."

"Power, he's very powerful in the department. No apology necessary. He does strange things to me, too."

Carr frowned, "Sometimes, I wish I could be half so . . . intimidating."

"Sometimes, I'm sure he wishes he could be less intimidating."

They returned to the work at hand, forgetting the

37

others outside for the time being.

"She wasn't killed here," Sybil told Don Carr.

Carr hadn't had Sybil's experience. He was capable in the lab, but his field experience had been limited much more than her own. He believed her, but asked, "How can you be sure?"

"She died in a confined area without oxygen. As tight as this place is, it's not airtight."

"You're saying on the basis of what you see here, that she died of suffocation?"

"That's about right."

"Look, I know what I said to Kelso's got you ticked, I mean I as much as contradicted you, Doctor, but it won't help going out on a limb and—"

"I'm not going out on a limb, Doctor."

Carr grit his teeth and pointed to the corpse. "Not a single mark on the throat, and we'd have to open it to be sure, to rule out strangulation or severe irritation from poison."

"Don, I think it's neither laryngeal edema nor a fracture of the cricoid cartilage—"

"No way you can tell that without cutting, Sybil."

"Then let's do it."

"Tonight?"

"Tonight, as soon as she's transported."

"Why? What's the rush? You pushing for a—"

"Hey, didn't I just hear Kelso give you departmental approval?"

"But I've got to log it tonight, after working all day—"

"Budgetary constraints, huh? Shitty way to run an investigation."

"All right," he agreed, "if I can get the department's okay."

"No way to run a pathology unit."

"They sign my paycheck. You got it easy with Dr. Grant's operation. Pretty slick, complete independence from the judiciary and law enforcement agencies. Might even call that criminal."

"The only way to fly, and speaking of flies, let's get out of here, and let's do something for this poor kid," she indicated the deceased. "How young do you make her?"

"Same as you, too young."

"To hell with you! I'm too young? You're just—"

"No, no, I didn't mean—I meant, I think same as you that she's too—"

But Sybil was up and over the top of the dumpster, feeling the jutting, metal edge tear at her smeared, white coroner's oversuit. Outside, watching Carr climb out behind her, she ordered the body retrieved and transported to the M.E.'s office downtown.

He smiled at the customers, swapping stories and neighborly concerns and advice with them as they came and went, the bell on the door tinkling their comings and goings. Midway through the morning he checked the newspaper. There was no word of any discovery of the body. At lunchtime he closed the little shop, a relic of its kind, and went down a few doors to Mr. Ahmsted's delicatessen, where a big beef sandwich, potato salad, and a glass of wine slaked his hunger. He traded anecdotes with Ahmsted, an old

Jew of Dutch heritage who traveled back and forth to Amsterdam where he had family. Always he spoke about his family, but all the old fool had were pictures of people on the street there in Amsterdam, people who might be anybody and who were certainly, like Ahmsted himself, nobody. The world was spilling over with nobodies.

At first he hadn't needed it *every* night. At first he had gone slowly, believing that not only was it prudent to do so, but that Solomon wanted it that way. Solomon worked in mysterious ways, and seldom revealed himself directly. But he came in some form almost every evening, whispering in his ears for sustenance, for the breath of life.

Ahmsted had to nudge him to get his attention.

"Do you? Well, do you?"

"What?"

"What, are you going deaf? I want to know what kind of sausage you can sell me. I give you top price. Louis, you sure are acting strange again."

"One seventy-nine a pound."

"What? That's robbery!"

"You want it or not?"

"Louis, sometimes you are like your old man— a *shit*. A real shit old Malinowski was, too."

"Don't start on my father."

"Your father! Were you ever sure he *was* your father? Maybe not. Treated you like gutter—"

Louis knocked over his plate when he grabbed the older man by the shirt, his eyes glaring red, "Say another word and I'll kill you!"

"Easy, easy, Louis, it's me! What's this? You treat your only friend like this? The only friend you got,

40

Mr. big-shot butcher, you remember that? Remember that!" Ahmsted shouted as Louis Malinowski rushed from the deli. "I'll send one of my boys around for the sausage."

But Malinowski was gone and people all about were staring after him. "Big Polack's got a short fuse lately, that's all. Moody, a moody man," said Ahmsted to his other customers. "He don't mean nothing by it."

Ahmsted brooded over the episode however. He remembered how old Malinowski had died in that butcher shop down the street. He remembered the blood all over the walls, and the kid standing in the middle of it, in a state of shock the doctors had said, unable to speak or remember what had happened. His old man had taken the carving knives to his mother right in front of the boy, and was about to go to work on the boy when police shot him ten times over to bring him down. But now he was a man, and a man, Mr. Ahmsted felt, must face up to the truth of the matter, however painful. How else would Louis ever exorcise his demons?

Back in his shop, Louis Malinowski left the Closed sign on the door a bit longer. He needed time to gather himself together. The old fool's words had made him crazy, made him see red, as if his eyes were soaked with blood. Everything he recalled about his parents' deaths was told to him by others. He had no recollections of it. But when he truly was made angry, his mind raged with a blood-red world before him.

He went to his apron, spattered with the blood of animals. The animal blood ran from half and quarter carcasses hung on meat hooks in the rear in tough vinyl bags that held in the freshness and were protection from freezer burn. The blood of objects like carcasses didn't trouble him. If he saw a bleeding cat or dog in the street, he went into a near catatonic state of fear and quaking that began innocently enough as goosebumps and developed into a chill and a strange kind of perspiration which, if left unchecked, threatened to send him into a faint. It was stronger and worse with human blood. Couldn't stand the sight of it. Couldn't stand the sight of his own. It was a downright disgusting thing if he should accidentally cut himself. He was a joke in the neighborhood as a result, the butcher who faints when he sees himself cut.

A doctor once told him it was not uncommon, and that given the incident of his father's having literally butchered his mother before his eyes, it was not at all surprising. The surprising thing was that he remained a butcher. But it was all he knew how to do. He was good for nothing else. That is, until he met Solomon.

Three

The body was prepped by a technician while Sybil Shanley sat at her desk taking in great breaths of air, the dead girl on the autopsy slab ten yards away who had been denied the breath of life. Someone had locked her in an airtight place and she'd slowly strangled on her own exhalations, asphyxiated by her own body's conversion of life-giving oxygen to death-dealing carbon dioxide.

But for what ungodly reason? And was this just the tip of the iceberg, as Sybil feared? How many wrongly diagnosed asphyxiation cases were being reported as diabetic shock, some form of hepatitis, pancreatitis, and heart failure, like Fowler's young dead man scheduled for exhumation tomorrow?

How far out on a limb could she go—she, a Deputy Medical Examiner with only a few months experience? She'd fought a long time to get where she was, and now she was risking it all for this terrifying suspicion of hers. She wondered what Dean would do in her place.

When she was in medical school at the University of Chicago, Dean was teaching forensics at the Hospital for Special Surgery. She eagerly signed on as his technician, knowing she could learn from this man. At the time she was rooming with Anna Melton, a toxicologist in Dean Grant's office, then a bureaucratic arm of the Chicago Police Department. Anna and Grant's influence turned her toward pathology and, in particular, forensics. She worked as an assistant medical examiner in St. Louis, and later for a short time in Dade County, Florida. But her home was Chicago, and when Anna Melton left Dean's office to take on the medical examiner's job for Wichita, Kansas, Sybil jumped at the chance to rejoin Grant in Chicago to continue working alongside him.

She was a driven, sleepless woman who reveled in her commitment to her work. She prided herself on knowing all the newest developments in her field. She took to new gadgets like a computer hacker. She brought a lot of the new technology into the office. She found her niche here when just after Christmas, as a sort of belated gift, Dean announced that he was making her his Deputy. It was an honor that increased her standing in the field as well as her paycheck. And she knew she had deserved it; that she had earned it.

How much pain could a guy like Dr. Fowler cause her now? Did it matter? Would it have mattered a scintilla before she'd become Deputy M.E.? Not likely. Screw him, she told herself and got up, taking a look around the facilities.

Scintilla, she kicked over the melodic word for

trace or minute elements. That's what they did here in the crime lab: they coolly and sometimes desperately searched for that scintilla of evidence buried deep within the labyrinth of the inert body that might prove or disprove foul play. They determined cause of death from facts imprinted sometimes microscopically upon the corpse, as honest as the fingerprint or the DNA of a man.

The glare of bright fluorescent lights outside her office revealed a stark, clinical realm. There were three main autopsy rooms, and three more for special cases—those of an infective nature, including a decomposed corpse. One of these was already prepared to accept the John Doe she'd scheduled for exhumation in a few hours.

They'd moved into the new offices earlier in the month thanks to the fabulous funding that followed Dean's successes with all their attendant publicity.

The exterior of the building at 100 Wabash Avenue, only a causeway from their old digs, was white-glazed brick with aluminum panelling. With six floors aboveground for administrative offices and divisions, the autopsy rooms and body storage filled the easily accessible, well-lit basement. A sub-basement contained air-conditioning and heating equipment and supplies. The special autopsy rooms were kept virtually germ-free due to the constant flow of air. All autopsy work was centralized here, and a unit of the Missing Persons Bureau of Chicago's Police Department, with its people and computers, had been located in the building at Dean's insistence, to better coordinate IDing bodies.

The entire building, including the autopsy rooms,

was comfortably air-conditioned, a feature that helped everyone—including bereaved people who were called there to view the remains lying in one of a hundred and thirty-eight refrigerated compartments that lined the basement walls. Each shrouded body on its individual tray was easily reached, the stainless steel door opening, the tray careening forward on automatic casters.

Sybil also could see from her office the large, walk-in refrigerator with shelves for storage of children's and infants' bodies—her least favorite area, which brought on great pangs of sadness. She'd had to do autopsies on many, many children in her years. Some of those autopsies had placed the parents in prison.

Seventy-five hundred autopsies would be performed in the coming year in their new building, or so it was estimated. This from a total of about thirty-two thousand cases accepted each year for investigation, only a third of Chicago's ninety-five thousand annual deaths.

On the floors above, administrative offices worked with such figures, offices filled with stenographers, typists, administrative clerks. On the "high ground" directly overhead was the lobby with marbled walls and a picture of the Mayor of the city, alongside the enormous symbol of the medical profession, the cross and a pair of symmetrical snakes coiling upward. Above this a Latin motto prescribing silence in the face of death. The lobby and reception area fronted for an identification room with five desks, the Missing Persons Bureau of the CPD, a kind of communications and clearinghouse for the hundreds of thousands of MPs reported annually. Each desk area was shared by a cop and a clerk. The accounting clerk dealt in numbers and figures, names and addresses, cataloging and storing information on computers—information cops dug out of people and sometimes acted on. In this way, clerks received and dispatched notifications of missing persons from five quadrants of the city. It was a kind of lost and found, with dire consequences should the party be found. Opposite this was the Medical Examiner's large business office, working in close conjunction with the MP people, handling the cases of the day. Even when the autopsy rooms were empty, the morgue silent, the activity in these offices was always high, and they remained open twenty-four hours a day, seven days a week.

Beyond this, another large office, sliced into cubicles by an unfriendly partitioning that created a maze, took up the rest of the floor. Here typists with iron-clad stomachs transcribed the autopsy findings from tapes. Others in this office filed, compiled, and collated records. The secretarial pool was also called on to put together long-forgotten, past autopsy reports and records for an impending trial case which either Dean, Sybil, or some other M.E. with the department might need. Death—and murder—kept a lot of people on the payroll.

On another floor were offices for statisticians, the death-toll accountants whose job it was to not only record the numbers but to classify data gleaned from the numbers. Facts such as that most traumatic deaths were alcohol- or drug-related, or that most homicides involved handguns.

The other floors of the building were primarily

devoted to laboratories. One toxicology lab was already running tests on the Jane Doe's blood, searching for the obvious—alcohol content—and the not so obvious—poisons that might have stopped her heart or her respiratory organs. The sixth floor was for the public, a kind of morbid museum of death, a series of displays that formed the Dean Grant museum of the most fiendish murder cases—Chicago's own Museum of Horrors. The walls and showcases were filled with murder weapons and documents Dean had assiduously collected for years: hatchets, scimitars, blunt instruments, lead pipes, explosives, a plumber's well-publicized blowtorch, alongside specimens from autopsies, ranging from knives embedded into skulls to slides depicting arsenic poisoning the viewer could see under a microscope. The halls here were lined with demonstrations of various identification techniques, from the ancient in which a man might be wrongly convicted on the basis of animal blood on his clothes, to the modern and incontrovertible evidence of human gene identification.

The sixth floor also housed a complete medical and legal library. An M.E. could spend a lifetime in these two places, but Sybil couldn't recall the last time she'd had time to visit either.

Don Carr's arms shot up in a gesture of despair. He'd been waiting patiently for her, but the patience had grown thin. "You ready, Doctor?" he called when she opened her glass panelled door.

"I am. Let's get to work, Doctor."

"You know, it wouldn't hurt to call me Don."

"All right, Don."

"So, may I call you Sybil?"

"Can we talk about it after the autopsy?"

"Sure."

She was cool, her mind riveted to the task before her. She had to focus completely and tightly on the job at hand. She didn't care for any distractions save the learned, habitual one of music during the autopsy, something Dean liked to have when he worked in the autopsy room. He'd seen to it that music could be piped in, but it must always be the best, Bach, Schubert, sometimes Strauss. It must be kept to a minimum pitch, so that when the stenos went to transcribe the autopsy report, they could hear Dean or Sybil's voice and directions clearly.

Sybil clicked on the music and the tape at the same instant on entering the autopsy room. In a curt voice, she gave the stenographer her name and title, letting the title hang there for a moment, as if savoring it, Carr thought. Then she gave Carr's name and title, Police Pathologist and witness, and the fact he was attending in the autopsy of an unknown female, Jane Doe, giving the deceased the requisite tag number. She then barked at a young lab tech, "James, did you examine the exterior bruises and discolorations?"

"Yes, Dr. Shanley."

"Anything unusual, out of the ordinary?"

"Cuts, bruises to the lower left leg, upper right thigh, not enough to cause deadly injury. Some scratches across the chest, collarbone area, back—"

"Reddening?"

"Some, yes."

"Anything else?"

"Fingers on both hands."

49

"Yeah, we know," she said, eyeing Carr. "Anything out of the scrapings we took at the scene from either of our labs yet?"

"Takes time," said Carr, "and apparently, you're in much more of a hurry tonight than anyone else, doctor."

"Obviously." She went to the legs and examined these bruises and scratches first. She did so rapidly, coolly, examining them in the manner of a carpenter examining a poorly lined beam, almost tsking, but then rushing on. "Nothing to show any wounds to the head or neck, James?"

"None," the young assistant said tentatively.

"Yes or no?" she prodded him roughly, her little words like an electric shock to his ego, making him avert his eyes away from Dr. Carr's before answering.

"No visible signs of such injury, Dr. Shanley."

"Right, okay . . . And you looked closely for needle marks? Icepick impressions?"

"I've had plenty of time, yes," replied the bespectacled young man showing a little sarcasm.

"You've taken sections for histology?"

"Yes, Dr. Shanley, that's my job."

"Any results? No, I assume not."

"There's been no time. Hour maybe—"

She waved him down. "All right, let's open her." She said it with that prepared indifference to the aura of death that Don Carr both understood and used himself, but detested in a woman. Somehow, it made a woman less a woman, a man more a man. Maybe, he reasoned, it was just his upbringing, some male chauvinism that he'd never get over, embedded deep within.

"Ready, Dr. Carr?"

Carr nodded, and together they began carefully to peel back the layers of the woman's earthly shell, the noise of the power tools they used trapped by the tape recording. They pierced the breast bone and below the fluorescent lights searched for signs of violence. As they worked, Sybil talked softly, as if in consort with the melodic Blue Danube, which had been interrupted horribly by the ear-splitting and bone-cracking sounds of the saw.

"I didn't want to make too much of it earlier, Don, but did you notice the condition of the legs as opposed to the rest of the body?"

"Lividity, you mean?"

"Exactly."

"Somewhat odd," he conceded.

"I think the record should show," she said loudly into the microphone, "that hypostasis shows the lowest portions of the body pulled the blood due to gravity. In other words, the victim died in an upright position."

"True," said Carr to her, "but blood settling can move to a new position, if the body is moved."

"Report stands," she replied, "as an oddity we don't often see. In fact, I've never seen it. Have you, Dr. Carr?"

"Once . . . case of a guy who was skewered to a wall with a bayonet, when I was serving in Vietnam."

"And you don't think it's unusual in this case?"

"I think it's damned unusual," he countered, pushing up his wire-rimmed glasses. "I just don't think you can build a scenario around lividity, especially when we know she was not murdered where she was found."

"At least you suspect murder, Don. I was beginning to wonder."

"Sure, I suspect murder . . . have all along, but proving it is another matter, one that takes careful preparation and time, Sybil. You're rushing it."

"Yeah, well suppose the killer's rushing it? Suppose the bastard responsible for this—" she pointed to the corpse with her scalpel catching the light, "is out there somewhere right this moment, doing this to some other woman?"

"So, let's get on with it."

The chest was open to them now and by peeling back the large breast flap, Don could place his hand inside and locate the larynx. "Throat is good, no crushing, clear passage," he said, "and no swelling."

"We have to cut, *see* it with our own eyes," she said.

"Waste of time," he countered, "and just another scar for her to bear."

"Oh, you're concerned about that are you?"

He stared across at her. "Damned right I am, doctor."

She fixed him hard inside her hazel pools. "Yeah, I guess you are. Sorry, I only meant that we have to be sure."

"I am sure. She was not choked to death, or given poison or borax to drink that'd cut off her air supply when the throat irritation closed off—"

Sybil's scalpel swiped open the throat.

"Yeah, right . . . do it," he finished. "It is your autopsy, Doctor Shanley."

She placed a large magnifying glass on a moveable arm across the top of the incision, and with forceps peeled back the throat flaps to reveal the intact, healthy larynx. It was speckled with blood flecks. "Does that tell you anything, Doctor Carr?"

He only gaped and shook his head and again eyeballed the telltale conditions. Sybil had been right. The incision spoke of blood bursting from small arteries for lack of oxygen, in miniscule fashion escaping to grasp at air at any cost. No large irritation or ugly swelling, no growths or laryngeal edema, no sign this woman had choked to death, except in the spotted discolorations around the larynx, easily overlooked. These were similar to spots on the retinas and the whites of the eyes, where microscopic arteries spit forth pepper dots of blood which, when viewed through a powerful microscope, would look like upside-down exclamation points.

"Lungs're perfectly healthy, doctor," said Sybil a few moments later. "Would you agree?"

"Agreed, but deflated."

"Unusually so, would you say?"

"Some air always remains except in the case of asphyxiation wherein *all* air is depleted, and in cases of respiratory illness . . ."

"But here the lungs show no sign of prolonged scars, no blackening from cigarettes or cancer. I want a section taken, James. Draw some blood, skin, the usual."

James moved in with a scalpel and efficiently took the sample she could have snipped off herself, if she weren't playing at Deputy M.E., Carr thought. Or was she studying James's technique as part of her job?

Next she took out the heart, had James weigh it and take a section for tests, and then it was returned, stitched to a wall and cradled into place. The right ventricle was flush with blood.

"Jane has a few scratches on her wrists, left side of her chest, other smaller ones at the back, left side, other marks on the legs as earlier indicated. There is a graze over the right collarbone, near the front of the shoulder." Sybil lifted the woman's hands which were both scarred, the nails jagged, broken, and in some cases torn away. She noted this. "All these minor cuts save the legs show a *vital reaction*." She turned to James and asked, "What do you make of that, James?"

"Leg bruises came after death . . . others while she was alive."

"When she was dumped, her legs caught on the dumpster," said Carr.

"No vital reaction or puckering or reddening about the leg injuries, although plenty of blood. That's where all her blood had gone," replied Sybil. "The vital reaction and the reddening around the other areas if conclusive; these were inflicted while she was alive. The ones most interesting are these," she said, holding up the fingers of both hands.

"She was scratching at something hard," said Carr, "a door maybe, wood or metal."

"To get out, yes."

"Horrible."

"Yes."

54

"Let's have another look at the eyes."

"Something else, Don," she said, stopping him.

"What?"

"Notice anything about the skin?"

"You mean the dampness?"

"I'm willing to bet a month's pay that James's histology report on the skin will show water, a lot of water, and, maybe traces of alcohol."

"Water . . . you mean . . . melted, as in crystals formed under the epidermal layer, and then disappearing over time inside that hot box."

"I think she's been on ice for a while, yes. And since it wasn't here, where?"

"Let's have a closer look at the eyes."

They did so. There were fly eggs embedded there, especially in the left eye, as the other had been turned a little downward. But none had had time to hatch into maggots. There was hardly any decomposition of the body, indicating again the possibility it'd been on ice and had "thawed" in the dumpster.

In the eyelids there were thousands of miniscule but telltale pretechial hemorrhages. These tiny blood flecks suggested asphyxia.

"No compression marks about the neck," she was saying into the microphone. "No ligature. No outward sign of strangulation. Still, it is the considered opinion that the body before us died of some form of asphyxiation. With regard to the gastrointestinal tract, the stomach was filled with a large amount of recently ingested food, extending from its upper opening to its lower end. Our considered opinion, Dr. Carr agreeing, is that the time of death after the last food was ingested was of a period of fewer than two hours before death. The contents will be examined and catalogued at a later date."

Even James knew that if a person eats a meal and lives on quite normally, the rate of digestion and emptying of the stomach progressed in a fairly regular manner, depending on the kind of food ingested. It was usually within two hours. This was especially true in young healthy people who digest and move food along rapidly from the stomach. In the case of Jane, the chewed, swallowed, and softened food hadn't even time to be propelled out of the stomach into the duodenum—the first part of the intestine—where a different kind of digestive process begins.

The whole process was altered, often frozen, in the event of trauma, assault, fright, illness, mental disturbance, or going into a state of unconsciousness. A stomach jammed as full as Jane's left no doubt whatsoever that the food was swallowed not more than two hours before death. What kind of food it was, where she had eaten it, could place her at a given place at a given time. Many a killer had been brought to justice on such evidence alone.

"I'll do the lab work on the stomach contents myself," Sybil told James and Don Carr. She didn't want to leave anything to chance, and what she couldn't recognize under a microscope, simply didn't exist. "James, I want you to photograph the exterior scars to further corroborate the conclusions we've made on which were inflicted before and which after death."

"Yes, Doctor."

"No mistakes, nothing left to chance, understood?"

He glared his affirmative.

"How about tomorrow, five or six?" James asked.

"Yeah, I guess you have been here a long time. See you late in the day tomorrow, unless you want to assist on the exhumation."

"What exhumation?"

It was Carr's voice but blended with another, deeper, and overwhelming voice, an ordinary drum inside a bass drum, she thought. Asking at the same instant as Carr was Dr. Dean Grant who stood in the doorway to the autopsy lab. He'd finally decided to return from Hammond. He now went about putting down his full vial case, tossing his coat aside, his face both a massive question mark and a reflection of fatigue.

"And what goes on here?" he asked, then said, "Hi, Don, Jim. What've we got here, Sybil?"

"Asphyxiation victim, Chief," said Sybil. "Just completed the autopsy and Carr here will tell you, this woman's death is abnormal by anyone's standards. I'll have the full report on your desk tomorrow morning."

"Asphyxiation, huh? Don, what do you say?"

"Have to admit, Dr. Grant, it looks like Syb—Dr. Shanley's right on with this one. Eyes, larynx both speckled with—"

"Ever see napalm victims? Of course you have. Could be a poisonous gas that cuts off vital organs, shuts down the lungs and heart→"

"No, lungs, heart all look normal, and the throat is clear of irritations."

"I see."

"Admit it, Dean, we've got another psycho on our hands. It's like the country breeds them, the city nourishes them, and 1989's a bumper crop," said Sybil.

He gave her a concerned look and a nod, followed by a deep, tired sigh. "I've just come from a house that proves that much, Sybil. Look, ahh . . . it's almost three in the morning, and we're all tired. I'll read your report on—she got a name?"

"No ID."

"I'll read it tomorrow. Now, what's this about an exhumation? Don't tell me it's the Fowler patient, Sybil. I couldn't deal with that tonight."

"All right, it's not the Fowler patient."

"Who then?"

"Another John Doe I got suspicious about, that's all."

"You wouldn't be lying to me, would you?"

"I might be."

Grant's expression grew stern and he clenched his teeth. "Damn," he muttered, "Don, goodnight . . . you, too, Jim. Dr. Shanley and I have some talking to do."

"Sure, sure," said James, delighted at the thought Dr. Shanley was about to get her comeuppance at last.

Carr picked up his belongings and with a glance back from the door, saw that Grant was pouring both himself and Sybil a crystal clear shot of Scotch. He'd heard a great deal about Grant's management style, but this was the first time he'd ever seen it in action. He wished for the moment he could be a fly on the wall. Stumbling out, he gave a friendly wink to Sybil who brought herself up bravely to face Dean.

She knew that when Dean poured himself a drink, it was serious. She knew he was angry with her for going against his judgment, but she wasn't a little girl anymore, and she was never a mindless flag bearer. "Look," she began.

"No . . . no, *you* look, Sybil—"

"Are we, or are we not independent of the politicking shit we used to be faced with when we were part of the cop operation under the mayor?"

"That doesn't change the fact we get funded through the city. Now, your exhumation tomorrow's going to cost us friends in City Hall, on the board of governors, with the aldermen, all those people."

"All those old, fat men. Fowler has that much power?"

"Much more than *this* fat man." He drained his Scotch and thumped it on the desk between them. She did likewise, choking on it a bit.

"So, what're you going to do? Make a few phone calls, put a stop to it before it's too late?"

"Sybil, you're being impractical—"

"Because the guy that's buried out there in that potter's field is a nobody, a John Doe, we just sweep the whole thing under? Pass the paperwork and sharpen our pencils?"

"Hell no, that's not what I'm trying to say, Sybil."

"What then?"

"We're only independent as long as we fight to keep it that way. We can do a multitude of good in these new walls and with our new status, only if we can remain autonomous. I'll fight for that. I'll even fight you for that. I'm tired, and not making myself very clear here but—"

She interrupted him, "Oh, you make yourself very clear, Dr. Grant. You and Kelso have paid your dues, so now it's time to lean back, maybe cut loose on a golf course some place, meanwhile—"

"Sybil, that's bullshit and you know it."

She raced for the door ahead of him and he hadn't the strength either to chase her or answer her. Dr. John Fowler was head of Cook County Hospital, for Christ's sake, and she was questioning his diagnosis on a John Doe who'd died previous to any hospital care! All over a fixation about strangulated or asphyxiated people she seemed to be producing all around her. She was his concern as much as the behind-the-scenes difficulties Fowler could hoist upon the office. He'd be telephoning Dean—if he hadn't already—demanding that Dean let Dr. Shanley go. It was as inevitable as rain. And no way in hell would he let the rain fall on Sybil Shanley.

Meanwhile he had to get some sleep. He had a vial case full with samples and sections taken from the Schletter place. He'd have to see to them in the morning. He had to phone home, explain he was sleeping here on the old, reliable black couch in his office. That he had an exhumation to attend tomorrow, thanks to Sybil. Not to mention a keen interest to see what she had on the Jane Doe that James had carefully put away in a compartment before he'd left for the night.

Dean laid down in his already rumpled pants and shirt, the tie somewhere on the floor. He was a bit chilled but didn't have the strength to get up and

60

search for the pillow and blanket he kept in a file cabinet somewhere nearby. His mind faded off into welcome sleep instead. He didn't hear Sybil return. he didn't feel it when she placed the blanket over him. He didn't know it when she took his phone off the hook, dialed his own office and placed it on hold to keep out the calls.

Four

Dean Grant was slowly awakened by the movement of people in the outer offices and labs, the sound of trays being plunked down, murmuring of people's voices, the general hum of life. Lab technicians were going about their duties, and doctors were dictating to assistants the day's workload and order of priority.

Dean was tired already. he was bleary-eyed and weakened by thoughts of a long day ahead and the hard-to-swallow realization that nothing had gone away. That it had not even been partially a nightmare, all the business in Hammond and all the trouble with Sybil the night before. It all stood in stark reality about him, like the mysterious covering he fought to remove, and the pillow. He couldn't recall having snatched them from the file cabinet.

The bulging vial case he'd brought back from Hammond sat across from him on the floor and stared back at him as if the damned thing breathed. It held all the samples and slides taken from the

63

Schletter house. It looked as if it had been moved from the position where he'd dropped it by the door. Materials inside it would tell a morbid, disturbing tale, the sequence of murders, and in what order their parts went down the pipes. Dean wanted to do all in his power to insure that Emil Schletter got exactly what he deserved, but modern law would balk at an eye for an eye in this matter. Who would dismember the man and place him piece by piece into the industrial-sized disposal in the building? Still, what a pretty sound it would make, the *whoosh-grind, whoosh-grind* against the bloody murderer's flesh and bone. Not likely . . . not in a civil society with law and order and courts and places for the insane to be shut away.

A man like Schletter, a triple murderer, if he ever *was* taken into custody, had a better chance at an insane asylum than the fellow who finds his girl in bed with someone else and kills one of them.

Dean got up a bit too quickly and felt a wave of pain rise and fade deep inside his head. He went into his private restroom where he threw water in his face and stared for a moment into the mirror. He looked as tired as he felt, his eyes bloodshot and heavy, the lids drooping. More water to the face.

He hadn't much time to do what he must do before the scheduled 9:00 a.m. exhumation Sybil was determined to have. He knew he could not countermand her order, so he must do the next best thing. In order to do it properly, he must rush, but he couldn't rush to the detriment of an honest appraisal of her night's work over the Jane Doe.

He returned to his office. Trying very hard to

ignore the Schletter material that screamed out at him, he got on the phone and located James Remmer. Remmer was a first-year pathology student who did odd jobs and got credit for time spent learning the workings of the Office, as well as soaking up its atypical atmosphere. As low man on the totem, he was also the gofer.

Dean called for coffee and anything edible, "A doughnut, toast, anything that looks good in the cafeteria."

"Dr. Grant, nothing in the cafeteria—"

"Please, Jim, *anything*, and rush."

"Yes, sir, right away, Dr. Grant."

Dean then located his change of clothes and hung them out in the restroom which he'd had equipped with a shower for such occasions as this morning. He started the shower and allowed the clothes to steam a bit.

The phone rang.

It was his wife, Jackie, calling from home, preparing to leave for the hospital where she worked.

"So, when'll I get my husband back?" she asked.

He ran rather brusquely down the long itinerary of things he must do. She was at the end of that list, and he knew that must hurt her. "You understand, I know . . . like when that arson fire kept you busy with patients for forty-eight hours."

"Yeah, but your so-called patients aren't going anywhere." She relented, asking, "What's this about Sybil's exhuming a body?"

Dean explained.

"You sound worried about her."

"Well, you've heard of Dr. Mortimer Fowler."

"Cook County."

"Head guy on surgery."

"Headhunter's more the word in medical circles, a real—"

"Prick, I know. Anyway, the body being exhumed, it's one of his?"

"Right."

"Oh shit. He made a mistake?"

"Hey, what doctor doesn't make mistakes?"

"Hey, what doctor wants his buried mistakes *unearthed?*"

"In this case, I think the mistake's Sybil's. She made her diagnosis purely from paper!"

"So, she's got to examine the corpse. You'd do the same if it were you, if you had a doubt."

Dean stared down at the dossier of information Sybil had left on his desk dealing with the Jane Doe of the previous night, and tests on two others that she had concluded were asphyxiation victims. He thought a moment about Sybil's recent behavior—behavior he'd unofficially begun to think of as obsessive and detrimental—and yet it was true that he had taught her to be passionate about her beliefs and to maintain faith with incontrovertible evidence. Did she have doubts about herself in this matter? None. Did she have the evidence? Don Carr seemed to think so last night. Had Dean been too caught up in his own ghastly case to see what was going on?

"Maybe, Jackie, maybe you've got something there. We'll see. Anyway, I've left the shower running and I've got to get in it and shave and have breakfast."

"I'll see you later then. And Dean, good luck. I've missed you."

Before he could get his shower, however, breakfast arrived. So did Don Carr. James Remmer began to pour coffee for Dean. Remmer was a polite, hard-working kid still trying to make up his mind about forensics as a career. He was happy to shut off the shower at Grant's request, then leave the room.

"What brings you around so early, Don?" Grant asked, then gulped down his black coffee.

"Dr. Grant, I'd like to ask a favor."

"Oh? What a coincidence. I have a favor to ask of you, too. I'd like a third opinion on Sybil Shanley's suspicions of homicide in these asphyxiation deaths, and whether they're related or isolated cases." He pointed to the paperwork before him. "Sybil suspects more, but these are the ones where she's found some correlations. Now she's looking for another match-up."

Carr nodded the entire time Dean was talking, his round face and glasses bobbing as if his spinal column were rubber. Somewhat easily intimidated, Carr was young and new to the Chicago Police Force, and fearful of mistakes. "I know," he began, "and I'm interested, too. In fact—"

"Now, what'd you want of me?"

"An okay to be at the exhumation."

"I have no problem with that, but what do you hope to gain by it?"

"Autopsy'll be performed at a nearby mortuary, I understand, Gundersen's off Pulaski?"

"I guess so, I haven't looked, but if you say so."

"Anyway, if Dr. Shanley's right about this being a serial killer, well, then it becomes a police matter . . ."

"And you want it? Take it off our hands, so to speak."

"No, I'd just like to work with you, in consort."

"I see no problem. We'd have referred it to Chief Kelso as soon as we were in agreement and had enough physical evidence to make a case anyway."

"I believe in early involvement."

Dean nodded. "I like your enthusiasm, Don. Sure, no problem. Now, I've got to get that shower. Use my desk, or the one just outside, but look these over. See if you agree with Dr. Shanley's assessment."

Carr nodded, lifted the folders, and took them to the desk in the outer office, feeling a bit more comfortable with that arrangement. Coffee in hand, he began reading. Dean disappeared into the shower.

The warm, pulsating water revived Dean, and for a brief time he thought he might stay beneath it forever. For in a moment all the hideous thoughts and suspicions and realities of what awaited him beyond the shower had washed from existence: vaporized with the steam surrounding him.

Dean Grant once more summoned young Jim Remmer from the lab into his office. Remmer looked worried until Dean told him to relax. "I've got a case here filled with highly sensitive, very important materials connected with the Hammond case—the Schletter business."

Dean handed the heavy, black leather bag over to the young lab assistant who said, shakily, "And you want me to relax? Please, tell me you're not putting me in charge of this."

"Not in charge, no . . . not entirely. But all my key people are quite busy, Jim, and so, I'd like you to oversee the administration of the necessary tests. They're all listed and outlined here," Dean explained, handing him a typewritten sheet he'd had prepared by his secretary. "I'm counting on you, Jim. Think you can handle it?"

Remmer covered his lower lip with the upper and looked for a moment as if he were about to say no. "I'll do the best job I can."

"Good, I knew I could count on you. Most of it's routine. The tough stuff, maybe Dr. Phillips can get to tomorrow? Your job's simply to route it and keep damned close tabs on it."

"Got it." Remmer said, nodding. "Will that be all?"

"See you later, Jim."

"Thank you, Dr. Grant."

Grant then turned to Donald Carr. "So, Don, what do you think of Sybil's case? Has she made one?"

"Her work's usually . . . ahh . . ."

"I know, more complete, more everything, right."

Carr nodded. "Sorry, but I think it's patchy in parts." Now that Dean had let the cork out on his own assessment, the safe Carr did likewise, almost with an eagerness. Was it eagerness to please Dean? Or something else? Was there a rivalry that had developed between his and Kelso's M.E.s? Dean ran a hand across his freshly shaven face. He had put on a clean white shirt and was now putting together his dark blue tie, trying to get it right, as he spoke. "Still, Sybil Shanley's instincts are very good, excellent, in fact," he said in her defense.

"Perhaps, but you can't prosecute on instincts."

"No, no, you can't."

"I mean, I know that the cause of death in the cases she has taken time to itemize is asphyxiation—"

"Slow asphyxiation."

"Okay, slow . . . anyway, she's created a kind of what-if situation here."

"What-ifs are important in criminal forensics, my friend. Don't ever forget that."

Carr nodded noncommittally, as if feeling his way. "What is it you want me to say? That she has an airtight reason to suspect all these cases are related somehow, and that we've got a serial killer on our hands who has devised some excruciating means of torture and—"

"That's what she's talked herself into. I just wanted another opinion, based on what evidence she's collected."

"Based on this," he said, tapping the top file, "I'd have to say it's patchy at best."

"But she's convinced each case has the classic, characteristic signs of asphyxiation."

"I understand that, but a lot of those same characteristic signs can mean a lot of different things, Dr. Grant."

"Agreed. At least we know what to look for during the exhumation."

Carr frowned and shook his head but declined to say anything. Dean pressed him. "You have reservations about this exhumation?"

"What'll it prove? A body that's been in the grave for so long? It could just lead you astray."

"Depends on the condition of the body," said

Dean, eyeing Carr suspiciously now. He wanted something, but what? "Still, it hasn't been under earth so long as to make much difference, if we're careful. Ever exhume a body from a potter's field, Dr. Carr?"

He took in a great breath of air and shook his head. His eyes were on the carpeted floor. "No, no sir, I have not."

"Be surprised what a cadaver can tell you, pine boxes and dampness notwithstanding . . . sometimes. Other times, well . . . there's a certain amount of gamble involved."

"Truth be known, Dr. Grant, I've never attended an exhumation of any sort before. That's really the reason I'm here, sir."

"Oh? Well, no teacher like experience, Dr. Carr."

"Well, I'm game, Doctor."

"Good," said Dean, feeling more comfortable, believing that this was all that Carr wanted from their interview. "Best get moving then. I'll just tidy up a few things, grab my coat, leave word with my secretary, and I'll meet you, sir, at the elevator."

"Thank you, Dr. Grant. I appreciate the opportunity, and sorry if I can't agree one hundred percent with your Deputy M.E.'s workup here."

"No need for apologies, not when you give your honest opinion. See you outside."

In ten minutes they were on the elevator together.

"I assume you've seen a lot of exhumations," Carr said, by way of making conversation.

"Too many," Dean replied. "Frankly, they put me off my food for awhile. You, too, most likely. You look into the face of death all day long in a well-lit

71

lab like ours here and it's one thing. You stare into an unearthed box in the ground and it wells up at you, claws at your eyes and nose and worse, your mind. Takes a lot of stamina, Don.''

"I'll be all right," he said.

In forty minutes they were pulling up to the enormous graveyard on the outskirts of the city proper, some miles distant from the intersection of Pulaski and Interstate 294. Here unknowns shared space with felons and people shot dead by the city police, anyone unclaimed by family for proper burial with rites. A great number of suspected diseased felons and drug addicts were now incinerated, but the majority in Chicago were simply given a four-by-six square foot of real estate here in Mount Orchid Cemetery, popularly known as Boot Hill or the potter's field. It was older than all the surrounding suburbs, a cemetery with the ancient appearance of one found in rural Ireland, long ago bought up by the city for its continuing and pressing needs.

It wasn't well kept. Crabgrass enjoyed life here, as did moles, mice, and other vermin that burrowed in the ground. Grass grew wildly in patches that hadn't been mowed in months. Vines, weeds, and occasional wildflowers climbed over the city government-issue headstones which were mere markers, some with names, others with only numbers.

An ancient, gray fieldstone cottage, too small for one man to live comfortably in, sat like a squatting, headless gargoyle at the center of the field. The place had a dingy little brown sign with modern lettering on the door: Property of the City of Chicago. It had become the caretaker's tool shed, filled with mowers, rakes, shears, edgers, and assorted digging tools. The only tools without cobwebs upon them were those most put to use, digging tools. The caretaker didn't live on the grounds but he doubled as a grave digger, helping to keep abreast of the numbers. His wages were higher by far than city workers in comfortable, clean, and warm offices around the city. His dress and manner of speech as well as his habit of spitting every few seconds as if to get the dirt out of his lungs, marked him as a former railroad man. He wore coveralls of a vintage style, suspendered at the shoulder, pockets every few inches surrounding his waist, almost as many cubby holes in his outfit as Dean had vials in his bag.

Dean had left the Schletter specimens in capable hands at the lab for analysis. Most of the work was routine now, and with a few suggestions to his young assistant, he felt confident all would be well on that score. Meanwhile, here he was, with Carr in tow, walking across a graveyard without paths, over the graves of men, women, and children, to get to the group of doctors and uniformed officers ahead of them. A hearse had been allowed to drive in on a back road through a back fence to get as near as possible to the grave in question. The simple etiquette of not driving over graves was being observed due to the fact that so many important people were here today. Dean saw tire tracks about the field everywhere.

Dean and Carr were late, trying to make up the time by hustling, when they saw the caretaker who'd walked off from the exhuming party where Sybil was at the center. The caretaker was shaking his head, muttering, cursing under his breath like an old crone. "Never seen so much stupidity in one place . . . dogshit . . . dig up this one they say . . . do it, and whatcha thinkya got? Wrong-un!"

Dean knew the thick-necked, heavyset digger by name and called him over. "Mr. Gwinn, what's the problem? What's the hold up."

"They had us diggin' in the wrong place!"

"Wrong place?" Carr was flabbergasted, but Dean put up a hand to him, indicating he'd handle this.

"You have your records, Mr. Gwinn?"

"Damned straight I do, after the last time."

"It's happened before?" asked Carr.

"Go get your records, and we'll sort this out," said Dean.

Gwinn hustled after talking to Dean. He found his box of records with names and numbers, dates of burials and corresponding gravesite number. He also had a map with the site numbers of each individual buried. Whole sections of the map were filled, just as in a parking garage.

Now, together, they reached the confused group standing around an exasperated Sybil Shanley who was telling the other grave diggers to please just return the body of the dessicated remains of a woman to its resting place. In the 11:00 A.M. sun that bore down on the eyeless corpse, the brown jello clinging to the bones looked and smelled like bear shit. But rather than cover the corpse—the pine box having withered away to a splintered hull—the grave diggers were arguing with Sybil, with the cops, and with one another.

"Shut up, shut up!" shouted Gwinn when he returned.

74

Dean's eyes met Sybil's and she came to him, a bit shaken by the surprise of events. "It's not going well."

"So I see, but one thing's in your favor."

"Yeah, no one from Fowler's side showed up."

"Maybe they're just late, like Don and me."

"Hi, Don," she said, "I didn't know you'd be here, either of you." But Donald was staring fixedly at the corpse.

"Hey, what're friends for?" asked Dean. "And Don here could use the experience, wouldn't you agree?"

There was a strange edge to her voice, Dean had noticed, but he chalked it up to the harrowing situation. Beside them the caretaker, the diggers, and the cops were trying to sort out the picture. The diggers still shouting that they wanted overtime and that Gwinn of all people ought to understand that, since they'd been on a graveyard shift with bodies lined up since the day before when the final results of a gang fight had come rolling through the gates from three city hospitals. Nine gangland chiefs—hardly kids—were dead of gunshot wounds, their bodies left unclaimed.

"All right, you'll get overtime," shouted one of the cops.

"You don't know that," said Gwinn.

"Time and a half," said one of the diggers.

"Double time and half," said the other, "or we go now!"

"You know that takes a call to downtown, guys."

"Christ, let the assholes go," said the second cop. "We'll do the digging, but this time—"

"Whoa, partner, *we'll* do the digging?" asked the

first cop. "Nothing in the police academy or on my job description anywhere about grave digging."

Dean stepped in and silenced them all with his powerful voice and presence, "We're all going to dig in and get this job done! You city workers, you ever hear of a man named Harry Ernst?"

They stared at one another, and even Gwinn gulped and said, "We don't want no truck with ol' Harry. That big German bastard'll make life hell for us."

"He's a very good friend of mine," said Dean. "In fact, I married his niece. By the way, I'm Dr. Dean Grant, Medical Examiner for the City."

"You hear the man?" asked the cop who didn't like the notion of having to dig.

"And another of my best friends is Chief Kenneth Kelso, Chief Inspector with the police force," continued Dean, jabbing at this man.

The other cop said, "Okay, can we get on with this now?"

"Mr. Gwinn, have you located where the right grave is?" asked Sybil.

"It's here, the one beside. Tags got written down wrong, that's all . . . coulda' happen' to anybody."

Dean thought glumly over the sad fact it happened to *this* body.

Carr and Dean looked over Gwinn's shoulders and saw the error he indicated. "Suppose it's the grave to the left of her instead of the right?" asked Carr.

"Then we could be here till nightfall," said Dean.

"Are you sure, Mr. Gwinn?" said an exasperated Sybil.

"Yeah, it's got to be this one to the right."

76

"Okay, dig," ordered Dean and the men went to work.

"Kind of like a shell game out here, isn't it?" Sybil said, trying to dig some humor from the humorless situation. "Uh-oh," she added, making Dean look up.

The driver of the hearse from Gundersen's Funeral Home had come up on them, and hearing and understanding what was amiss, he said formally and with great practiced dignity, "I have observed the time it takes to exhume one body. I will return at mid-afternoon, at which time I'm sure the hearse and my services will be useful."

"That'll be fine," Dean told the man. "In the meantime, we'd like to come over to Gundersen's to see if he's put in those additions I've asked for."

"As you wish."

"Join me?" he asked Sybil.

"Right."

"Carr, maybe if you remained, these men will work a bit faster."

"Sure, not a problem."

Five

At Gundersen's the lighting wasn't close to perfect and the facilities were only so-so. The place met minimal state requirements in all its operation, and this appeared to apply to the amount of wattage in the bulbs. Dean was used to the morgue setting of a parlor's back room with its combination slab and sink, space-saving cabinets beneath for naptha, solvents, chemicals, the portable aspirators, and suction devices. And the endless supply of Perma-glow, the sickening pink fluid reminiscent of Pepto-Bismol that was used to inflate the body via the arteries, replacing the blood so recently flushed out and washed down the turrets of the table and out the grill on the floor. There were the requisite plastic gloves and plastic bags, containers and a porcelain scale. The place smelled of formaldehyde and a strange mix of odors that had accumulated over the years, out of dampness and darkness, blood and mildew.

In one corner was a portable machine on wheels

that pumped the Perma-glow into the cadavers. Using another switch on the machine, it reverted to a suction machine, vacuuming out the vital fluids. Plastic tubing snaked about the machine on two sides, the tubing looking like serpentine arms. Plastic tubing also coiled about well-anchored hookups along the lengthy table. In a sense the place had the atmosphere of its boss, the same feel toward the empty shells that passed through this car wash for human bodies. Gundersen was all business when he went to work back here, and to him the thing on the table may just as well be a sausage that required just the proper ingredients and stuffing. Dean didn't like Gundersen and he didn't fully believe anything the man had to say. In fact, Dean often felt he'd do better to do an autopsy in the street outside than in here with Gundersen carping about the body being the husk, the soul being the corn.

Gundersen was the type of mortician who'd failed medical school. He turned to undertaking as an alternative, motivated, Dean believed, by money more than anything else. Unable to hack it as a true doctor, he was what in olden times was called the hacker. Many a mortician was a would-be doctor; some were scavengers, Dean felt. An absolutely necessary breed, they were not as easily categorized as some might assume. Gundersen was a fat, jolly man with lots to be thankful for—or so he incessantly said. He was a self-proclaimed minister as well, using his parlor for congregations whenever no cadavers were about to muddle the Word. He laughed at anything. His eyes shone bright, but seemed insincere. His gestures seemed studied. He believed that the body, after death, was as wood cut from a tree, the soul long since departed with the life, and in this spirit he actually "ministered" to people who wept at the funerals he orchestrated so well.

"Purchasing all that equipment, Dr. Grant, isn't going to help the bereaved out there," said Gundersen now, pointing to the front, laughing as if it were truly a good joke on the high and mighty, and lately famous, Dr. Grant. "Nor's it going to bring a man's soul back to the vessel! Tract lighting, all right, it's comin', but all those other items . . ." He stopped to laugh again. "My, I priced them!"

"You do what you think's best, Mr. Gundersen, but your place comes up for review in two weeks, and proximity to the graveyard notwithstanding, we're not doing any more business with you, if we don't have an adequately equipped room. Last time, we were held up over the lack of a microscope! *And* because you have only one table! That's below standard. Minimal is two."

"Where's the room?"

"Knock out a wall!"

Dean took Sybil by the arm and they left. "We'll be back. Have the room free."

"How long?"

But Dean and Sybil were gone. Already it was nearing two and they hadn't eaten. "Let's get a bite," he suggested.

"Sure it's a good idea?"

"Something light, a salad maybe. I know a place nearby."

"Fine." She was curiously silent. Dean thought he knew the signs of anger when he saw them. She was angry with him. He remained silent, until they got to the restaurant and ordered and then he said over the checkered tablecloth in the Italian place, "What's bothering you, Sybil. What is it?"

"You, Dean, you and Carr."

"What's that supposed to mean?"

"You two are skeptical. All right, I can accept that. But did you bother to read my reports at all? No, you gave them to Carr to read."

Dean stared across at her, realizing that Remmer must've said something in passing to her. She must have telephoned in. Jim must have made some remark about Carr's having been there earlier and it led to this. "I see. Well, Don dropped in—"

"Just happened to drop in!"

"No, he came to ask if he could be in on the exhumation, and he seems to believe you may be onto something."

She took this in with the water she began to drain. "He concluded this from the reports?"

"That and last night's autopsy."

She shifted uncomfortably in her seat. "Then at least one person is on my side."

"I'm on your side, too, kiddo."

"I went against your wishes, hurt your ego and your friendship with Fowler."

"I have no friendship with Fowler, but as for my ego, I suppose for a while I did feel let down."

"Blind faith and obedience, huh, Dr. Grant? In the end, all male doctors are alike."

"You do understand, Sybil, that I have had my hands full, too. Now maybe the exhumation's not necessary, and maybe it is. Either way, I have not put a stop to it. Either way, I'm on your side in this, as in all fights. You see, I do have faith in you."

Her chin quivered a bit as if she might cry, but instead she managed a smile and said, "Blind faith?"

"I'm a bat working on radar."

"Just hoping not to fly into a mountain with me at the controls, right?"

"I trust your judgment, your skills, and your intuition, Sybil. After all, I trained you."

"Then why are we fighting?"

"We're not." The salads came, hers a huge chef's salad and his a Greek salad. "We're eating, breaking bread not heads. Enjoy."

They ate and drank in silence for a while when Sybil asked, "What if I'm wrong about the boy out in Boot Hill?"

"Then you're wrong. You think I never made a mistake?"

"I've never seen you make one."

He laughed and shook his head, "Come on, it took me *years* to catch on to that crazed nut that wanted to drown everybody and sit and watch them float. I denied the possibility while a friend of mine tried to open my eyes to it. Believe me, I'm more cautious now about denying anything . . . anything's possible. And when I begin to think otherwise, that nothing more horrible than the last could possibly occur, I pick up a newspaper and read about the latest and worst horror on the front page."

"Thanks . . . thanks, Dean."

"For what?"

"For being here when I need you."

It was dusk by the time they finally unearthed #129865.

The wind had picked up, taking on a strange feel as it licked about Dean's neck, lapped at Sybil's skirt, made a lung for Carr's pants-leg, after which it skimmed about the lonely death field, finally deciding to execute a full vortex that seemed to center on the open grave.

This sent up a whirling dervish out of the hole. The poor light only added to the intense moment when the grave diggers pried loose the coffin lid, not about to raise the box from its resting place until a light was shone on the face to prove it was at least close to being the body in question. They'd made the error of lifting out two other rotting pine wood boxes already and had had to replace them.

Dean did not in the least blame them for their grumbling which remained mostly between them. They spoke like churlish old witches around a boiling pot down in the hole. "Haven't worked this fuckin' hard since boot camp."

"You oughta' come over ta' my place any Saturday."

"Your place, that pigsty?"

"No worse than yours."

"My Sally cleans up after herself, 'least."

"'Sat right, well—"

"Pop it!" shouted one of the cops, his clothes filthy

from having helped with the digging.

"Can it, you mean, don't cha?"

"I mean get the damned lid off, and damn it, Gwinn, if this isn't the right stiff, I'm arresting you for . . . for idiocy!"

The lid came off willingly, as if pushed by the gases inside. Inside, too, was the body of a male with dirty brown hair. Even from where Dean stood, he could see that it was a full, round, rather featureless face, like a blank, that of a youth who had not been given time to form character lines, save for a scar over his temple, a knife slit along the ear. Dean made instant and immediate mental notes.

A full head of hair, outer epidermal layer a clay brown, eyeless, the cadaver in the box was raised and finally transported by the motley crew of pallbearers in reverse, to the hearse. In between this unearthing, there had been yet another wrongly raised. Everyone's nerves were on edge and Dean did not have to tell Sybil that another reason he hated exhumations was the carelessness with which they were handled in the instance of an unclaimed body. It made Sybil wonder how many in this field were unclaimed and how many simply lost.

Now they were back at Gundersen's, the body hefted upon the slab. Donald Carr looked ten years older by this time, but he was hanging in. Sybil and Dean stood over the body and Dean put out a micro tape recorder with great range, turned it on, and after announcing themselves and the purpose for the exhumation on the John Doe, they got their hands dirty.

The body'd been handled carelessly both on burial

and now by the diggers. The sandy hair which had continued to grow after death was caked with dirt which Sybil had rinsed out in a basin, pouring the sediment into a flask and labeling it. She also took several strands of the dead man's hair, tucked these into a clear plastic envelope and labeled it.

Dean, as was his nature and as they'd agreed, took charge at this point. It would look better on record this way. Sybil knew he was right.

The autopsy began, as always with Dean, with a search of the exterior. His eyes told him a great deal. He spoke his thoughts for the recorder.

"No eyeballs to show bulging or blood spots. But tongue's protrusion, while most certainly due to gas pressure, may also indicate cause of death as asphyxial in nature."

Then he suddenly said to Sybil, "Look here, what do you see, Dr. Shanley? Dr. Carr? Look closely."

Carr and Sybil saw only the chest, discolored to a greenish yellow with brown centers coming slowly together to soon cover the entire body. "What do you see?" Dean almost shouted.

Carr pointed to the sternum and said, "Darkening . . . mapping out of superficial veins . . . that's all."

"Light in here stinks," complained Dean. "You, Officer Wyatt, you have a powerful flashlight in your squad car?"

"Sure."

"Get it."

"Right away, Doc."

Dean turned back to Sybil and asked again, "What do you see, Sybil?"

"Syanosis," she replied quietly, as if pronouncing a cure. Sybil ran something dartlike through her mind, and then seemed to tuck it away for future reference.

"I don't see it," said Carr.

Sybil pointed with gloved fingers to the left cheek, high, below the eye socket, and then traced a line down to the neck where the aqua blue of syanosis was more prominent.

"Could be," Carr muttered, unsure still. "But then why wouldn't the doctors at Cook have noticed?"

"Sometimes the blue rises out of the skin long after. They just didn't stay on it long enough," said Dean.

"But this isn't enough to prove—"

"The light!" shouted Dean, when the officer returned with the long tube already lit. "Now observe," Dean told Carr, just as Sybil saw what he meant.

"Obscure but definite pinpoint hemorrhages freckling the neck, chest, and shoulders."

Sybil moved in with a minute scalpel and scraped the interior of the dead man's mouth with it. She deposited the matter caught on the blade onto a slide. Carr added fixative and a top. This was labeled and put aside. She then did the same for the nose. Dean could see from her expression that she was confident the sample she'd just taken was the blood-tinged mucous typically ejected in an airless agony.

Externally, the man lying dead before them on Gundersen's table exhibited a condition as typically asphyxial as that of the woman on Sybil's table the night before; perhaps even more since time had given the body a chance to respond to the assault it had endured. Most noticeably, internal bleeding from tiny burst arteries filled the microscopic cavities hidden by the flush of life even days after death. But given time, the discoloration, like bad fruit on a kitchen table for too long, reared itself and spread. Not even embalmers like Gundersen could eradicate it completely. It was a certain sign of death due to lack of oxygen.

But Dean wanted more evidence still before pronouncing the cause of death. Pronouncing it aloud in Sybil's and Carr's presence might make it official, and anything further they might do to John Doe superfluous. But it also made Dean feel suddenly queasy, as if some old wound had split open to suddenly squirm, stir, and throb. Around them the air stirred and throbbed with a near palpable and pyschic thought they all shared at once, a not very pretty thought co-mingling with the facts before them.

Dean's hands worked over the corpse now with fleet, deft ability of the sort Don Carr loved to watch. Carr believed that he could never be as good as Dean Grant, whose hands played over the corpse like those of a master pianist over the keys. Satisfied there were no exterior wounds or abrasions great enough to cause death, Dean made the first long cut from sternum to waist, and the second straight across the pectoralis area, easily done since the body had been autopsied by Dr. Fowler's pathology lab at Cook. The stitch work was adequate, Dean observed. Next, the two square upper flaps were scrolled to the armpits and fastened there. In a matter of a few minutes, Dean had hold of the lungs and he massaged each in his hands. "Take a biopsy here," he said, slicing off a minute piece, handing it to Sybil who deposited it in a vial. "Left lung," he said and they repeated the operation. Carr saw how well they worked together, that they were on the same wavelength.

"No way to tell how much blood was in the lungs."

"Too much according to Fowler's autopsy," said Sybil.

"And the right side of the heart?"

"Ditto."

Dean raised up, stretched, and looked at the skull. "They didn't bother to look at the brain, I see."

"No," she replied. "Why bother when they already knew the cause of death, right?"

"Gotcha."

"One look and they'd have seen subcutaneous hemorrhages there."

"Or so we might assume from what we've seen here and now."

"Are we finished?" asked Carr.

"Not quite. I'd like a look at the larynx," said Dean who already had his hands on it, his arm extended upward through the chest cavity. "Throat next," continued Dean, his fingers searching and recording. "All seems intact. Hyoid bone intact. Open it up, will you, Sybil?"

Fowler's crew hadn't bothered with the throat, and perhaps understandably so. There were no ligature marks, no bruises. Sybil had it open for inspection before Dean had wiped his hands.

"How's it look to you, Dr. Carr?"

"Intact . . . some hemorrhaging."

"But not concentrated to the left where the thumbs of most murderers are applied," said Dean.

"Shall we remove the skull cap, Doctors? Or are we all satisfied at what we will inevitably find there?"

"Blood deposits left behind when the brain was filled with it during oxygen starvation," said Sybil. She had already seen this condition three times recently.

"We're agreed," said Carr, a bit of reluctance seeping through.

Dean looked up at him. "You're sure, Dr. Carr?"

"Sure, yes."

Slitting a piece of the larynx for the lab, Dean continued. "I'd say we're done, then. We'll continue in the lab after tests have been run." He cut off the recorder. "We've got to make this as airtight a case as possible, Sybil."

"Understood, Dean."

"On the surface, kiddo, you're batting a thousand. I admit, I was skeptical until I saw the face and neck. Almost makes you wish you'd been wrong after all, doesn't it?"

"No, I haven't had time to look at it that way."

"Carr, what do you think?"

"I'll hold judgment for the tests."

"Chicken," said Sybil.

"I wish you'd be more cautious, Sybil," said Dean.

The cops had been relieved by a second duo, and now these men were tired. Gundersen was to see to the return of the John Doe to the cemetery and burial the following morning. Dean thanked the officer with the light, and as he was returning it, the policeman spoke to his partner, asking him to come closer for a look at the stiff on the table. The other man didn't want any part of it, but his partner urged him on.

"Look good. Couldn't that be the one on that artist's sketch, wanted for robbing the 7-Eleven on Grand and Ogden?"

"Damn," said the other, "could be."

"Could be just a fluke likeness, but . . ."

"You think you know somebody that can ID this guy?"

"If it's the kid we're talking about, his name's Jory Bemis; bad news kid, in and out of detention homes, got a sister who put out a missing person's on him a few days ago. She waited so long 'cause normally Jory'd turn up, she was sure."

"Turned up, all right," said the other cop.

"Get her down here to make the ID," said Grant, "and then maybe we can find his murderer."

"Murdered, doc?"

"How?" asked the other one.

"Asphyxiated."

Sybil and Carr left out the back, taking the sample cases with them. Dean wanted to wait around to see if the sister could be located and brought there. In the meantime, he found a telephone and called Chief Ken Kelso.

With Kelso on the line, Dean told of his bizarre day, and he voiced his and Sybil's darkest suspicion: that there was a psycho of the worst sort committing multiple murder in Kelso's city.

"Worst sort, Dean?"

"The sort that enjoy themselves immensely. The kind that likes to watch another human being struggle and suffer."

"You suspect asphyxiation in these cases. How long can a guy suffer if he's asphyxiated?"

"Ken, I suspect, based on the number of indicators and the depth of destroyed tissue in some of these cases, the guy . . . the guy doing the killing doesn't just suffocate these people, that he *very* slowly suffocates them, toys with them."

"Christ help us."

"Then you believe me?"

"I learned long ago to heed you, my friend, and with the added backing given this one by Sybil—"

"Sybil saw this long before me."

"She's come along quite well, hasn't she?"

"The best."

"Trained by the best."

Dean asked if Kelso'd join him for when the dead boy's supposed sister arrived. Kelso did so unhesitatingly.

Outside Gundersen's Sybil and Don Carr got into her car. She'd promised him a lift back to the lab, to home, or to a bar. "Your choice," she had said.

Carr smiled for the first time all day. He wasn't usually so glum. Must be the exhumations, she reasoned. He'd bargained for one, but had gotten three. Like a man who is suddenly told his wife's had triplets, Don was stunned. And perhaps he was also stunned over the notion that there was, somewhere out there in the dark three million Chicago arteries, a killer bent on slowly taking the breath away from his victims for no sane reason, a serial killer that thrived on the dying breath of others.

The thought was indeed chilling and the questions legion. *Why* was seldom tantamount to understanding an insane killer bent on destruction for the sake of destruction. The sane mind cried out for motivation, even if a sick motivation. The easiest catchword, insanity, didn't cover it in such bizarre cases. Very often the killer had worked out some fabric of whys and wherefores, blessing and rewards and punishments that fed his aberrant fever. Was there anything remotely like this at work in the mind of this horrible excuse for a man. A man who locked people into a death chamber both icy and mind-numbing, to watch them succumb to a death as painful and pathetic as that of a disease victim? She shuddered in her seat at the thought of a bubble chamber somewhere, a wizened, ugly man at the controls reducing the oxygen level a smidge at a time, torturing his captive with details of what was to come next.

Carr placed a hand on her shoulder and said, "You all right?"

"Yeah, as well as can be expected."

"You have to get these specimens back tonight to the lab?"

"I do. I mean, I planned to, yes, and to get you back."

"Why not tomorrow? It's been a long and trying day."

"Why? What do you propose?"

"I thought we might have dinner, get to know one

93

another better."

"Why, Don?"

"I've been watching you all day. You're good, better'n I'll ever be and—"

"Whoa-up there, cowboy," she said, "that's a nice thing to say, but wrong. You've got to give yourself time and a chance. Watching Dean work, now wasn't that something?"

"Yeah, really."

"I like you well enough, Don, but if you don't mind, a little more confidence in yourself, a little less kowtowing to guys like Kelso, and maybe I could really like you."

"Kowtowing?"

"You know what I mean."

"But damn it, the system stinks and now—" He stopped himself.

"Now what?" she asked.

"Forget it, never mind. Look, can't the tests wait? How much sleep have you had in the last two days?"

"Not enough, I grant you."

"You should go easier on yourself. Suppose you came up ill?"

"All right, I'll lighten up."

"When you do, I'd like to be around."

She put a hand up to cover his hand on her shoulder. It felt good to hold onto his warm, strong hand after working on dead flesh all day. "I know a place not far from my apartment where we could get some wine and a bite, if you're really interested."

"Sounds great."

Sybil had never thought of Don Carr in a romantic light. She regarded him now. Beneath the glasses and the innocence, there was a strong, good, and warm man. His eyes were a sincere blue, the color of robin's eggs. The face was squared at the jaw, flaring at the cheeks, James Dean at thirty-five with that characteristic wild and sandy hair with a life of its own. Before, she'd allowed his officiousness and his chauvinism to color her impression of him. Now, in the dark, sitting close by, his hand still in hers, he was suddenly attractive and available, and the tests could cool in her freezer at home as easily as at the lab after all.

Six

It was the search that was the least exciting part of the evening. He stalked neighborhood shelters, bus stops, sometimes a church stoop where someone was huddled against the night. Soup kitchens, all-night shelters, and the occasional emergency shelter all provided fodder for his needs. Tonight he was at the Salvation Army's shelter for the homeless. He went about the cots and looked from one small staked out territory to another. He required someone alone. Male, female, it didn't matter. Age didn't much matter either, although he was developing and testing a theory that the younger his victim, the more potent and powerful the transfer of energies when he breathed them into his own body at the moment of release, when they gave up their dying breath.

There was a flinty, smelly old man who raised his hand out toward him as if he recognized him from some distant past. Malinowski moved on. The room was stuffy and it smelled of perspiration and aged rags and bedclothes. Box springs whined like stricken animals. Children cried softly.

His eyes scanned the people for that special one, that one who would go willingly with him. He had had prostitutes, young men barely out of their teens, homos—it mattered little enough to him about their sexual proclivities—so long as they were breathing.

There was a dirty-faced boy sitting alone, but as Malinowski approached him, an older man joined the boy. He went on, sifting through the human marketplace until his eyes fell on a woman, perhaps in her early thirties or younger. Life, obviously, had not been kind to her. She had stringy blonde hair and her face was drawn tight about the bones, the nose a mere beak, the eyes darting in a frightened bird way. She sat against a wall on a cot, huddled and silent, staring and thinking and smoking.

Malinowski went to her, taking off his hat and asking her name.

"Who're you?" she wanted to know.

"My name is Malinowski."

"You one of the shelter people?"

"They know me. They know I come to help when I can. Tell me, do you eat good here?"

"Eat good?" She made a gesture of gagging, placing her bony index finger down her throat.

"You want to eat good?"

"What do you want? Me to spread for you, or you want head? How much you willing to pay?"

"No, I want nothing from you. I want to give . . . to give you something, something to eat."

"Like what?"

"Steak . . . when's the last time you had good red meat?"

98

"Red meat, you want something all right."

"I'm a butcher, and you have no idea how much gets wasted each month, right out my back door. I give it to you *for one thing.*"

"Now we get to cases. What do you want in return?"

"Just that you dine with me. I only wish you to spend time with me. I am a lonely man, but no sex, I swear it."

"You're a liar, but I've slept with worse. All right, Malinowski, take me home . . . I'm yours."

Not yet, but soon, he thought.

Later, in the apartment over the butcher shop, she was beginning to believe he was for real. Malinowski, who asked to be called Louie, opened his freezer to reveal hundreds of cuts of prime meat, one of which he selected and placed in the microwave on defrost. He then pan-fried it for her, saying repeatedly, "All for you, dear . . . all for you."

"Aren't you having any?" she asked.

Malinowski was a big man, heavy and a bit overweight even for his size. He patted his stomach and said, "Doctor's orders, but I join you for wine."

"My name's Cleopatra," she said with a shrug.

"Really?" He laughed lightly. "Cleopatra."

"What's so funny?"

"Nothing, really, just that . . . well, I've never known anyone by that name. It's an . . . an interesting name."

"Liar!"

"Oh, but it is—"

"Perfectly awful name. Friends call me, Cloe, for short."

"You have a lot of friends?"

She frowned. "What's a friend? Come right down to it, no, not really. That's why you found me in that shelter." She stopped talking long enough to finish chewing and swallow. He watched the action of the mouth as the meat went round about, up and down with the grinding of her crooked teeth. Her large lips pursed at the moments before swallowing, almost as if throwing him a kiss, but not quite.

Malinowski calmly poured wine down his own throat, his thoughts on what was to come. He tipped his glass in her direction, and this made her lift hers and they toasted nothing in particular with each of their mouths forming uncertain, half smiles. "You are very pretty," he told her.

She blushed and shrugged. Malinowski sipped more wine while she continued to chew and swallow her last meal. The meat was laced with sedatives, enough to subdue her. He really didn't care to fight her, disfigure or hurt her, or to be hurt himself. He didn't care for scratching and biting and struggling, all adding up to a disturbance that could bring neighbors. He merely wished to have her body downstairs and placed neatly in the bag, hanging beside the sides of beef and pork, where she'd die of suffocation long before she would die of cold. He'd already preset the controls to bring the temperature up above 35°C—long enough to keep her alive, brief enough so as to have no spoiled meat on his hands. Mustn't have his victim dying prematurely of prolonged exposure to cold; hypothermia would only spoil the opportunity he faced of reaching his ultimate goal. Inside his stomach, at the back of the rectus abdominus, or belly button, and all along his spine, there was a tingling sensation aroused by the anticipation of it all. This part he liked.

She drained another glass of wine, and so did he. He watched her become animated, when she smiled the dire look in her eyes left her. In a moment, still chewing a lump of the steak in her mouth, choking and spitting it up, she slumped over the table and was silent.

He left the meat, dishes, and wine sitting out, took her in his arms, cradling her like a baby, and made his way down to the store. No one had seen her come in with Malinowski, nor leave with him from the shelter. He'd gotten her to admit she had no one in the city. No one would miss her.

Knowing every inch of the shop. Malinowski didn't need to turn on a light, and inside the huge freezer, the light came on automatically with the opening of the door. There were no windows here, no chance for prying eyes or curious neighbors wondering about lights in a closed butcher shop. Here, too, the cold worked to de-sensitize both victim and killer for their mutual benefit: she to feel nothing, and he to reach into that higher realm of being he sought so desperately.

He stripped her nude, saving the clothing to replace later when he must discard the carcass. For that was what she'd become, just another carcass. God, he was about to liberate this wretched soul from her carcass. He removed her faded blouse and dingy, washed-out bra and panties, tossing it all aside, unaware that in one hand she clutched a matchbook. The effect of his touch against her bare skin, the cold

101

that made her shiver, and the fear that filled her brain, made her fight the drug that held her captive to weakness and uncaring.

"Wa-lla yew dew-n? Wadder yew doin'?" she whimpered weakly, unable to form words coherently, or to use her limbs in any but random gestures of self-defense. She sensed danger, sensed the cold, and would do so until the cold and the lack of oxygen claimed her totally.

He removed her faded blouse and dingy, washed-out bra and panties, tossing it all aside, unaware that in one hand she clutched a matchbook—all in her mind? Or had that just played out in real life and real time? She squeezed the matchbook. It felt real. She tightened her grip on it and held fast.

A butcher's table awaited her. Atop it lay an enormous, thick-skinned cellophane bag, the zipper running the entire length its most prominent feature. The shiny, metal zipper appeared two inches wide and four or five feet long with a clasp at the top where it locked. Another odd feature of the bag was the strap atop it, dangling now over the edge of the butcher's table. This strap was like the straps from which dangled the forest of meat here in the dark "oz" she'd discovered.

"No, no, no," she whimpered repeatedly, but could not be sure the words were getting out of her. Her stomach turned over and she felt the pain of retching.

Big bag, unraveled, laid out and waiting, open and unzipped, prepared earlier for her. She felt weightless. He lifted her right onto the table and into the body-length, clear polyethylene bag. Her body felt as hard as the tabletop, rigid with the cold, and her breathing was coming hard. And he was looking down over her . . . enticed, enthused, excited, and terrifyingly pleased. For a moment he placed his mouth over hers, not in a kiss, but in a strange gesture of sucking at her breath, squeezing her cheeks as he did so. He whispered some sort of loving words into her ear just before she heard the *zrip-rip-rip* of the zipper being raised up and up.

He shivered at the finish, like a young boy with his first sexual encounter, and then he hastily finished sealing her into the bag, locking the hasp at the top.

Over the stainless steel table hung a thick cable, and on it a pulley on a universal joint. He snatched at this and it brought forward a huge hook. Sitting her upright, and seeing her eyes fix onto the hook, he connected bag and hook and pressing the automatic pulley once again, she was lifted and moved off.

Her mind began screaming inside her skull, inside the bag. She had no doubt any longer: the nightmare was real. Her true scream came out as a muffled roar and could not be heard beyond the freezer. The automatic pulley apparatus moved her young, frail body into the next holding position, and when it came to an abrupt stop, the whine of the mechanism suddenly silent, she was between an enormous slab of bacon on one side and a beef carcass on the other.

Malinowski did his best to ignore the clawing and screaming coming from inside the body bag. He went to the next step in his program, going to a nearby hook on the wall and taking down a brown clipboard with a pencil attached. He then pulled up a stool before the dying woman and sat before her there in the bag and began jotting down notes. He mostly just watched, though, for it fascinated him to watch the writhing, the clawing, the gasping of the helpless a few inches from him as if she were drowning in a sea of perspiration, body fluids, and exhalations. Already, the bag was frosting over on the outside and steamy inside, due to the variations in temperature and the exhaled breath in the bag. Once it reached a certain cloudiness, and the occupant became subdued from lack of oxygen and strength, he'd unlock the hasp, slip it open a crack at a time, peek in, and view the perspiration and damp, the plastered hair against the scalp. At this time, he'd allow in enough oxygen to keep her alive a little longer. At this same time, he'd inhale some of the so-called bad air from the bag, filling his brain with her excretions in order to reach completely the high he sought. Soon now . . . soon he'd open it up, when she was at her weakest. But the waiting was difficult now that he could see so little of her through the haze and film covering the bag. He wiped away at the condensation and frost outside, but could do nothing about that on the inside.

He wanted to open it now, but he knew timing was everything in this. Too soon and she'd be clawing at his eyes. Too late, and she'd be dead. A happy median was called for. He must wait.

The bag remained still. She'd put up only a moderate fight. She likely wouldn't last the night. No heart, he thought. How disappointing Cloe was proving.

Unable to wait a moment longer, he slipped the zipper down a bit, allowing some of her out, some oxygen in. Just enough oxygen to keep her alive . . . easy, easy. She looked like a trapped bird, drained and soaked with perspiring. He sucked at the slit he had created, filling his brain with a heady mixture made up primarily of her CO_2. Already, he was feeling a bit woozy on the stuff, and inside the bag, in her fluttering eyes, the dark centers rolling back, he could see dancing little figures, galaxies, misty moors, and fire. He even heard the flames licking and his cheek whiskers were singed! All before he realized that the little crackling noise had been the striking of a match. The fire was real!

She'd lit a match and then a book of matches, pushing it through to his sucking lips, burning away the gift of oxygen he had given her in an instant of retaliation! *Bitch!* He shot the zipper back to its hasp and shut her off with the burning matchbook inside where it had fallen to her toes. With his hands, from outside, he crushed the fire against her bare foot and it was out. From inside he could hear her coughing and choking. She'd been playing possum until the moment he opened the bag.

Perhaps he'd misjudged her after all; perhaps she would provide him with more excitement than he had expected; perhaps she would last the night. But next time, before he dared open the bag again, he'd give her plenty of time to expire; all the way to the point of utter weakness and helplessness. He really didn't care for fighting and biting and kicking and clawing and screaming. He derived no pleasure from such things.

He got back onto his stool after he shut off the fire inside the bag. He jotted down the special occurrence just as it had happened. He filled in some blanks on the form he had made for the work. Then he sat back to watch some more.

He knew what she was going through, knew it intimately. He'd been the guinea pig once himself. He knew just how soon the roaring in her ears would begin, the loss of sight, discoloration of the face, blocking of the blood vessels, and unconsciousness. He would normally then slip down the zipper, allowing his victim to come around so he could do it all over again.

He knew of the experiment intimately because his father had punished him in just such a way years before, locking him into a freezer. How old had he been, he tried to recall, how young when it started. All he knew for sure was the utter lack of sensations. The complete dark, the complete unfeeling, the whole of nothingness when his father would rob him of his breath. It had been no miracle that he had survived his childhood; the murder had saved him. For when his father killed his mother, he was at last free of his father.

Now he was the one in control, and never again would he be manipulated in the manner of his victims. Twisted? he asked himself as he stared into the writhing form inside the polyethylene bag. Maybe, but not so twisted as his victims.

In fact, Cloe was twisting about at the moment like an eel caught on a hook, wrapping herself round and round, striking out uselessly at the bag which held fast. The bag was so constructed as to withstand much more pressure than she could ever hope to apply. He smirked at her useless battle where it raged inside the

106

bag. She'd grow weaker and weaker still until she'd become the pathetic, little carcass he sought, and nothing more. All else, all that was of any use, *coming from inside her,* would join with him to enlarge his power, strengthen him, and keep him.

Meanwhile, so others might understand, and even follow by example, he kept detailed records of his actions and his victim's reactions. But his records were in fact a homage to his gods, detailing his complete conversion to them, and how, in the end, he converted the internal gases of his various victims into brain food and fuel for his body and soul. It was the record of a symbiotic relationship. They gave to him, and he gave them a better life, a life joined with his own, each strengthening and elongating the other, for he was now convinced that he could live forever, a vampire that fed on the exhalations of his victims.

And why not?

She continues now a snakelike twisting inside the bag, he wrote, continuing his journal of details on the experiment. *Most enjoyable to see. She's at the bag with her nails, ripping them on the inside of the zipper. She is fading fast after this and I'm so excited by her that I almost forgot to save her for one more time.*

He put aside the pencil and clipboard once again and got down off the stool. He went to the bag and unlocked the hasp. He just opened it an inch, enough to inhale her gases. He shivered with every nerve ending. She was subdued, yet alive; he was in complete, utter control of another life. Control. He wanted to enjoy her till morning, easing off on the asphyxiation just enough to keep her going; he wished to come back to the well again and again, fill himself, and then and only then, would he allow her death. Somewhere—perhaps from his own lips—he heard the words, "That he may smother me with kisses."

Malinowski was no longer Malinowski. No longer the butcher in back of a failing butcher shop, he was no longer just mortal. Using the dying breath of the woman in the bag, he had reached a mental state of anoxia and anoxaemia, a dangerous deficiency of oxygen in the tissues, and a deficiency of oxygen in the blood. This simulated the death of his partner in the bag. It brought on asphyxic symptoms: buzzing of the head, muscular inco-ordination, deterioration of vision, vertigo, blackouts, sweating, unstable emotions, loss of judgment, and beautiful hallucinations. He saw things scurrying all about out of the corners of his eyes. He saw as if he had more than two eyes. He saw dark and powerful shadows looming over him, shadows that liked him, the shadows of powerful beings that infused him with power.

He had self-induced his own carbon dioxide trance through CO_2 intoxication. He was now a visionary, a mystic experiencing mystical sights and sounds and smells. His visions even had an odor, the odor of meat and blood. His visions spewed forth hundreds, thousands, millions of words, as if a dam had burst between one dimension and another, when unintelligible ringing and gibberish was suddenly understandable.

Malinowski remained in this state for most of the night until his own oxygen-starved brain and tissues were revived. When he came to, around 3:00 A.M., he was bitterly disappointed, as always to find himself cold and shivering still inside the damned freezer surrounded by carcasses, many and various in size and shape and origin. Disappointed that the enormous shadow beings hadn't taken him with them when they left.

Disappointed, too, because he must give thought to this world and pressing concerns. It would be daylight before he could fully function again. The bodies in the shop were piling up. He'd have to clear them out some way, some how . . . tomorrow for certain.

Seven

Seven

Dean preferred waiting with the corpse to waiting with Gundersen, and as he awaited Kelso's arrival, he considered the corpse on the table. This "thing" was believed to be surrounded by a sacred and yet dangerous contagion in the past. This especially so to friends, relatives, and mourners, or anyone who had physically approached or dared touch it, for instance a coroner. Such people were shunned until they had ceremonially purified themselves—and a good thing, too, in ancient societies, especially in tropical regions. Little wonder that attendants, pallbearers and the like were a class apart in such places as Egypt and India, where a man like himself would be despised as an untouchable, no matter his training. For not only was the physical body contaminated by the dead, but also the spiritual self.

The dead like # 129865, a young man named Jory, were believed to emanate a highly potent psychic aura that resided in the body itself. Corpses therefore had to be ritually turned over to the elements of earth, fire, or water, or given over to birds and animals to pick clean. Yet witches, sorcerers, magicians, and shamans the world over resorted to human cadavers for the success of their sabbats, at black mass, and in necromania. The fat of dead men, the charred bones of felons, the fingers and toes of dead children to stop the spread of an ulcer, to stew into a powerful aphrodisiac, all of this was once "science." And today, a corpse was just a corpse, the most useless of materials on the face of the planet. Except in the case when modern science was allowed to work its miracles: organ and tissue transfer. Snatching life from death. And most recently, improving the quality of life via the earlier discarded, often incinerated fetal tissue.

The cop named Wyatt and his partner returned with a thin, washed-out woman who looked like a model for an Andrew Wyeth painting: mousey, frail-boned, despondent expression of fear and pain. A contradiction, she was both easily hurt and long on endurance and acceptance. Dean saw that she shivered beneath her cloth jacket as she neared the remains under the sheet on Gundersen's slab. Conditions for the occasion were horrendous.

She raised a hand to her lips, half expectant, half denial that the thing lying stretched before her was her missing brother. She seemed totally unaware of Dean's presence, or his eyes that were riveted to her. Dean fixed on her for a dual reason. He watched her for her reaction, in order to verify her story on the one hand, and to help her should she need it, on the other. She'd obviously braced herself for the worst, but her knees buckled anyway and Dean grabbed her along with Wyatt. They took her out to a settee near the entrance. Gundersen's office was locked tight, even against his own son who was minding the store tonight. Wyatt shook his head over the young woman and said, "Looks like an ID, huh?"

"Yeah, but she has to say so," replied Dean.

Ken Kelso then stepped in, taking in the situation at a glance. "This the dead kid's sister?"

"Appears so. She fainted."

"Can't say as I blame her," said Wyatt. "Thank God she didn't look beneath the sheet."

"What's her name?" asked Kelso who took her hand in his and began patting it and rubbing heat into it. "She's cold."

"Bemis, Janet Bemis," said Wyatt, a thin, good-looking man in his uniform. "Brother was Jory Bemis."

"Punk kid with a sheet longer'n my arm," said Kelso. "Any number of people might've iced him."

"We've established the guy was asphyxiated, Ken, in a horrible, agonizingly slow way. Multiple signs, fairly certain it could have a connection to others who've died in a like manner."

"Sybil tried to warn me, but I wasn't buying it."

"Me either at first. Maybe we just didn't want to believe it, because now that we do it seems we've brought it into existence."

"Getting superstitious in your old age, Dino?"

"Older I get, the more validity I find in old superstitions. Don't ask me why."

Janet Bemis was coming around. The three men fawned over her until she was sitting up, crying.

"Are you absolutely certain it's Jory?" asked Kelso

113

in his kindest voice.

"It's him all right."

"How . . . how can you be certain?"

"Scar over his eye. I . . . I give it to him. Cut on his ear, that come in a fight with a drug dealer he was once mixed up with."

"That seals it for us," said Kelso. "You want to have the body shipped to a funeral home near your place, Miss Bemis?"

"Can't afford it. You just put him in the ground. I just had to know. Some ways maybe it's best this way. I . . . I can get on with my own life now."

Wyatt led her out, telling her that the department could raise the money to bury Jory. She turned and stared at Kelso and said, "No, nobody's to do nothing for Jory. He never did anything for anybody in his life, except get little kids hooked on drugs. No, don't you all waste a dime on him. He was trash all his life. He's just that now." She rushed away.

"I'll get her address and later sometime we'll talk to her about Jory's hangouts, his latest friends, where he might've been the night he was killed."

"Maybe Jory can do more good in death than he did in life. Who knows? There's a tavern down the road, Ken. Let's have a nightcap."

"Sounds good. We can do some catching up."

"My thoughts exactly."

Together, Dean and Ken Kelso left Jory Bemis's corpse to Gundersen's people. In the cool night air, Dean took in a great breath, filling his brain with oxygen in as pure a state as he might expect in Chicago. As he did so, he heard Kelso's lighter flick open. Kelso had taken up cigars again, despite the

114

nagging Dean had given him about the nasty habit. Once he lit up, and they walked toward the neon sign down the road, Kelso said, "Dino, do you really think this Jory Bemis creep is worth Sybil's job?"

"You heard about Fowler's concern in all this, huh?"

"Fowler, yeah, and all the mix up out at the digs. Doesn't set well, making the department look like the Keystone Cops."

"Hey, it isn't exactly front page news."

"It is when you get involved. You seen the evening rags?"

"No, no I haven't."

"Seems Carr shot his mouth off to a reporter who came by to see what was up."

"Came by the cemetery?" Dean figured it must've occurred when he and Sybil were at Gundersen's or to lunch.

"Came by the cemetery, yes," replied Kelso, flicking the cigar, puffing. "Came by with a camera and a notepad."

"Sonofabitch."

"Who, the reporter, or Carr?"

"Fowler, damn it."

"Fowler, huh?"

"He didn't bother to show up because he decided to send a reporter by instead. Damn him."

"What does he hope to gain?"

"Embarrass the M.E.'s Office. Force my hand, I suppose."

Kelso laughed outside the bar where they now stood.

"What's so damned funny?"

115

"Funny? No, not funny," he said, getting control. "Just that I've never known anyone to force your hand, at least not politically."

"We're at a sensitive impasse with this new direction, Ken. After all these years, finally we've got a truly independent office, and it's still not independent because jackals like Fowler are always nipping away at it."

"True. So, what're you going to do? Back off? Not likely."

Dean pushed through the door, saying, "I'm going to have a drink."

Kelso ordered a whiskey neat, Dean a Scotch. He was going through a Scotch phase. They found a table near the rear, the regulars staring fixedly at them. Kelso, used to being stared at in such places, ignored this.

"I can't believe Carr talked to the press."

Kelso shrugged. "I plan to bounce him around about it, but you know how persistent the press guys can be, and he's not been in this game as long as you and Sybil."

Then it hit Dean. "Did you ask Carr to spot us on this exhumation, Ken?"

Kelso drained his glass. "I did."

"Why?"

"You know damned well why."

"Why?"

"We're interested."

"That's *it*, that's all of it?"

"You getting paranoid now that you're over at Wabash all by your lonesome, Dean, you and Sybil and your army of—"

116

"Listen, Ken, since when do you sneak around with me?"

"I didn't order Carr on the autopsy. I just told him he could learn a lot from you and Sybil. I didn't sic him on you for Fowler's sake."

"Then who did?"

"Same prick that sent the reporter. Fowler."

Dean dropped his gaze. "Sorry, Ken. It's been a grueling two days. First the business out in Hammond, and now this."

"How're things going with the Hammond shit?"

"Don't know. Haven't checked in with the lab, and don't plan to until tomorrow. I have to check in with Jackie."

"Smart move. Been awhile since I saw my lady, too."

"Anything on the whereabouts of Emil Schletter?"

"Still hounding the man, but nothing concrete as yet. FBI's on it now, since we're pretty sure he's flown out of the country. Left a zigzag trail. Must've spent a week on planes. Flew from here to *Wyoming!* From there to San Francisco, back east to Oklahoma, down to Florida where he booked an international flight on two different planes and must have put someone on the second plane in his place. Both destinations are being pursued."

"What are they?"

"One to Armenia—"

"Damn, planning a defection is he?"

"Other is to Buenos Aires."

Dean looked deeply into his friend's eyes. "Dr. Carol and I theorize that what may have set Schletter off was one of the daughters."

117

Kelso nodded knowingly. "Yeah, oldest one was pregnant."

"How'd you know that?"

"Hey, pal, not all police investigation is limited to your goddamned lab. A little old-fashioned foot work and pressing doorbells, that's all." After seeing Dean nod, Kelso went on. "Seen an aunt who confided that Schletter would explode at family gatherings for no good reason, calling his wife horrible names. You know, the usual, slut, bitch . . . suspected her of having an affair. Lot of fights in the home. Oldest then gets pregnant, and when he found out, it looks like his cap blew sky high."

"Lot of supposition in all that."

"Yeah, until you and Carol prove it."

"We'll see."

Dean finished his drink. Kelso asked, "What do you plan to do about Fowler?"

"Actions speak louder than words."

"Go get 'em, Dino."

They parted where their cars had been left near Gundersen's. As Dean drove for home, he wondered what he could say to Dr. Donald Carr, the guy in the middle, squeezed hard, no doubt, by Dr. Mortimer Fowler. Despite everything, despite the fact Dean knew Fowler had far-reaching influence and had probably more or less blackmailed Carr, Dean found himself wanting to punish the younger man first. It seemed the higher Dean climbed, the fewer men and women he could trust. It always seemed to come down to a handful: Jackie, his wife, Sybil, his second in command at the Office, and Ken Kelso, his best friend and fellow crime fighter. These few people seemed the only steadfast and sure things in the galaxy.

"And I couldn't believe it when you let me pay for the check!" Sybil told Carr as they entered her apartment.

"Hey, you make a hell of a lot more with the M.E.'s Office than I do with the department."

"A man who can accept that in a woman! Don, you continue to surprise me."

He took her in his arms and kissed her. She came away breathless. "There's something else about me that's going to surprise you," he said.

"I can see that," she replied, returning his kiss.

He pulled away, looking suddenly troubled. "Sybil, I—"

"What is it, Don?"

He shook his head. "I don't know how to tell you this."

"Try straight out. I make you nervous, don't I? Everything's happening too fast?"

"No, no, you're . . . you are wonderful, the best . . . just that . . ."

"Don, what is it?"

"I should have told you earlier."

"Damn it, Don, tell me what?"

"Fowler."

"Fowler? What about Fowler?"

"Sybil, I was at the exhumation in Fowler's place."

She backed instinctively away from him and he pursued her. She found the sofa chair and sat on it, hunched together in an outward show of disgust and anger, trying desperately to understand. "Why . . . why're you telling me now?"

"Because, I'm . . . I feel sick about it. At the time, I was just thinking about my job. He's got me over a barrel. Dug up some crap on me—"

"What kind of crap?"

"Exams. Six-year-old crap. I didn't exactly pass with the scores on my resume."

She bit her lip, a tear welled up and escaped her eye. She missed when she rubbed at it. "You bastard, and all this was just to set me up for a fall?"

"Fowler sent a reporter to the exhumation. I told him about the mess up in the bodies. Afraid I gave them plenty of fodder for the A.M. slop they'll hash out."

"Damn you!"

"I'm telling you now, because I never really wanted any part of it, and because—"

"Get out! Don't say another ugly word! Just get out."

He dropped his gaze, pushed his glasses up, turned, and began to go. He stopped at the door. "I knew it was wrong all along, but I really knew it after watching you and Dr. Grant perform the autopsy. Fowler was wrong, and I'll say so on my report for the department."

She leaped from the chair, rushing at him with an epithet and pushing him from the room. "And that's supposed to make it all better? Your damned report?" She slammed the door and locked it. She leaned against it, sliding to the floor, allowing the tears to come. All the words he'd said, all the moves he'd made—it all made perfect sense after all. She was to blame, not **Don Carr** or anyone else, only she. She'd foolishly allowed herself that most dangerous of luxuries—to open up to someone, to trust someone—and now she was paying the price.

Don Carr stood on the other side of the door, just staring at it for a long time, hearing her quietly sob on the other side. He'd lost her before he had her. But he couldn't let her come unprepared to face the facts when she lifted the morning's *Tribune*. That would have been far and away more devastating than hearing it from him personally, especially after spending the evening with him.

The little free time they had spent together had been captivatingly refreshing. He'd had emotions and thoughts not felt since his earliest memories of dating. Sybil Shanley had excited him in every way, intellectually and physically, as well as spiritually. He'd been completely wrong to take the steps he had taken, and what little consolation he had was in the fact that the M.E.'s Office had unquestionably proven its point—Sybil's point. That's what he'd like to tell her now, what he had wished to add at the end, the second before she leapt from the chair and threw him out.

Maybe tomorrow. Perhaps somehow he could make it up to her. Flowers? Too cliché. A card? Not enough. His head on a platter? Maybe . . . but she'd only dissect it.

"Damn you, Carr," he cursed himself for having allowed himself to be used.

On his way down the street to a busier avenue

where he might find a cab, he picked up the early edition of the morning's paper and dug through it, wondering how much damage had been done.

When he found the story, he groaned. The headline read: Chicago's M.E. Clowns with Death: Unnecessary Exhumations Tarnish Grant's Crown.

When he got into the cab, he told the driver to take him to the river where he needed to jump in. The driver laughed and said, "Hey, it couldn't be so bad! Least you got your health, kid. Me, I got a back problem on top of an ulcer you wouldn't believe, and somedays, like today, they both kick in at once and zowie!"

Carr gave the driver his address, then flinched as he made out the print beneath the headline. It characterized Grant as an overbearing Baron of death, and Sybil as his doting Cattle Queen. Fowler was not once mentioned in the article, although the body so long searched for and missing was mentioned as a John Doe that had died at Cook County of arteriosclerosis. Neither Carr nor the city workers or the CPD got any of the flack from the antagonistic reporter.

The final upshot of the article was blessedly brief, but even more damaging, explaining that the M.E.'s Office was no longer answerable to any power in the city. It made perfectly clear that the extravagant expense of a useless exhumation with its subsequent disastrous add ons, due to Grant's inability to pinpoint the target he'd wanted at Mount Orchid, was too much for the average taxpayer to stomach.

Fowler had gotten the right man to cover the "body snatching" as the reporter put it.

Carr wanted to crawl under a rock, and he wondered how he could face either Dean or Sybil ever again.

Louis Malinowski heard the bell at the back of the shop where the alley met the poor excuse for a loading platform. Deliveries so early? It didn't seem likely. It was the middle of the night, wasn't it? The bell again, sounding louder than before, and some muffled shouting. Whoever it was, they would wake the whole neighborhood, and at such an hour. But a glance at his watch told Malinowski that he had been in a trance, and that it was in fact later than he realized. Time might just as well stand still when he was enjoying himself and keeping his records here in the freezer. It was 7:13 A.M., a new day, and the girl named Cleopatra was dead for the last time. Now someone was ringing the bell out back, persistently and insistently, like the building was on fire. Who could it be? What did they want?

He wasn't particularly worried because he allowed no one entry into his freezer anyway, and the body would keep now that he'd re-set the temperature gauge. In fact, the carcass would be frozen solid soon if this disturbance at the back door took very long.

Whoever it was, he was persistent, the bell rang and rang.

He gathered Cleopatra's clothing and stowed it inside a box with a lid on it. He closed the freezer door as a further precaution, and then he calmly went to the back door.

It was the kid from Ahmsted's, his youngest boy—

the one who worked as if it were more fulfilling than sex for him. He made his older brother appear to be a bum by comparison. What was the eager beaver doing here now? Malinowski stared a hole through him, trying to recall his name. Suddenly it came to him.

"Robbie, what in heaven's name you want, boy?"

"The sausage, sir."

"What the hell're you talking about, boy?"

"You're 'spose to sell us some Vienna! I come by last night, but nobody answered here or upstairs."

"All right, all right, I forgot is all. Hold on, wait here."

Malinowski stepped back in, leaving the door ajar. Inside the freezer, he searched for what the boy's father wanted, vaguely recalling something about the deal they had struck the day before. He had to rotate the moveable hooks, the sides of beef, and other portions swaying like the *danse macabre*, round about like clothes at a cleaner's. Then he saw the links he was looking for and took them down. When he turned, he saw the boy staring in.

"Jesus, boy! I told you to wait outside!"

"Could you teach me your trade?" he asked, surprising Malinowski who looked over his shoulder at the carcasses. The dead woman inside blended in so well with the others that no one could distinguish it at this distance.

"You, you want to learn my trade? The butchering business, from me?"

"My father ought to have his own freezer like this. It's neat, the way you got it back here, push-button. If he had a butcher's set up, a decent one, and a good butcher—that'd be me—he could be making twice, maybe three times as much at the deli, I know it."

"You're right, but you got school and you work at your father's. You don't have time, Robbie." He led the boy away from the freezer. Robbie stared in as long as he could. But Malinowski was certain he had seen nothing. If he had, he'd be hysterical.

"I won't tell the old man until it's done, until I got the learning part of it down. I'm smart, Mr. Malinowski, and I pick up on things real fast."

"I've seen that."

"And I work hard."

"I've seen that."

"Then what do you say?"

"What do *I* get out of it, satisfaction?"

"I'll pay. I got savings."

"Tell you what, I don't think your father would approve."

"But he will . . . after, I mean, when it's done."

"You won't tell him until then?"

"No sir."

Malinowski shook his head. The neck was stiff, the temples pounding from the night before. "He'll wonder where you're going nights."

"He already does that. I got friends and we visit back and forth, and I go to the arcade, the mall, and to the movies all the time."

"You'll give all that up?"

"Hey, Mr. Malinowski, I'm like almost eighteen. I've got to take on more responsibility, and maybe I'll get a raise from dad."

"All right, tonight then."

"How much?"

"What?"

"How much for the lesson?"

"We'll talk about that tonight."

"I can't afford too much."

Malinowski finished with the Vienna sausages, and handed them, fully wrapped, to the boy. Robbie handed over the money and for the first time since the boy had known Louis Malinowski, he didn't count the bills. He just thanked Robbie and said, "Tell no one about our arrangement. One person in this neighborhood knows, everybody knows. No one, you understand? You promise? I don't want your old man mad at me, and tell him . . . tell him I'm sorry about losing my temper with him before."

"Ahhh, he's forgot all about it. Said he had it coming, said he shot off his mouth about your father."

Malinowski's eyes darted fire at the boy who started a bit. Bravely, the boy ventured on. "I never quite understood what happened. You ever want to talk about it . . . well, listen, I better get going. See you tonight."

"Yes, Robbie, tonight, and if you want to learn more about my father . . . maybe, just maybe you will."

Malinowski waved the boy off, his mind filling with a plan for clearing out his freezer. Not only was Cloe's body in there now, but the turgid carcass of another victim he'd killed several nights before. He'd placed it deep in the freezer, far to the rear, among those of animals. Frozen over solid in its bag, it looked like any other bag of meat there. But now it was evident the bodies must go, this morning.

The freezer should not be used for such long periods. It was too dangerous, too foolhardy. New deliveries were scheduled today or tomorrow. He hadn't a moment longer to procrastinate, nor did he have time to dress the dead, not here, not now.

His own delivery truck sat parked out back, close up on the door. The back of the truck was the place for the two human carcasses. He bent to the work, bagging up clothing, getting the pieces scrambled and caring very little that he did so. He threw the bag into the van, returned, and hefted the first dead woman over his shoulder. She was stiff and heavy and near invisible inside the bag that had frosted from both within and without. He had to squint to make out the features.

He loaded in this one. It was before hours. He had perhaps one hour to return to the store. He returned to the freezer and took down the second corpse, Cloe, who was not so solidly frozen. He rushed her back to the van where he unceremoniously tossed her atop the other one. The thud and rattle it made against the metal floor was like an ice block against a drum. Anyone watching would chalk it up to an early morning delivery, which, in a sense, it was.

Malinowski locked up his shop and rushed back, climbing in behind the wheel, mentally going over possible dumping sites for the bodies. The outside temperature was already thawing the bags behind him, already uncovering his secret cargo.

He headed for the deserted area of Ogden and Hubbard, where failed factories and out-of-use train tracks shared space with weedy lots, viaducts, and street gang battlegrounds; a bit further along was the blackened stretch of deserted track that eventually ran to Union Station and the Chicago River.

He decided one body would go into a deserted loading dock amid the ghost town of failed factories, the other into the river. Water would cover the cause of death nicely, he thought. In any event, it was an hour's distance from the shop, and he'd miss opening on time. It was a change in habit that could come back to haunt him. He worried over the detail far more than he did about the two bodies thumping against the sides behind him.

He pulled the van into the weed-ridden, concrete dock he'd selected. No one was about. Climbing into the back, he snatched off the body bag with some difficulty. Part of it had plastered itself to the skin where it lay atop the bag, and the zipper stuck. It came, however, and he began to dress the body in the clothes he remembered this one had come in, paying little heed to undergarments as they were nearly the same. Both young women had been homeless street people. He thought again how his work cleaned the streets of such people, how he was doing everyone a big favor and getting no recognition for it, nor caring to.

Finished, he unceremoniously kicked the body out the rear of the van and watched it roll down the length of the incline to come to a stop below the dock. The sun was creeping down toward her in narrow rivulets of light.

When the gear box stuck, he revved the motor and cranked the gears noisily before he was gone, heading toward a secluded, ugly spot along the rail line and the river where some shrubbery would hide him. A look at his watch and he feared he'd be later than an hour getting back. Cursing, he forged ahead. He bumped along the dirt railyard road and came to a stop where the brush and river met, backing into the area when he saw a man walking a dog. Miles from anywhere and some jackass was out here walking a dog. He hadn't a moment to lose. For now the man was far enough off that he couldn't possibly read the sign on the truck, or make out what Malinowski's cargo might be.

He hadn't time to dress the woman, and he wanted to be done with her clothing as well as her body. He racked his brain for an adequate solution to his mounting problem, hearing the dog bark some distance from the van, the other side of the stunted trees and brush where he'd backed the van on this silent stretch of river. The sound of the dog made him look out. The damned beast was bounding his way, off his leash, the man coming up the rear. Malinowski searched the van and his mind for some solution to his problem: leave immediately, dump the body elsewhere, or sink it below the water before anyone could see. Inside the van were several bricks, and he stashed these, along with Cloe's clothing, into the body bag with her. He zipped it open halfway so it would fill with water and quickly sink with the weight of the bricks. It seemed plausible and possible. The dog's bark sounded again. He snatched out the body when he saw that the dog had bounded back to its master and both seemed to be keeping their distance for the moment.

Malinowski pulled the body and the bag to the river's edge. There was a sheer drop off, no shallows.

It stood to reason that the bag would simply and quickly disappear. He hated to lose the expensive bag, but there seemed no other way. He launched Cloe into the Chicago River, the bag making a dull splat two feet below the top of the retaining wall. He watched it begin to bob and take on water, and when it was half out of sight, he saw that the man and the dog had become agitated. He could faintly make out the old man's shouting at the dog and then he saw the dog racing straight for him. Malinowski rushed to and through the van, got into the driver's seat and took it out of idle, hitting the gas and careening away so as to not be recognized.

Behind him, in the river, the bag which originally had looked to be sinking, held enough air inside to cause it instead to float at one end. In this manner, Cloe, her thawing facial expression changing with the sunlight as it beat down on her, floated off lazily toward the bridges of downtown Chicago. As it did so, the man walking the dog, a railroad detective, shook his head over the littering he had witnessed, cursing himself he hadn't gotten close enough to the van to make out either the insignia along the side, or the license plate number.

He watched the garbage deposited on the river float off. He was too distant from it to make out much. Looked like some sort of furniture to him, a mattress maybe.

Jake Fisk was a stumpy old sort who liked rye when he could get it, and was not adverse to using it on the job. The life and work of a railroad dick wasn't much more than that of a hobo, he reasoned, except he drew pay for bumming about the tracks with his dog, and he got to wear a little badge inside his coat. No guns, though, not any more. Lots of changes in Chicago since he was a boy. He moved on down the line, a look of consternation on his rugged, deep-cut face, his only companion his dog, Brownie. Then he heard someone scream. It was a distant, almost ghostly sort of scream, hard to track down exactly where it was coming from. He looked all around before he followed the dog's eyes. Brownie was barking up at someone on the overpass where cars zipped by. A few pedestrians had gathered up there and some were now pointing down to what floated in the water.

Jake realized suddenly that it wasn't just trash the van had dropped off at the water's edge. He and Brownie raced for the clump of plasticky matter lazily moving away from them.

When he got to the water's edge, out of breath, he shouted for Brownie to haul the body in. He was aghast at the discovery. Police were already zooming in all around him, and it suddenly occurred to Jake that they thought he'd done it, and there was no one to say otherwise.

The cops came out charging, their weapons drawn, and Jake, his hands skyward—looking guilty as sin he supposed—with Brownie barking a blue streak, tried to tell his story. They thought it was bull. It sounded like bull. A white or gray van pulling up a mile or more up, dumping a body into the river in plain view of him.

One of the cops knew Jake and told the others to calm down. "Jake, you armed?" he asked.

"Hell no, just my switchblade."

"Let's have it," he said.

Jake frowned. "Powell, your name's Tom Powell, right?"

"That's right, Jake. Use to ride with Walt Tabori."

"Old friends, him and me. Look, son, I didn't in no way have not a thing to do with . . . with that," he pointed to the body being hauled ashore now by other men in blue. "I swear. It happened like I told you. I know it sounds like bull, but—" he stopped, handing over the knife.

Another cop locked Jake's hands behind his back. The dog snarled. "You want to shut that animal up, mister, or do we do it for you?" Powell began reading him his rights.

"'Fraid you're going to have to tell it downtown, Jake," Powell said to him, then continued reading his rights.

"But I didn't do it!"

"Some people on the bridge say you were the only one in sight, and she ain't been in the water long," said another cop. "Come along peaceable."

"What about my dog?"

"Pound'll take good care of him."

"Anything happen to my dog and I swear—"

One of the cops shoved him into the door, bloodying his nose. "Get in, and no more threats, old-timer!"

Jake clambered in to the sound of Brownie being choked, straining against a leash somewhere.

Eight

Dean had gotten the call from Ken Kelso first, the phone shattering the peace he and Jackie shared in their bedroom. The news a corpse had been discovered floating in the Chicago River, wrapped in some sort of cellophane bag, had him instantly, if groggily, alert. He listened to the synopsis of what had occurred, where, when and presumably how. A man was in custody, always a good sign. All the answers seemed suddeny to be coming out in a flood, except why . . . why does a man go on a rampage of serial killings to asphyxiate fellow human beings? Still, he cautioned his own anxious desire for an answer to the riddle. The incident at the tracks must be thoroughly investigated, the suspect questioned, witnesses—if any—must be interrogated. The scene must be gone over with meticulous care, all physical evidence examined.

"Call Sybil Shanley, and get a car over to her place. She'll want to take charge and she's earned this one."

"Your decision on that score, Dean."

"I'm on my way."

Dean rushed to dress, Jackie groaning and complaining from the bed. "You'd think you were the only M.E. in the whole damned city."

Dean didn't bother to shave. He'd make a stop in at his barber's downtown later. His tie swinging loosely over his shoulder, he finished by slipping on his shoes and kissing Jackie farewell.

When Dean arrived at the scene, it was littered with police cars and flashing lights. Dawn had broken over the river a half hour before and people littered the bridge overhead, several policemen going among them seeking witnesses. Dean saw Sybil in the center of the excitement, shouting orders.

"Goddamnit, don't touch anything, back off from here before you contaminate the scene any damned further!"

"Contaminate her, hell, she's dead," said one rookie cop.

"Couldn't be much older'n my girl, Nanc," said an older cop.

Dean then saw what they were staring down at. His mind reeled with the sight that sent him into a paroxysm of ugly memories about a series of murders by drowning. Kelso had been on a radio nearby and watched Dean's reaction, and now he came to him, saying, "Take it easy, Dean."

Dean's eyes were riveted on the amorphorous body beneath the crinkled, wet plastic, nude and cold and "drowned." The victim had drowned in her own exhalations, locked inside the bag. Her hair was wet, not from the river, but from a feverish perspiration that had plastered it there. Her eyes bulged like two

134

doorknobs, the sockets unable to contain them, the pupils gone from sight, leaving only the fishy white. The tongue was lolling over the lips like a serpent searching for any sign of moisture and oxygen. It was a bloated tongue, the tongue of a large calf. The body looked formless, without skeletal support, almost watery, as if melting before them. It was partially the effect of the bag which seemed to have an enlarging effect. Her breasts sagged to each side looking as drained as Dean assumed her lungs to be.

Sybil looked up at Dean and said, "This is how he does it. Bags his victims up like garbage, traps them inside, slowly allows them enough air to keep them going, then denies them again and again; turns them into his special party favors.

"Guy in custody, Ken, is he a reliable suspect?"

"I doubt it. Had a reason for being here. Walks the rails for the Milwaukee Road. Combination rail inspector and dick."

"Had a dog with him," said a young police officer.

"Any priors on the guy?"

"Not a one, Dino, but don't forget, there wasn't any on Emil Schletter either." Kelso added, "Still, this guy doesn't feel right, Dean."

Dean knew what that meant. Kelso had a second sense about people he'd personally interrogated.

"How much time'd you spend with him?"

"Fifteen minutes."

"And no witnesses?"

"One, but she's shakier'n a redwood fence. Contends that the railroad guy was the one who did it. But she didn't see him throw the body into the water,

135

and she didn't see him go near the body until he and the dog raced to it, *after* she screamed. Tell me this, if you'd just dumped a body and somebody screamed, which way would you run from here?" Ken looked around for effect. "Steps going up to street level that way. Places to hide over there, and presumably that's railroad property from the sign, and this guy had a mitt full of keys and a badge."

Dean got control of himself and knelt beside the body where Sybil worked the zipper loose. "Hold it," he told her. "Take a look." He pointed to the inside of the zipper and the interior flap. There was a crusty patch of material, brown and scabby, nettled into the teeth of the zipper. It flew away at the touch when Sybil inched the zipper down. There was also a patch of plastic, about three inches in diameter, ill-shaped, that appeared to be covering a burn right next to the zipper.

"Yeah, I see," replied Sybil.

"Where's Carr?" asked Dean. "I'd have thought he'd be here."

"He's about a mile off, Dean. We got another body over that way."

"Another body? Where?"

"Doesn't appear related," he said. "Just coincidence is my guess. No plastic bag."

"Just how close is it?"

"Three-quarters of a mile, a mile and a half, what would you say, Powell?"

The young uniformed officer said, "The old man said he saw a van dump the body. If there was a van, maybe there were two bodies in that van."

"So, you sent Carr down that way? Okay, we'll

136

watch closely for anything that might connect the two—"

"Or disconnect them," said Kelso.

"I think we ought to take this one back to the lab just as she is," said Sybil, indicating the dead girl in the see-through bag. Dean found her more difficult to look at than the exhumed body of the boy the day before.

"You're right. Ken, have you ever seen a see-through body bag before?"

"No such thing. This wasn't manufactured for bodies, Dean."

"What then?"

"Any number of things, I suppose."

"As in?"

"You name it: trees, lumber, marble, glass, mannequins, anything perishable or easily scratched or damaged by humidity or other conditions. Anything requiring shipment. Shit, could be a long list. I'm already working on this angle, but it will take time. I've got men checking with plastics companies and manufacturers of bags like these in particular."

"Soon as we're done with the bag, you can have it."

"For now, I'll just take this," he said, slitting off a manufacturer's tag with his Swiss Army knife. As he did so, flecks of what Dean had guessed to be blood snowflaked off the zipper and onto the corpse.

"Looks as if the killer was kind enough to return her clothes to her," said Sybil.

"We'll check for sexual molestation."

"You won't find any," Sybil said with certainty.

"We'll check anyway."

"This creep gets his kicks in a way that perverts would call perverted," she added.

Dean gave a nod to the police photographer who moved in and began flashing. Not a mile distant, a second pathologist and police photographer were doing the same for a second victim. It begged the question Dean dared ask himself now: had the killer's appetite for violent death increased twofold overnight?

Many items of equal importance awaited them at the lab. Tests had been run on samples taken at the Schletter place in Hammond for Dean, all of it bearing Dr. Sam Carol out.

Biopsies and tests on the Jane Doe that Sybil and Don Carr had autopsied together had piled up. And now Sybil arrived just ahead of the latest corpse in this continuing nightmare, with a case full with samples and slides taken from Jory Bemis's exhumation, that would necessarily hang fire now, whether Fowler planned any further damage or not.

She had seen the newspaper article on the exhumation and she blamed herself for being so completely blind to Carr to see him for what he was. Now she had caused serious problems for Dean, and yet Dean seemed to be taking it lightly enough when he learned of Carr's confession of the night before, and when she pushed the article into the Chief's hands.

"We've weathered worse, much worse, haven't we, Sybil?" was all Dean had said on the subject before he began popping questions. They'd returned in separate cars, since she was the M.E. of record on the latest case, and so must travel to and from the scene in a squad car. It was a formality adhered to for the sake of protocol and to avoid criticism of the sort that might call into question the integrity of the evidence gathering later on. For the same reason an officer from the CPD had to be on hand during any autopsy. It was time-consuming and wasteful in the long run, but it was seen as tough-love training by the uniformed cops, the rawest recruits always pulling the duty, except in rare occasions, as when Carr joined Sybil. Had he been working for Fowler as early as that, Sybil wondered, and knew she needn't wonder. As far back as the inside of the dumpster, Carr had been looking for mistakes on her part, trying desperately to latch onto just one that he could report to Fowler.

She didn't care if she never saw him again.

Coffee was perked and the scientists went to work over the body of the new Jane Doe as soon as it was wheeled in, still in the ugly sack, like a cocoon or the silky gauze of a spider's sack.

Sybil grabbed up a barber's long-bristled clothes brush, and sprinkling baby powder over the surface of the bag, she began brushing it all toward the center. There flecks of dust particles, strands of hair, and dirt all congregated. She tweezered this matter from the powder and deposited each into a vial, James Remmer labeling each. Dean slit a tiny patch of the bag itself for analysis. He then did the same for the burned section. Finished, Sybil held a tray on the inside of the bag, her knuckles touching the deceased at the breast, while Dean slowly brought the zipper down. Flecks of blood were caught and accumulated on the glass tray, fixed onto a slide and ready for the microscope. Remmer was now busy with taking several blood samples from various locations of the body, labeling each, while Dean and Sybil carefully removed the clothing items which even included the woman's shoes. Each item was neatly put away, each in its own small bag now. They next began to work the body from the bag, the men lifting it, while Sybil slipped it from beneath like a magician attempting the tablecloth trick. She succeeded and folded the long thick bag as if it were a sheet fresh out of the laundry. But it was filled with air pockets and didn't lie flat. When she put it down, it grew in size and shape, making a crackling sound.

When it bubbled up, Dean saw something trapped inside which they'd missed, a matchbook, crispy and flaky from having burned itself up. Sybil saw it too now, and she also noticed the second splotch of burned plastic at the bottom of the bag.

"She tried to burn a hole in the bag," said Sybil.

Dean bit his lip. "Looks that way. Only succeeded in using up the oxygen content more quickly."

"Maybe she wanted it that way."

Dean nodded, then said, "Let's cut the bag here for the matchbook. Looks too far gone to help, but we've got some miracle workers in documents who might be able to salvage something there."

They did the work and stowed the piecemeal evidence in its own container. "Have to get the bag over to Kelso," Dean said before going to an intercom, hitting the button, and asking for a technician in the next room to drop what he was doing in order to run the bag over to Precinct One, for Kelso only.

Sybil flashed a light into the dead eyes and saw the telltale red pinpoints, near invisible to the naked eye. "We'll want some microphotos of the eyes, James," she told her assistant.

"Right away." He went for the equipment a few feet away. In a few moments, Dean and Sybil were perched over the Jane Doe's legs, she saying, "See what I mean? Hypostasis in the lower regions. You saw the loop at the top of the bag. This woman died upright, suspended in that bag."

Dean nodded and shook his head in a single gesture of agreement and disgust. "After we finish her," he indicated the corpse, "we've got to look at the one Carr's taken charge of."

She nodded and frowned all at once. "You're right. If there's a connection—"

"We've got to prove it. If not, we've got to prove that, too."

"I think you can do that very quickly, Doctors," said Donald Carr who'd stepped into the autopsy room.

"Carr, what've you got there?"

Carr held up a pair of women's panties inside a sealed plastic bag. They were soiled and the waistband worn. "These belong to her—your body."

Sybil shook her head, "Thanks, Dr. Carr, but—"

"Here," he said firmly, holding up a second, stamp-sized plastic envelope with a few strands of pubic hair. "Taken from the panties, but they don't match my girl. If they match your girl, I'd say we have a double murder here in which the killer has gotten the clothes confused."

"What're you waiting for, Sybil? Place it alongside the slide you've got on our girl."

"I haven't made one yet of the pubic hair."

"Then do it. Carr, let's have a look at that under the scope."

Dean did so and when he was satisfied about the appearance and structure, he looked up for Sybil who was there with the second slide. Using a comparison microscope, the strands could be viewed simultaneously.

"Well?" said Carr, anxious for the small victory.

Without raising his eyes from the dual eyepiece, Dean said, "It's a match all right, I'd stake my career on it. Sybil, we'll need atomic tests to prove it unquestionably."

"Let me do it," said Carr. "I'd like to take on that job. I'm . . . I'm good at it. Get results to you two as soon as I possibly can."

Carr left abruptly without another word, and he failed to glance back from the door, as had been his custom. Dean had felt the tension between Sybil and Don, but none of them had time at the moment for personal problems or the mistrust caused by Dr. Mortimer Fowler.

"Sybil, are you ready to continue?"

She stared for a moment at Dean and said, "This brings the number of suspected deaths by our serial killer to six . . . six that we know of. I suspect it's far more."

"Right now, our concern is this one."

"Yeah, she was a fighter, trying to burn her way

out, and look here." Sybil held the dead girl's hands up. They were scarred and bloody about the nails which had been rubbed raw against the metal zipper.

Chief of Detectives of the Chicago Police Department had its up side and down side. Downside, Kelso had too bloody much paperwork to please him. Upside, he had power, the power to pull men and resources off ongoing cases, like vice and drugs, which weren't going to go away, and onto something like this. He had the authority even before he had the filthy murder weapon, a four-foot-high length of pure polyethylene which Dean Grant would likely analyze out as polyurethane instead. Kelso's hand played over the rugged, inch-wide zipper, its teeth cutting his thumb. He next looked closely at the reinforced, double-strength seams, and he wondered if it was a bag that was commonly made, or custom-made. He knew for a fact that you could get anything in this world made to specs, if you were willing to pay for it.

He now had before him a great deal to do. There was no longer any question, only the solution. He didn't care why this maniac was doing what he was doing, he only cared, like a bulldog or a Chicago Bear linebacker, to bring this mutant human being down, to put him out of his misery before he brought on more misery to others.

Kelso had already pulled together a special investigative unit, drawing on men with whom he had worked well in the past, as in the pryo case when a man with a different kind of burning obsession had very nearly killed Kelso's firewoman sweetheart, Kristie Howlett—and Kelso, as well. Ken had seen his share of freaks. You didn't get to the top of the CPD and retain the respect of the men below you by ignoring the realities out there. But for a time, when Sybil Shanley had first stumbled onto the horrific possibilities, he'd done just that. He simply didn't want to face the facts. Now the fact was in his hands in the form of a most gruesome instrument of murder, one Dean likely would request some day for his little horror show over on Wabash. But for now Exhibit A was going to be making the rounds of every plastics manufacturer in the city if need be. He'd already had a list of questions distributed to his crack team of detectives, and when they zeroed in on the handful of manufacturers, or the single manufacturer that had made this bag, he'd have another list to run down, a list of buyers, and from this list, one by one, they would narrow it to the man who purchased this particular bag.

The tag he'd slit from the bag earlier had been useless, save for a number, an inventory number which was waiting for Kelso in some computer somewhere in the city.

Kelso hadn't been able to sit idly by anymore this morning, however. He had called his special unit together and had displayed the bag to them. They could see for themselves the film left over the interior by the victim's carbon dioxide. They could see it, touch it, examine it all they wanted, he'd told them.

Now he rang for an assistant in uniform to get him a suitcase.

"A suitcase?"

144

"Or large briefcase for that damned bag."

"But, Chief, I don't have any suitcases."

"Get one from the cage, anywhere! I don't care, but get me something to put this damned bag into."

"Might take awhile."

"Fifteen damned minutes!" shouted Kelso. "I want it in fifteen minutes."

Sometimes it worked, his blustering, and this was one of those times. He had the case, a rather poor-looking one, inside twenty minutes. He told his officer assistant to place the bag into the suitcase. The young man worked it in after much difficulty.

"Thanks, Krieder," he told him, picked up the suitcase, and said, "I'm gone for the day."

Officer Krieder stared after him.

Kelso wasted no time getting across town into what was popularly referred to as Plastics Row where many of Chicago's largest plastics distributors and manufacturers were located. He'd chosen Falcon Plastics Distribution for two reasons: they had the very largest ad in the yellow pages section on plastics, and they seemed to distribute absolutely anything made from plastics. He'd telephoned ahead and made an appointment with a public relations guy, telling him he wanted to speak with someone that knew—really knew—all there was to know about their plastic bags. Right away the guy assumed Kelso was buying and he started pitching, until Kelso set him straight about the reason for his visit.

Nick Kimble, the publicity man, along with Falcon's bag and sheet plastics man did not keep Kelso waiting. They took him on a tour of the place as they talked. All around the machines men were moving, darting here and there, filling orders from shelves stacked to the ceiling in the noisy, bustling warehouse. The bag man was Jerry Lawrence, and not a bad PR man himself, grinning too much, gabbing too much as he took Kelso around, Kimble fading behind them.

Kelso held the suitcase he'd come in with tight in his hand. "I just want to know if you can identify a specific sort of heavy-duty polyethylene bag, Mr. Lawrence."

"Which you've brought with you," he said, pointing to the suitcase.

"Yeah, inside." Kelso had seen none like it on the shelves.

"Let's have a look."

Kelso opened the suitcase.

Lawrence studied the bag. "We don't carry these as a rule, but we could, whenever anyone special orders. Costly to stock, you see."

"You know who makes them, then?"

"Oh, maybe four dozen companies."

"In the state?"

"In the city."

"Who do you get them from?"

"Depends on what price we can get. Come on, I'll show you."

Kelso fought with getting the bag repacked, gave up, and held the case closed, part of the bag sticking out. Lawrence guided him to a small office hardly large enough for two men, let alone three. Kimble took the opportunity to excuse himself, saying he had much to do before closing time.

While Kelso fussed with the mess of the bag

146

spilling from the suitcase, Lawrence located and opened an enormous book. It was his list of suppliers. "I'd have to go through the whole damned book to pinpoint every company that makes that kind of bag, and some may be making it that I don't know about. Can only deal with so many salesmen, you know."

"It's very important."

"Yeah, so Mr. Kimble said. Something to do with a murder investigation? Say, that wouldn't be the girl they found in the river this morning? I read about it in the paper. Yeah, they said something about a—"

"That's it, Mr. Lawrence. Now, can you help us?"

"Work here's up to the ceiling," he mumbled, looking over his cluttered desk. "But what the hell. How many times does a guy like me get a chance to help the Chicago Police Department solve a murder? Can maybe tell my kids all about how—hey, what's the bag got to do with it?"

"She was locked in the bag, Mr. Lawrence, and asphyxiated."

He blanched and Kelso had the sense that some of his emotional pain and suffering was passing from himself to another human being. He was glad to be rid of it. "Will you help?"

"I . . . yes . . . I'll do what I can."

"Can I expect a list by tomorrow?"

"Tomorrow, yes."

Kelso had overcome the bag and suitcase problem and now stood, reached out a hand to the frailer man in white shirt and tie, shaking it. "Thank you, sir. And now, if you'll fill in a couple of blanks for me, I'll be out of your way. Who do you buy this sort of item from the most?"

"That'd be Linmeyer's."

"I see, and where's that?"

"Not two blocks down. One reason we do so much with them, proximity to product."

"And this," said Kelso, handing him a slip of paper. "Looks like an inventory number. It came off the bag."

"You . . . you want me to check our files for it?"

"If that bag came through here, I want to know it."

"I'll see if it matches anything we have on file."

"One other thing, Mr. Lawrence. What're such expensive, custom-made bags for?"

"Well, that one has a loop attachment, for hanging up things, like clothes—"

"You need that kind of construction for clothes?"

"You get what you pay for. But, these bags, well, they could be used for an endless number of purposes."

"Like?"

"Storage of anything."

"Mannequins?"

"Yes, anything you'd want to preserve."

Kelso nodded, "And that covers a lot of territory."

"It does indeed."

"To whom do you sell most of these bags?"

"Wholesale to hospitals as body bags. They're rather in vogue nowadays, and may surpass the dark bags one of these days."

Kelso wondered if the killer was a medical maniac. Lawrence continued. "Seems the see-through feature helps poorly trained hospital staff, ambulance attendants, and all that to keep tabs a little better on who's who."

Kelso frowned. He hadn't heard of such nonsense from Dean and wondered if Lawrence was reading from memorized lines off a brochure somewhere. "You have any literature on these bags, their uses, etc.?"

"I'll dig out what we've got. Maybe in the catalog."

"Who's your second largest account for bags of this size?"

"This size and larger would be department store mannequin makers. They ship their stuff in 'em."

Kelso tried to imagine a mannequin maker who stuffed life-sized replicas of the human form into plastic bags. He could see some whacko getting off on fantasizing about putting a real girl into the bag. In any event, every answer Lawrence gave him opened another hundred or more avenues that required pursuing.

Not going to crack this case soon, he silently told himself. "Okay, thanks for your time, Mr. Lawrence, and I'll hope to hear from you tomorrow."

Lawrence's smile was gone, but he nodded as Kelso closed the door.

Nine

Tonight, Malinowski told himself, tonight, he would enjoy himself once more by reaching out to and touching, with Solomon, the heights to which his own soul could soar when freed by the trance, a trance that would be induced by Ahmsted's boy. It was too good to pass up. No loitering about the street, no stalking through shelters. This time his prey was coming to him.

Only two people knew that he'd opened late this morning—an old bitch named Kunkel that lived down the street, and the delivery man, Gus. But Gus was settled down by a rack of ribs that Malinowski pushed into his hands.

He rushed to the freezer now and laid out the bag that would receive Robbie Ahmsted, laid it out along the length of the stainless steel table he'd just cleaned of fat, gristle, and blood. He zipped it down the four foot length, the thick zipper teeth nipping at his fingertips as he did so. The zipper made a noise like a purring cat that wished to be scratched. He arranged for the waiting hook to be close at hand, and he set the temperature control to just above freezing.

All finished downstairs, he took the interior stairwell up to the flat over the shop and to his freezer. Here he snatched out two prime cuts of meat, both filet mignon, except that one was marked with a penciled X on the label. This one was for Robbie. He unwrapped each, keeping Robbie's meat always on his lefthand side. He defrosted the meat in the microwave and then placed them alongside one another on a skillet. Ready to explode with nervous energy, Malinowski found a box of dehydrated potatoes. Following the directions, he got them as close to prepared as possible. By that time it was almost six fifteen. He wondered if he had time for a shower. He hadn't had an opportunity to do so all day.

He dare not risk it now. The boy might come and go and he wouldn't even hear. No, instead, he sat down and ran his hands anxiously over each other, wondering if the boy had been serious, wondering where he was, wondering if the boy had been putting him on, a great kidder that one. He sat anxiously wondering, and getting up and peering through the window at the street fronting the shop every three minutes, when suddenly at twenty to seven, there came an abrupt knock at the door. He was here, just the other side of the door, standing in the hall. Suppose someone had seen him come up? Standing at Malinowski's door?

He opened the door wide and put on a better face, a stiff smile showing beneath the whiskers. The boy stepped in, talking.

"I'm here. Told you I was serious. When can we start?"

"You told no one?"

The boy hesitated. "No, no one."

"You're sure, now?"

"Can we get started?"

Malinowski would like nothing better. "I haven't even eaten yet. What about you?"

"I grabbed a candy bar."

"Swiped it from your old man's counter, huh? But that's not enough for a growing boy. Look, I gave our deal thought all day today. You know I live alone, and it gets so quiet sometimes my ears ring in here, even with a radio on. So, part of the deal is, you and me we have supper together. What do you say to a nice steak?"

"Oh, no, I couldn't—"

"Look, I've already put one on for you." He showed him the frying meat.

"Looks good, all right, but that can't be cheap."

"You pay me back with talk, with just being here tonight. It's good to have another living soul in the place, believe me."

The boy frowned at this, hunched, and said, "Well, it smells good."

"How about a little wine, too?"

"Wine? Sure, okay!"

Louis Malinowski smiled again and this time Robbie felt it was genuine. "You know, Mr. Malinowski . . . You're not so bad after all."

"Thank you, Robbie. I know I am not an easy man to know." He poured the wine. "Steaks are almost ready."

When Malinowski turned back to the stove, he was horrified to see that Robbie had turned the steaks for him.

"Tell me, Robbie, when you turned the two steaks, did you set them down the same way, on the same side of the pan, I mean. It's important."

Robbie shrugged. "I think so. Why?"

"Mine must be free of salt, doctor's orders."

"Well, one taste'll tell."

"Yes, yes, of course." He poured more wine into Robbie's glass.

"Well, let's eat and get started. I'm really ready." Robbie Ahmsted was beginning to feel small and guilty over this idea of his brother's that they were carrying out. "You tell the mean bastard that it's something you want to do against Pop's wishes, and he'll jump at the chance," his brother had said. "Once you learn the basics from him, we'll do our own damned butchering and we won't need him or anyone like him." At the time it had seemed like a good plan. At the time, the old man's lip was still fat where he'd hit it against the counter when Malinowski had grabbed him. At the time, Malinowski seemed to deserve to be lied to and tricked. But now, Robbie wasn't so sure anymore. He wondered what his father would say to Malinowski's serving him filet mignon and wine.

The meat and potatoes were placed on the table and Malinowski forked Robbie's steak over to him, saying, "Enjoy, eat up." Malinowski, however, only nibbled at his own food.

"You okay, Mr. Malinowski?"

"Ulcer sometimes flares up at the worse times, that's all. I worry too much."

154

"About what?"

"About life, death, taxes, the upkeep of this place," he said, looking at the ceiling but watching the boy out of the corner of his eye, certain he himself had gotten the steak laced with the potent sedative. He took a bite of his own steak, to make it look good. He commented on the quality of the filet. "What do you think, Robbie?"

Robbie looked across at him as if he didn't understand the question and Malinowski recognized the symptoms.

"Are you all right, Robbie?"

"Yeah, think . . . so. Did it get hot in here?" His eyelids dropped downward and he valiantly fought against them. "You're right. This place . . . so quiet . . . it sort of makes your ears . . . ring."

"Just the vibration from my freezer downstairs. Gets to you."

Robbie mumbled something unintelligible, his head nodding forward.

The wine and sedative mix hit him hard now. Malinowski watched as Robbie's head slumped into his potatoes. From somewhere far, far away Robbie heard Malinowski laugh. It struck him as strange. He'd never heard Malinowski laugh, not in all the years he'd grown up in the neighborhood, not even when the butcher was poking fun at Robbie's father. Then Robbie didn't hear it anymore. He went quietly to sleep, giving no thought to the completion of his mission, or to his moment of remorse, or to where he'd wake up. In his mouth was the taste of meat.

* * *

The one test in particular that Sybil Shanley had held out on the Jane Doe of the day before, she today had run back to back with the Jane Doe of today. Hairs and fibers were fine, but stomach contents often helped trace the last moments of a victim's life. She'd run a detailed chemical analysis on the women, and in both cases, they had virtually the same last meal: a green-leafed vegetable, either spinach or parsley, and a rich meat, most likely grade A steak. One had some noodles.

Reluctantly, she telephoned Carr and asked him if he'd run any tests on the third victim's stomach contents. He had.

"Would you kindly read the results to me?"

"Sybil—" his tone was apologetic.

"Doctor, please," she remained formal. "The results?"

He read them off. "Carrots, most likely canned, chewing gum, and some meat."

"Can you be more specific on the type of meat?"

"I didn't go into it closely."

"Would you please?"

There was a moment's silence. "Okay, phone you with the results. How long're you going to be there?"

"An hour, maybe more."

"Get back to you."

She put the phone down and stared at it as if it were Don Carr's head. Dean was watching and couldn't help but hear the cryptic conversation. "You two ought to patch it up, kiddo. You're both professionals."

"How can you be so casual about what he did to . . . to us?"

156

"I didn't sleep with him."

"Neither did I!"

"Oh, sorry, I guess I better keep my mouth shut."

She stormed back to her lab.

Moments later, Dean peeked in and said, "You ought to run a test on the stomach contents for unusual chemicals, like slow-acting poison or—"

"Sedatives, alcohol, I know. That's what I'm doing."

She was angry and tired and snapping at everyone. She'd made James Remmer stay to help her. "Look, its really late, Sybil. Maybe the rest ought to wait until tomorrow."

"Tomorrow someone else will be dead."

He saw that she was adamant. "Well, I've had enough of the lab to last me awhile, and we're all getting a bit careless and bitchy."

She darted an angry look in his direction. "You don't have to stay, Dr. Grant. I can manage."

"Sybil, be careful. When you become too emotionally involved, you make blunders. I know, I've made them."

James Remmer was staring at Dean and then he looked at Sybil and back to Dean with a frown. "Jim," said Dean, "go home."

Sybil continued to run her chemical test on the meat, certain she'd find a trace of some element that ought not to be there.

Dean returned to his office, telephoned Jackie, and told her he was on his way with Sybil in tow. "She needs to be around people in a normal setting. It has been a very difficult time for her."

"Sure, bring her," said Jackie. "I've got a guest of

157

my own coming over."

"Oh?"

"Old friend from my days at Rush-Presbyterian, Dr. Taylor."

Dean pictured the psychiatrist who had helped Jackie recover from an awful experience of the year before. Dr. Marilee Taylor was a woman with many interest, well read, her knowledge of her field and associated fields from sociology to police forensics making her an excellent friend to Dean as well as to Jackie. With their busy schedules, none of them had seen one another in several months.

He'd give Sybil time to settle down and then he'd go back and insist she come home with him.

A half hour later, Dean returned to Sybil, proposing she spend the evening with good wine, bread, and companions.

She relented long enough to ask, "What companions?"

"Jackie telephoned to ask you over to join us for dinner, along with Dr. Taylor—Marilee Taylor, Jackie's friend."

"Shrink, you mean. You think I'm on the verge of some sort of breakdown? That I need a shrink?"

"Damn it, Sybil! It's just an evening off which you have earned! There was a time when I'd have to make you stay. Now, I have to make you go!"

"People change."

"Kid, you need time away from this case. Maybe then you'll see things more clearly."

She rubbed the back of her neck and stared away at the corridor through the glass partitions running the length of the labs. "Maybe . . . maybe you're right.

I'm starting to see spots before my eyes."

"The lab, the work, it'll all be here in the morning."

She nodded, giving in. "Look, I want to go by my place, freshen up. How's eight o'clock sound?"

"It's almost eight now. Look at your watch."

"My God, so it is."

"Come on, you don't have your car here. You can freshen up at our place, you know that. Our place is your place. You've got a change of clothes in your closet here, don't you? For tomorrow? You can stay over, and Jackie won't mind in the least."

"Okay, okay, sold."

"Good." He took her hand in his. "You know. Shanley, you're one of a kind."

"Thanks, Dino."

"Hey, only Kelso gets away with calling me that."

"So, I'm still just a lowly assistant to you after all."

"No, it's just that I never liked being called Dino."

She laughed and he joined in her laughter. She placed everything in readiness for the next day and together they left for the Grant condominium overlooking beautiful Lake Michigan.

Dr. Marilee Taylor always found Dean's cases fascinated her, especially those involving serial killers. She had once begun a study of aberrant behavior, abandoning it for another project. She told him now, over drinks, that she'd returned to the work and had been doing a great deal of reading in the field.

Sybil seemed to have come into her own around Jackie and Marilee, finding the feminine company refreshing. She had never met Dr. Taylor before, but she found herself hanging on her every word. It seemed to her serendipity that she should meet this fascinating professional woman just now, for what she was saying about serial killers was right on the money.

"What do you plan on calling your book if you finish it and publish it?" asked Sybil.

"I don't know, maybe *Bestial Behavior in Mad Men and Women,* or *Murder by Psychotic Design.*"

"What do you think about a killer who has chosen to do away with his victims through asphyxiation?" she asked.

"Strangulation, you mean?"

"I mean cutting off his victims from any source of air."

Marilee gasped, her pert, dark-haired head shaking, her eyes narrowing, as if trying to imagine such a madman. "Funny you should mention it."

"Oh, why?"

Now Dean was curious. He hunched forward, after dinner drink in hand, the ice tinkling.

"I was planning a chapter on strangulation murders. You know, the typical sort, Boston Strangler, ligatures, ropes, a morbid fixation with knots some people have. Anyway, I stumbled onto an obscure chapter in a book by an Indian psycho-analyst named Shakir. His theory about strangulation murders and asphyxiation by premeditation is quite bizarre, and yet seems to me to have some validity."

"Go on, Doctor," said Sybil.

"Yes, please," said Jackie, "such cheerful discussions we have in this house."

Dean took Jackie's hand and pulled her to sit down beside him.

For a moment, with them all huddled about the silent, unlit fireplace, they seemed like a group of children listening to ghost stories, except this particular tale was chillingly close to home. "Well," she continued, "Shakir believed that the reason a man squeezes or crushes life from another is to take on his victim's life force, through his hands, eyes, nostrils as he breathes in the presence of the dead victim. I know it sounds like Return of the Vampire or something. But Shakir had some insight into the minds of men who were unbalanced. There were actually cults in the East that practiced strangulation rituals."

"Did he say anything about a guy who shuts people away in an airtight place, to watch them suffocate?" Sybil asked.

"I do recall something along those lines. An ancient cult . . . practiced a macabre version of genocide that involved a room filled with people standing toe to toe, packed in tightly, sealed off from air. Left to die of air starvation."

"That's sheer lunacy," said Jackie.

"What did they hope to gain? Was it a Jonestown sort of thing, where the followers went along with suicide?" asked Dean.

"Worse," she replied.

"Worse, how?" asked Sybil. "Why worse?"

Dr. Taylor brought herself up from the slouch

she'd allowed herself. "When the room was opened up, all those so-called followers dead, the priest and his remaining followers would enter to fill their lungs with what they considered the 'holy' air of the dead and dying . . ."

Sybil was almost off the edge of her chair. "But why? Why? For what ungodly reason?"

"They derived great—" she paused, searching for the right word. "Pleasure, and I suppose, excitement, from the practice."

"The chamber would have been filled with deadly carbon dioxide," Sybil pointed out.

"Deadly in large, concentrated dosage," Dean said, "but there would have been air filtering in. There would have been enough CO_2 though to send them into an hallucinatory state."

"Controlled hallucinations," said Dr. Taylor. "For the times, perhaps the only hallucinogen known."

"How barbaric!" said Jackie, shivering with a mental image of the mass death.

Sybil looked across at Dean, "Do you think our killer could be of Far Eastern descent? Some kind of weird new form of this cult?"

"There's no way of knowing, unless we get a sample of his blood. So far, all we've got is that of the victims."

Dr. Taylor raised a long, slender index finger into the air like a teacher, "Don't get too literal about this man's religious preferences or descent. You see, your killer is motivated perhaps—and I stress perhaps— by a Jungian paradigm—"

162

"Whoa, whoa, Dr. Taylor, you've lost me," said Dean.

"A model, a plan, possibly created at a young age." Dr. Taylor took Jackie's hands in hers and said, "If it's not too painful for Jackie, let's talk about the killer who attacked her last year. The killer had worked out an elaborate cause and effect, a hierarchy of command, reasons, and purpose. The killing was the murderer's reason for being."

"And you're saying our present killer also has some elaborate, crazy reason for asphyxiating young people?"

"That's about it. Of course, however insane his plan is to us, to him it's perfectly rational. Maybe he's working out the solution to some great and grave problem, or he has been commanded by a greater power to do what he must do. Or both."

"Both?"

"Records show that sometimes it's both. A trauma in childhood sets the course, and later in life a stronger personality—or voices heard in a schizoid state—trigger the psychosis."

"She's right, Dean," said Sybil, "I don't know how I know it, but she's right."

"If I were to hazard a guess about this killer," Dr. Taylor went on, but stopped herself. "But then, that's really not my province."

Dean said, "Go on, hazard away for us, Marilee."

She took a deep breath. The circle had now taken on the nature of a seance, Dean thought, watching her, caught up in her melodic, calm, rational voice and frightening words. "Perhaps our modern breath-

163

stealer is not so different in his wish fulfillment need as those ancient thieves I spoke of. Suppose he has discovered that he can get a high from CO_2; and suppose he truly believes—as the condition of his brain would inform him—that he derives sustenance from the dying breath of others?"

The phone rang making Sybil start. Dean, to hide the fact that he, too, had been startled, jumped up, and took the receiver in hand.

"Yes, she's here," he said into the phone. Then to Sybil, "It's for you."

"Who is it?"

Dean clamped his hand over the phone. "Carr."

She took the phone and said, "Yes, Dr. Carr?"

"I have information for you."

"It was steak, wasn't it?"

"Yes, and it was laced with a potent dose of Valium."

"You're sure?"

"Trace elements found in the largest undigested piece."

"So, he subdues them with a meal first."

"Sybil, I'm sorry about the other night."

She said nothing for a long moment. "I'll get over it."

"If there's anything else I can do . . ."

"Thanks for getting the information to me, Dr. Carr. Good night." She hung up and reported the findings to Dean.

Dr. Taylor was telling Jackie that it had become late and she had an early conference. Jackie fluttered about her friend, finding her jacket and purse while the others said good night. Sybil stepped outside with Dr. Taylor with a pencil and pad she'd picked up.

"Can you give me some titles of books on this breath-stealing notion, Dr. Taylor?"

"No book goes into it wholly, but a few touch on it. See if you can locate these." Marilee Taylor jotted down several titles before saying good-bye again.

Dean welcomed Sybil back and Jackie arranged the guest room for her. Sybil was tired, exhausted in fact, and yet sleep would not come easily tonight. She thought of all the people who had no idea of the cruelty in the world. Ignorance is bliss was the old saying.

She said good night to the Grants, showered and dressed for sleep, but when she got to bed, she found herself sitting up with the pencil and notepad, jotting down a list of items they knew about the killer.

—He fed his victims.

—Fed them a ritualistic last meal of meat laced with a powerful sedative.

—He put them into transparent body bags. Dangled the bags somewhere. On a strong hook, causing the blood to flow downward to the legs after death.

—He slowly asphyxiated them over a long period of time.

—He kept them in a near-frozen state, as evidenced by crystals under the skin in the latest victim.

—He stripped them naked to watch all parts of them writhe in agony.

165

—He didn't molest the women or the men he had killed.

—His motive was asexual.

—He normally placed the clothing back on, but failed to when dumping one in the river. Why?

—His motive was a blank, perhaps partially filled in by Dr. Taylor's breath-theft theory.

—He didn't want their clothes or money. They didn't have any insurance bonds or bank account numbers, or power of any sort. So, what did he want? What did he take?

—He wanted their very *essence*. He filled himself with their most precious possession— their lives—via oxygen deprivation.

She had to put it aside. The case threatened to consume her. Dean was right. She had and still was investing too much of herself in it, losing herself in it. She seemed unable not to, like an anorexia victim incapable of helping herself, falling, falling dead away into a hole that had enlarged and lengthened and was without boundaries . . . falling into it forever.

She was asleep with the lights on, sitting up against the headboard.

Ten

"Do we haffa' do dis?" Robbie Ahmsted was asking, only half-conscious of what was happening around him, but coming to sooner than Malinowski wished.

He wanted the young man to come around. he confessed that part of his excitement was watching as the agony of the situation wrung from the body that desirable, internal power he and Solomon sought. It was the life force which had fused with the respiratory system at birth, where the original womb—so much more beautiful than the one Robbie was occupying now—saw him writhe. Now he would writhe again, and that eternal essence would flow out to escape into Malinowski's body, giving his mind easier access to Solomon's world, giving his eyes right to see Solomon, his ears to hear him speak more clearly. Indeed the Ahmsted boy would provide fodder for all of Malinowski's senses tonight.

"Col—clothes . . . cold in here . . ."

"You're all right."

"What're you? My clothes!"

Malinowski had to work faster. He completed the stripping and had placed Robbie into the giant freezer bag and was fighting with a sticking zipper. Robbie's hand came down and snatched at him, ripping, tearing, and drawing blood. Malinowski stared at the rivulet and exploded, slapping the kid so hard he bloodied his lips and knocked him cold.

The jammed zipper finally came. He hefted the kid to a sitting position on the table, pressed for the hook to come in on its trolley line. He snatched it, clipped it to the loop on the bag and pressed the button again, watching as bag, Robbie and all, slid from the table, jerked upright, and moved to the center of the freezer.

Malinowski himself now disrobed and sat shivering on a pad before the bag. He was ready to be rejuvenated.

He first reduced his own senses, depriving them and starving them almost to the point of unfeeling and uncaring. It was like when his father would shut him in the freezer here for hours with the meat carcasses to teach him a lesson. It had taught him a great deal. He learned that he could survive without feeling, reducing his own air supply, pulse, heart rate, sense of touch, right to the edge when Solomon took charge of his form.

Solomon had come to him as a child, too, but he'd never understood why before. He had never been strong enough to hear accurately, to see clearly the meaning Solomon had brought into the world. He chanted Solomon's name for a time in a litany of sound that changed the form of the name.

"Solomon, Solo-man, Sol-a-man, Sol-of-man . . ."

he chanted in mantra fashion until he finished with, "Soul of man . . . soul of man . . ."

By now, Robbie Ahmsted was coming to and conscious of his predicament. On either side of him he saw meat hanging in thick vinyl bags, and he realized that he, too, was hanging inside such a bag. He did the predictable. He urinated and he pleaded, clawed at the interior and pleaded more, screamed, cursed and pleaded more, using up the oxygen inside the bag quickly, the interior covering over with the film of his exhalations, distorting Malinowski's view. Malinowski had lain out his recording tools, the clipboard, form, and pencil, and he watched with practiced patience as Ahmsted's son began to display the typical signs of asphyxiation.

But Solomon knew just when to slow the process, to draw out the young soul from the body like a salve. It was a long process, but a most rewarding one in the end.

Malinowski noted the changes in the young man's condition, jotting these down. He stared for a moment at the form, searching for the right blanks and squares to mark. The form was a redone purchase order and checklist he used with his suppliers. The one article of clothing Malinowski allowed himself was his wristwatch, and he glanced at it occasionally, timing the youth.

Robbie Ahmsted's name was filled in on the blank space at the top of the form. Age, sex, height, and approximate weight all noted. Then he got into the "meat" of the survey. He counted inhalations per minute. Marked this on the form. He jotted down the length of the boy's breath retention, finding it weak, due largely to panic, he noted, asterisk atop this. His exhalations were torrents, coming out with flying curses. He then would hold the breath after exhalation, an interesting twist. Malinowski would add his findings to the master chart he kept upstairs below his bed later, when there was time. On this he could compare to within seconds how each "volunteer" handled each sequence. Not a one of them seemed to know of the restorative formula of 3-5-7-9 which Solomon had taught him in his youth. Three seconds on inhalation, five to hold, seven on exhalation, nine to hold, that was the ticket to a calmer departure or a meeting of the mind with Solomon.

On his form, Malinowski also had a box for rate of speed, whether slow or rapid, the depth of breath, deep or shallow; whether the air was breathed out in a single gasp or a long blow, sudden or prolonged, smooth or jerky, done with a humming or wheezing sound. Robbie even had variations of fitful coughing. Malinowski looked for "purposeful" coughing, yawning, hiccuping, belching, sneezing, flatus. It all went into his records, and Robbie was providing more kick and fuss and fight than many other, earlier experiment in biodynamic breathing. He involved his lips, nose, throat, stomach, diaphragm, lungs, brain, heart, and sex organs. In fact, the whole body from toe to crown.

Malinowski panicked, suddenly seeing the boy's epileptic paroxysm stop cold. He threw down the clipboard and pencil, snatching open the bag at the zipper, allowing air to enter, *holy air* to escape. He breathed in as much CO_2 as he could, building toward the meeting with Solomon, his secret and powerful friend, but he worried the boy had gone, and that it was over. He'd allowed the starvation to go on too long. Or had he? The young man stirred in his near-catatonic condition and a labored breathing started up again.

Malinowski breathed easier. It would go on, the gratifying work of this night. He silently gave thanks to Solomon who had allowed it to be so.

Suddenly the boy vomited over himself. His bowels emptied. "So much standing in the way of the soul," Malinowski commented, closed the zipper, and took up his position again. He doubted the Ahmsted kid would last long after all, despite his initial fight.

Malinowski regained his pencil and pad, jotting check marks against the lines that corresponded with the subject's bodily functions.

Inside the bag it is hard to see the killer's face, but it is out there, the eyes staring back, teeth set and lips pulled back in a grimace, possibly half in empathy of the dying, near cataleptic one inside. This womb is inescapable and a pleasant feeling of release rushes over the mind, dissolving feeling or sensations or sickening odors of perspiration and worse. Coughing and gagging is silenced and the rest is like floating upward, like weightlessness. It is over and nothing bad can happen again.

But then the skin breathes somehow, and chills are felt along with the touch of cold, hard plastic along the collapsed thighs and buttocks, pressing against the feet. You could almost taste the oxygen let into the bag. Eyes are bleary, unseeing, and the bag's interior filled with a sickening film and odor that assails the nostrils but you're alive . . . Alive . . .

Then the sound of a rough, immediate *zip!* And it starts again and you scream.

Sybil shot upright in bed, waking from the nightmare, breathing as she'd never breathed before, bordering on hyperventilation. She'd seen and felt herself locked into the killing chamber. She had felt the killer's inhalations of her dying breath and the nightmare had shaken her to her core.

As a child, she had had a phobia about crowds and closed-in places. She could not abide closets or doors shut against tight places. As she had grown older, the fear had quietly resolved itself to the point where she could walk into a linen closet, pull the door behind her, and feel no undue stress, but something told her all that had changed back now.

She could hear movement in the outer rooms, Dean and Jackie, both early risers. She realized she'd soaked the sheets with perspiring and that she needed to shower again. She did so quickly and dressed for the office. The shower and mundane little things calmed her considerably, but she'd quaked unnaturally in the stall of the shower, the old claustrophobia settling in even there.

She shared a quiet (to distraction) breakfast with Dean and Jackie, Jackie looking beautiful, even in the plain white of her nurse's uniform. Sybil wore a matching skirt and jacket, black with a mild pink blouse, her hair pinned back. There was morning chatter between the Grants but it was stilted, forced, as if they'd been fighting and were now trying to hide the fact. It made Sybil feel ill at ease; made her feel out of place—which she was—and maybe in the way. The awkwardness eased only after Jackie left. Sybil and Dean were out the door fifteen minutes later, heading for the office.

"She's upset with me," Dean confided when they were on their way. "Jackie's worried about *you*."

"Is the whole world worried about me? I'm beginning to think there's something wrong with me."

"You've inherited a few of my nasty habits, like becoming a workaholic. Jackie was angry because she felt I had forgotten the reason I'd invited you over, which was to get your mind off work. That, somehow, all we talked about was work, and that it was my fault."

"That's not entirely true. I asked Dr. Taylor to speak her mind, not you."

"Seems that I'm not taking care of you enough to suit Jackie."

"Hey, tell her thanks, but I'm a big girl now." Sybil frowned, her hand going into her purse where she had folded the notepad of paper on which she had jotted down her thoughts on the killer. She crumpled it deeper into her purse, not sure just what she ought to do with her meanderings. Maybe talk to Dean about them, or more with Dr. Taylor. She hadn't decided. "Look, Jackie could never understand me; never understood why a woman, any woman, would willingly work the autopsy end of medicine instead of where she's at, degrees or not. It's taken her years to accept the fact that I'm more like you than she is, that we share a lot of things you and she can't, or won't.

173

The fact that she's worried about me, coming from her, I think I'll take that as a good sign, that we're finally friends."

"Easy for you to say," he said with a chuckle.

"A year ago, she wouldn't have dared leave us alone in your house, and I wouldn't have blamed her. I had a big crush on you, and she knew it."

"Crush? On me? Come on."

The radio crackled into life and Dean picked up the receiver. "Grant here."

"It's me, Dino, you alone?"

"Yeah," he said with a glance at Sybil.

"We got another body turned up, and from the look of it could be asphyxiation."

"Christ. Where do you want us?"

"End of the tarmac, north runway, Midway Airport."

"High visibility, huh?"

Kelso groaned. "We got press over this one like flies. Hurry up, will you?"

"On our way, and no—"

"Nobody touch nothing, I know . . . I know."

"Looks like we're up to bat again," he said to Sybil.

Sybil rubbed her hands into her face. "I knew it . . . I just could feel it. I even . . . even *dreamed* it! All this time wasted."

"Stop it right there, Sybil!" Dean shouted, whipping the car onto the expressway and bolting down the on ramp, not six blocks from their Wabash headquarters.

"But it's true, Dean!"

"Stop this, Sybil, it's not true!"

"I tell you, I—"

"We don't commit the crimes!"

"We don't stop them either!"

"Not always, but we do all in our power—"

She said bitterly, "Not enough! Not against such evil, such inhuman evil!"

"All we can do is point Kelso and people like him in the right direction and pray—pray like hell—it's the right direction. We are not miracle workers, nor are we psychics or fortune tellers. Damn it! We're just a couple of scientists kicking and poking at the bare residue left behind by a criminal act. I don't want to hear about your precognition or women's intuition. I want reports on the deceased, correlations you may infer from those factual findings, tests done on the micro aspects, and—"

"All right, you've made your point, Doctor."

He relented, sitting back, the big car moving now at top speed along the Kennedy Expressway, crossing onto the Stevenson that snaked along the Chicago Sanitary and Ship Canal. Sybil sat in stony silence, staring out the side at the images of Chicago which sped by in quicksilver fashion, as elusive as the killer himself.

Sometimes in her work, Sybil had indeed felt like a miracle worker, when some clue, invisible to the eye, had turned an innocent man loose or placed a guilty man behind bars. But she knew what Dean had said was true, that they were, after all, only people, and there was only so much a handful of law enforcement people could do to stem the Red Tide of blood and

175

violence. Especially now as she and Dean stared down at the most recent result. It lay face up in the grass off the runway. A crowd of policemen and reporters stood about as jets soared over them, creating a deafening sound that made communication between the two M.E.s difficult.

"It's a young man this time!" she shouted as another jet roared past and echoed away.

"We don't know he's a victim of the same killer, Sybil."

She knew. She knew it instinctively, and so did he. He was just being stubborn, holding out a strange but hardly misguided hope that this kid hadn't died the way yesterday's Jane Doe had, gagging for his last breath in a sealed vinyl bag.

She held back the eyelids and shined a light onto them. Nearby, one of Kelso's detectives was recording basic information for a report to Missing Persons, estimates on size, weight, age. He wrote down the color of the hair, any distinguishing marks other than the tight curls, and as another plane passed he shouted into Sybil's ear, "What color's his eyes?"

"Brown," she replied, "dark brown."

The skin tone was yellowish with splotches of a lighter hue. "Ten to one he's spent time in a freezer," she shouted over to Dean who nodded.

Kelso, overhearing this, knelt closer and asked, "You say a freezer?"

"That's a fair guess, Ken, at this point."

"God, you sound like Carr!" shouted Sybil.

Dean stared at her until she dropped her gaze and went on with the preliminary examination of the body. As with the other victims, no wallet or other identifying objects remained. There was, however, a broken lip, a mark that was clearly fresh and so colorful as to be prominent.

This one put up a fight, Sybil thought, but decided not to say it. She knew she wanted a sample of the splat of dried blood at the wound, but she also wanted it to remain intact for microphotos that could raise impressions for a rough estimate of whether the boy was hit with the right or the left hand. Could come in useful later on.

She worked hard to tell Dean these thoughts as the planes came in and out and the wind blew her hair from its pinnings. Dean concurred.

They took some nail scrapings, did some brushing of the clothing for fibers and prints, remarked how much nicer this one's clothes were, fashionable and not cheap. When they were finally satisfied, Sybil told the waiting, outwardly bored ambulance attendants to come ahead for the corpse. In the meantime, Don Carr had arrived, and he upset the applecart by suggesting that the signs were clear, that they had yet another victim of the Suffocator, as he'd begun to call the murderer.

Pressmen rushed at Carr with questions, pressing him to explain the term Suffocator. Dean looked on in anger and downright disgust and pulled Kelso aside. "When are you going to muzzle that guy?"

"Hey, I've tried. He's a good man and works hours you wouldn't believe. But he does have one major flaw: he's what you'd call a little too forthcoming."

"Honest to a fault."

"When he wants to be," added Sybil, glaring. "Just easily led into saying—and doing—things."

177

"Can you please get him free?" asked Dean. "This matter is still *ex officio*."

"See what I can do."

At that instant, Sybil shoved the folded and re-folded note she had written to herself on the killer into Kelso's huge hand. "Dean says we should point you in the right direction. This might help, I hope."

One reporter shouted a question in Dean's and Sybil's direction as they prepared to leave the scene. "How many people have to die before you people stop this madman?"

Dean ushered Sybil into his car again and they continued their interrupted journey to the office where they would be followed by victim number seven. "Forget those bastards and their questions, Sybil," said Dean. "How many of *them* are working night and day to catch this killer?"

"I'm okay . . . really."

He wasn't so sure.

Eleven

By mid-morning Dean had escaped the autopsy room for his office. Still in surgical garb, he clambered behind his desk, pushed some papers out of sight, and read over the results his people had gotten on the Schletter business. It all lined up so neat and proper, just as Dr. Samuel Carol had predicted it would, just as if the old man had prior knowledge. It recalled what Sybil had been getting at. No, forensics specialists weren't magicians or voodooist, but they did build up a store of experience and knowledge over the years, even one as young as Sybil. Memorized horror in some cases. Every brutal scar, every single burn, gash, they all came back when the attending doctor stared anew at similar marks of murder, brutality, molestation. From knife wounds to gunshot wounds and down the line to hacksaw marks like those picked up on the Schletter victims, Dean had seen it before, and if he long continued in this macabre practice, he'd see it again. Perhaps the only certainty in his profession.

He was satisfied Dr. Sam's prognosis of the Schletter massacre was accurate. The old man had done it without half the equipment, and had in fact summed up the situation on the spot. Dean had pulled off similar re-creations of the crime at the scene, but he had learned from hard experience that such scrutiny and observation must and should remain in-house. He'd known on inspection of the young male in the autopsy room that he was indeed another asphyxiation victim, just as Sybil had. He'd known the moment he looked down at the inert form in the tall grass near the runways. But only now could he, with full freedom, make the call to the CPD.

He dialed the touch tone phone by hitting the memory selector for Ken Kelso's direct line.

Luckily, Kelso was in and, from the sound of it, eating something at his desk.

"You know that suspect you got in the asphyxiation case?"

"The rail man, yeah."

"Well, you don't have him anymore."

"Work of the same killer this morning, huh?"

"Precisely."

"Never thought that old-timer was guilty. Went on with the investigation as if certain of that fact. Some of my people didn't like the notion, but they'll be set straight today. Thanks, Dino." He started to hang up but then shouted, "Oh, by the way, tell Sybil that her laundry list on this madman's being typed, Xeroxed, and distributed to all my men. She's on target. I'd give my right arm to have her in my d—"

"Forget it, you don't have enough bucks to woo

180

her away. Besides, I saw her first."

"Sure, rub it in my face."

"Face it, you just don't know how to treat a woman."

"Tell you what, unless you've got something else, screw off."

"That any way to talk to a friend?"

"Got tickets to the Cubs a week from Saturday and Kristie can't go. How about it?"

"Sounds good, I'll let you know. Say, are we any closer to catching this creep?"

"Not a whole hell of a lot, no."

"Any news on Schletter?"

"You'll be the first to know, promise."

Dean watched James Remmer through the glass, ferreting around by some equipment where Dean had left materials not to be touched. He wanted to shout him away. "Look, I've got to go."

"Shalom."

The latest victim's death struggle signs lined up right behind the two Jane Does, Jory Bemis and the prior suspicious deaths, no question about it. Dean's caution aside, Sybil knew it was bad form to speak out of school on any case, that it wasn't the job of the Chicago Coroner's Office to supply the *Tribune* and the *Sun-Times* with copy. But since this morning's incident, coming as it did on the heels of the girl found floating in the river, the halls were buzzing with reporters and excitement. The press wanted and demanded disclosure.

Dean had provided for such incidents, creating

within the new structure a public relations firm and hiring the best bull-slingers in the business. The men and women of the PR department upstairs had learned their lessons in advertising and business. They knew how to put the best light on the darkest picture. They knew how to write copy that said everything and said nothing in the same breath. And now they went to work with Dean's input and some from Sybil to diffuse the panic and furor caused by Donald Carr's office in the CPD, which, to be fair, had next to no help in the PR area. Dean sympathized with Carr's position. It hadn't been so long ago that he was in that position, bombarded by the press daily, sometimes hourly.

Just getting out to lunch was a problem in those days, and today at Wabash it was not so easy either. The idea of the Suffocator, who cut off a man's breathing, was tantalizing and mind-blowing at once, the kind of story that made slavering hounds of reporters. It sold papers, and so catapulted careers.

Sybil was hounded out the door and for a block before she called a cop to rid herself of a reporter. Once free, she arrived at her destination, a twelve-block walk, the Chicago Public Library, a building that always made her feel small and insignificant. Inside, using her lunch hour, she looked up and located two of the three books Dr. Taylor had put her onto. When she went to check them out, she was told that neither book circulated.

She explained who she was and why she needed the books, but was politely put off again.

"Do you have a supervisor, someone I can speak to who has some sense of . . ."

The clerk buzzed someone in an inner office. An attractive man in his mid-to late thirties sauntered out. He wore jeans and looked like a refugee time traveler from 1969 in wire-rimmed glasses, shoulder-length hair, and a beard. The beard was a reddish brown, the hair a dark brown. Beneath it all the eyes shone like beacons of curiosity and interest. "I'm Terry Ferman. How can I help you, Miss?"

"Doctor, Dr. Sybil Shanley," she replied.

He beamed, "Really, good, very good. Then how can I help you, Dr. Shanley?"

She repeated her wishes, flashing her library card.

"I've been reading about this guy they're calling the Suffocator. Is that all true?"

"Close enough to true to make your skin crawl," she confided, "but I'm really not at liberty to discuss it. Now, about the books. They could be important to the case, and as the Deputy Medical Examiner of the City, I should think the City Library would not want to—"

"Take them. Miss Brandt, see that Dr. Shanley's card is updated as well." He smiled and said to Sybil, "Expired seven and a half months ago."

"Oh, well . . . we have our own medical library in the building."

"A fine one, too, I'm sure." He was openly flirting now.

"What precisely is your title here, Mr. Ferman?"

"Communications Specialist and Overseer, you might say."

She smiled now.

"Look, why don't you fill this out for us, so we're sure we've got all the pertinent information we need on you?" he suggested. "While Miss Brandt is taking the necessary steps to check you out."

"All right, anything to help the cause," she said.

His eyebrows lifted at this remark. "I suppose dinner would be going too far . . ." He let the suggestion hang.

"I'm sorry, maybe sometime when I'm not so busy."

He managed to rebound with a smile, saying, "Perhaps when you get your library card renewed?"

She laughed lightly. He said good-bye and returned to his office and computer console. On leaving she waved to him through the glass but she wasn't sure he'd seen her.

She hefted the two books and started back for the office feeling like a schoolgirl. At her desk, she started leafing through the books for the sections she was interested in, slipping slits of paper as markers between the pages she'd want to read. One book in particular looked readable, while the other was written in such obtuse language it was off-putting immediately. When she had narrowed her reading, she looked up to find Donald Carr tapping at her windowed door.

She waved him in. He looked like a boy come to confess to a petty crime. "How's it going, Dr. Shanley?"

"Not too awful," she said.

"I thought you'd like to know, I'm quitting the CPD."

"Quitting?"

He pursed his lips, raised his shoulders and

replied, "Stepping down gracefully before the bomb hits."

"Fowler?"

"Gosh, you're astute."

She frowned. "You're letting him run you out? Have you talked to Dean about this?"

"What's he going to do?"

"You don't know Dean."

He shook his head, "No point dragging it out, and I really don't want anymore flack falling your way."

"Hey, you forget something, Doctor."

He turned at the door, hearing that fight in her voice which he'd missed. "What's that?"

"I brought the flack on myself. You just got in the middle and didn't know that friendly fire kills, too."

He returned to her and slumped in a chair opposite her. For a moment they just stared at one another. "Sybil, I let you down."

"Yes, you did."

"I hurt you."

"You did."

"I hurt myself."

"Believe me, you did."

"So, why're you even suggesting—"

She threw up her hands, "You think I've never made a mistake? Or Dean? If it's not with the lab work, and you dance over minefields there, believe me, then it's with the politics of the game."

"I'm still Deputy here and Marshal Grant's got the biggest six-shooters."

Carr managed a laugh. Everyone knew that Dean Grant got results, and with people like Sybil in his corner, Carr understood why. And in a city like Chicago—a town that always asked the question, *What've you done for me lately?*—M.E. Grant was known as a man who could deliver.

Sybil continued to talk easily. "We'll just go talk to him. He likes you, Don. I don't know why," she jested, "but he does. Anyway, if anybody can put a gun to Fowler's head, it's Dean Grant."

"Thanks, Sybil. What're you reading these days? Awfully large book."

"Light reading," was all she said, a wave of distrust still flitting through her mind.

"Sybil, you think we can ever pick up where we left off?"

Grant buzzed her on the intercom. She picked up, "Dr. Shanley."

"Those final tests on our young man aren't going to complete themselves, Dr. Shanley. Remmer tells me everything's hanging fire waiting for you."

"Jim Remmer's got a big mouth. He's also incompetent."

"Think maybe you've been riding him a bit hard? Remember, he's not too keen on remaining in path work and—"

"Then maybe he ought to move on."

"Sybil, he tells me you gave him a vial of dirt and told him to analyze it."

"That's right, and he did it."

"Aren't we a little busy for that sort of thing?"

She took in a deep breath of air. "You asked me to train him. It was part of his training. I wanted to see if he could follow orders, make the test, and come out with the right answers. Call it a pop quiz."

186

"Well, now that graveyard dirt's sticking in his craw, atop all the necessary work around here."

"I felt it was necessary, Dean. He's sneaky and he rushes through things."

"All right, so did he pass the test to your satisfaction?"

"Except for going to you with it."

"You'll meet me in the lab?"

"Carr's here."

"Then the rumor I've been hearing that he's hanging it up at the CPD isn't true?"

She held down the button. "You want to assist or not?"

"I'm with you," Carr said with an eager nod.

"Dean, he says there's not a shred of truth to that lie."

"Good, bring him along. I've got a few bones to pick with him anyway. I also heard another rumor—that you're doing the work of Kelso's special investigative unit."

She thought of the list of suppositions she'd drawn up and pushed into Kelso's hand. Apparently, he liked what he had read and made it known to Dean. "Yeah, maybe I'll retire and become a private eye some day," she replied and signed off.

They got lucky in the lab.

Sybil's care with the bruise and blood from the latest victim's mouth revealed that minute portions of the blood belonged to a second person, very likely the killer's. There it was, below her microscope, the blood of a demon. What perverted course had the

187

DNA of this man taken to become such a satanic creature? Invisible even to electron microscopes, the cause of sadism might never be known to science. Still, the blood provided clues to the DNA of this man, and it could be tested against any suspect Kelso might take into custody. A matchup could end the horror instantly. The only problem, unfortunately, was that they had no suspect to match the blood with.

At the end of the day, with nightfall approaching, the same fear that had overtaken her the night before began to encroach on her state of mind. She was careful to keep it hidden. She finished out the day with a pleasant mask, said good night to Dean and Carr, leaving earlier than usual, saying she had some rest to catch up on.

Dean had been ecstatic over her discovery of the murderer's blood, so much so that she had to caution him by saying, "We can only assume it's the killer's blood, and assumptions can be dangerous."

He recognized his own words coming back at him.

"Oh, by the way, Missing Persons has made a possible match with a report," he said.

"On our young man?"

"Right, A *possible* father's on his way down here, but I can take care of it, if you like."

"My turn, isn't it?" she asked.

"Not necessarily, Sybil. You have nothing to prove to me."

"It's my case."

"So it is. Then you'll meet him? Name's Ahmsted."

"Ahmsted, okay. On his way from where?"

"Fullerton near Sacramento."

"Time for coffee?"

"You may have time," he replied. "Take Don here with you. Nothing in the rule book says you've got to face a bereaved father alone."

She nodded, "All right, Don. How about buying me a cup of coffee?"

"I'll call Joe Diaz to get the body into viewing."

Dean had seen to it that the area where the public came in to view a body for purposes of identification was as pleasant as human beings could make it. It was air-conditioned, reducing the odors and heat and chances of becoming faint as much as possible. The viewer stood before a thick window and the body was wheeled up to it. If the ID was made, and the bereaved relative wished to enter with the body, this was his prerogative; if he or she did not wish to, this was all right, too. The viewing area was equipped with comfortable furniture and good lighting. All that was spoken here was recorded on tape and everyone entering knew it beforehand. But no matter the precautions, the place was worse than any sick room in any hospital, and there was truly nothing anyone could do to lessen the blow of death to those remaining behind who cared.

On the other hand, for those not emotionally involved, the room worked like a charm. The ID work went efficiently in such cases.

Sybil knew the moment she met Ahmsted that he was a caring father, and if the dead youth they'd found at Midway was his boy, there was going to be nothing neat and efficient about this reunion. Ahmsted was shaking with nerves, another son trying to reassure him that no way could it be Robbie.

189

"Where is he then? He never stayed away like this!" He turned to Sybil who introduced herself, Carr doing likewise beside her. "My Robbie, he never pulled any crap. Nothing bad anyway! He didn't come home last night."

"Pop," the other boy was tearing up, "it's a mistake. Got to be a mistake."

Sybil explained in a calm voice what the procedure was, telling Ahmsted that his son must be over eighteen to view the body with him. "Joey's nineteen," he said. "Let's get on with it."

Carr went ahead of them and into the room where the body lay pressed against the window, the specially designed gurney tilted the length of one side to present the corpse fully to the viewer. Overhead, on a TV screen, a closeup camera shot of Robbie Ahmsted seemed to knock Ahmsted down as if it were a direct hit. He slumped and crumpled to the floor with a cry, going limp in the legs, his clothes looking like a sack around him. His other boy had grabbed him halfway into the fall and now lay with him at the center of the room. They hadn't said a word for the tape, but they'd IDed the cadaver.

"Oh, God, oh, oh! My baby, my baby boy!" Ahmsted cried.

Shaken, Sybil tried to help him. The one named Joey lashed out at her. "Leave him alone! Leave us both alone!" He held tight to his father's form. The man's gaze had a catatonic appearance and he began to jerk unsteadily. Sybil shouted for Carr to give her a hand and he came rushing forward.

"I think he's having some sort of seizure, cardiac arrest maybe!"

Carr hit the intercom and shouted for a medic team on the double, giving the location. Sybil tried to reason with the living son, "Lay his head back! Give him space!"

She tore away at the funny, out-of-fashion tie the old man wore. He was breathing irregularly. Joey was shouting for her to do something. She began mouth-to-mouth and CPR techniques. Don Carr was splitting the buttons off the old man's shirt and pounding on his chest when the medic team arrived with medicine and machines. Sybil and Don backed off and let the medics go to work. Carr came around to her and put an arm around her. She leaned into him and looked across at the stricken eyes of Ahmsted's older son.

Ahmsted was stabilized via injection directly to the heart, and the fluttering green line that had straightened at one point with a mechanical banshee screech, now became a healthier zigzag and beeping sound.

Twelve

Malinowski was disconsolate. He knew he should not have done Ahmsted's son. It was a mistake for many reasons, paramount among them was that he knew the victim, could be connected with him. He worried all day over this after he'd dumped the body, all day at the counter, wrapping chops and veal and grinding beef; worried over lunch at Ahmsted's where everything was in disarray and confusion, the old man completely at a loss as to the whereabouts of his son and the older boy staring a hole through Malinowski as if he knew.

Always before when he selected a subject for Solomon, he hadn't known them. With Robbie Ahmsted, he'd seen the boy growing up. For all of his cantankerousness, Ahmsted was a neighbor, a person with whom Malinowski had had dealings, association. He felt no remorse, for after all the young man had gone to serve a better master than his father, to fulfill a greater destiny. What he did feel was the creeping possibility that someone had seen Robbie enter his apartment that night, or had known of his plan to meet with Malinowski.

The worry was like a canker that began as a small enough irritation but got out of control. Never before had he to worry about his victim's family. None of the others had ties. Suppose they began asking questions. Suppose the police were brought in? Atop this concern was the stupid and rash dumping of the one in the river. He learned through the accounts in the papers that the body hadn't sunk after he had raced away. Suppose the man walking the dog had had even a glimpse of him? Today the police had no one in custody for the crimes. The newspapers and politicans and people were restless for blood—his blood—and so the police would only too gladly check out a story from whatever remote source that said maybe Louis Malinowski knows something about the disappearance of young Robbie Ahmsted.

He was shaken by the possibilities.

He sat in a corner of the freezer with his legs pulled up, giving it thought.

He imagined what they'd do to him if they found the records he kept. The world wasn't ready for his findings on oxygen deprivation and carbon dioxide highs. No one could possibly understand. No one knew about Solomon. No one would listen.

Suppose they found his master chart upstairs?

He pondered the possibilities. So fearful were these that he couldn't cope, could not function. He had to think this out and prepare for the worse case scenario.

He thought of burning his records, thought about it for some time.

So much time in accumulating them, however. He couldn't see sending Solomon's words up in smoke and ash!

He considered burying them, or hiding them in a place no one would think to look. He considered one hiding place after another. Perhaps a bank's safe deposit box. This seemed a good idea. He'd see to it tomorrow as soon as the bank opened.

He felt instantly better now that he'd thought it through and made a decision. He also decided his freezer needed a complete cleansing. That was something he could do tonight. He got up, located the necessary cleansing agents and rags and mop. He'd leave the freezer spotless, get the papers out of the house along with the wallets and purses he'd accumulated, and then just let them come . . .

He'd have to get a large deposit box for all the garbage upstairs, the largest available.

Carr saw Sybil to her door where he handed over the books she'd brought from the office with her. Carr, curious about the books, had read the titles and asked what she expected to get from such reading.

"Not sure. Not yet," she'd said.

"You take care, Sybil. Get some rest."

Sybil's place was the first apartment she had really settled into, putting her stamp on the place, sparing no expense for the furniture and carpets and drapes she wanted. All her student life, all her first years as an intern and the grueling years as a training autopsiest, she had had the lean and hungry years. Now she indulged herself with thick beige carpeting, white drapes, and a huge white sofa. Her bedroom had a white, airiness about it too. An old love and hefty cop, Carl Prather, had called her bedroom an "angel's den." She liked the connotations and thought of it still as such.

She fixed herself a light meal, macaroni and cheese, greens on the side, a tumbler of milk. As she ate, she began leafing through one of the books from the library. At the kitchen table, below the harsh lights, her feet sore from the day, she nibbled some, read some, nibbled and read on, until the food grew cold and she put it aside in favor of the book.

She moved into the living room, still reading, fascinated by what the book was revealing to her. Certain passages, she thought, could have been written for, about, or even *by* the killer—or was her imagination running away from her? Could Dr. Taylor, a complete stranger to the case, an outsider who knew virtually nothing about the physical evidence, be so keenly and objectively correct about the killer? Was it possible?

Under a section on respiration, she learned that the breath of men, especially the last, expelled when released in sacrifices was thought to draw down from the spiritual world the hidden potencies that resided there. From the emanations of the dying breath, discarnate entities supposedly built their apparitional shapes to make themselves visible.

There was a long section on breath-retention techniques that went into some detail on Indian and African wonder workers who practiced a kind of suspended animation during which all senses were deprived. They had such control over their breathing that they could suspend their breathing for two or three hours, and were allegedly buried for hours without harm. They retained in their lungs a small reserve of air—like a child fallen into a freezing lake—capable of feeding the brain and precious organs the oxygen in minute amounts.

She read of transpowering, the belief that one could take on the energies of another through various means, one of these being breath-taking in the literal sense.

She read of conspiration, or co-breathing, in which case the breathing of two people is reciprocally harmonized. Considerable pages were spent on conspiration in sexual magic. She went on, flipping ahead, her mind filling with wonder. How much of this fit the killer, how much described his horrible design?

She was a scientist first and last, and to her all things sane and normal and natural in life had a magnificent quality of *arrangement*. The natural aggregate of the parts of organisms, the clean orderliness, the relationship of the various patterns the parts formed to the whole and to one another was remarkable. It was seen in the movement of electrons in molecules, the order of the planets and constellations, the angles in a crystal, direction and curve of a spiral, the design of the shell, scales on a fish, and in the humble soap bubble. It was seen in the location of the roots, trunk, and branches of a tree, the pattern of leaves on a stem, and the veins within each leaf. In the whorls on a flower petal. But nowhere was the sanity and order of the world more evident than in the architecture of the bony and muscular structure, in the arrangement of human organs and limbs. It was so in the human brain. And when that order was disrupted, perverted, disarranged, this to her seemed the root of all evil.

She marked passages in the book she felt pertinent, possibly pertinent, and just bizarre enough to be pertinent to the case at hand. She did her homework until late and fell asleep on the couch with the second book couched in her arm.

When Ken Kelso learned of the positive ID on the latest victim of asphyxial death, and what had occurred over at Dean's viewing room, he thought of the earlier positive ID in the case, the Bemis woman who'd viewed her brother's unearthed remains without so much as a tear. Perhaps she'd shed too many tears over the years for the boy, for herself. At any rate, people were vastly different and unquestionably full of inconsistencies and surprises. After several days of bombarding Bemis's sister with questions, returning to her again and again, Ken's people had gotten very little return on their investment. The initial visit had been futile. She didn't know or care where Jory might've eaten a steak dinner. She wanted to forget Jory. She wanted to get on with her life.

Kelso wondered if they'd get anymore out of Ahmsted, at least a better picture of his son's habits, list of friends and acquaintances, where he might have picked up a steak meal that night. He wondered, too, if the old man and his other son would willingly submit to a blood test. To this end, as soon as

Ahmsted was listed as stable and capable of seeing visitors, he sent his men over. That was around midnight, and Kelso was being kept informed at home where he was spending a quiet evening with his live-in girlfriend, Kristie Howlett.

He had left word he was to be notified only if they came up with anything *useful*.

The problem, of course, was recognizing that which was useful and that which was useless. Almost ninety-five percent of information gathered on an investigation was superfluous. Often, if not always, the overflow confused more often than it helped, and sometimes it was by mere luck, or chance, that someone saw the five percent in the clutter that might actually be useful. And here he was asking men to distinguish between the two types of information before disturbing him with nonsense. It was like hanging out a Do No Disturb sign.

He didn't really expect to hear anything tonight. Still, for some unaccountable reason, he was edgy, half here, half elsewhere.

As for the plastic bag man at Falcon's who was going to get back to him, *zilch!* Kelso had gone to the manufacturer, Linmeyer's. They, too, were sympathetic to his problem and cooperative, and he was given a cup of coffee, but little or no answers. Other of his men were pursuing other distributors, manufacturers, all armed with a photo of the bag, the serial number, and list of questions.

Several of Sybil Shanley's suggestions struck him as psychic. The bit about the bodies being kept at a near-freezing temperature would jive with the bag's being used for storage in a cold spot, say for meats.

On more than one occasion now he'd been told that a lot of this type of body bag was used by the meat industry. They were sold by the hundreds and thousands to the meat-packing centers, like those lining Hubbard at Franklin. It could be a guy working out of one of these meat-packing companies, takes a few bags home, but then he'd have to have a pretty large freezer, too, according to forensics.

This avenue jived also with what was shaping up as the last meals of the deceased, a hearty steak.

Kelso kicked it over and over, not sleeping well once he did doze off.

But deep into sleep Kristie roused him, pushing and punching and telling him it was for him.

"What's for me?"

"Telephone, Ken. Your guy at the hospital."

He rubbed his eyes and took the phone in hand. "What've you got?"

"Nothing concrete, Chief, but something the boy said."

"The boy?"

"The dead kid's brother. The old man didn't know much, but the brother seemed to think a neighbor could be involved in Robbie Ahmsted's death. I tell you, Chief, this kid was a gem. Brother tells us that he was taking some lessons from a guy down the street, and get this, it's a butcher."

"A butcher?" Kelso tried to keep that excitement in his voice in check. It could just be a coincidence. Investigative work was chock full of coincidence. The older he got, the more he saw it. He didn't want to get either himself or his detectives racing down a blind alley and so wasting more time. With a serial killer of this type, time meant more bodies dropping from out of nowhere. "Okay, so what's this guy's name?"

"Malinowski, Louis Malinowski, but the old man he doesn't see it, doesn't believe Malinowski capable of killing, and says he had no reason to harm his boy."

"What sort of deal did the boy strike with this guy?"

"Wanted to apprentice in the trade."

"Butchering?"

"So says the brother, but the father says he don't know nothing about that."

Kelso scratched his chin. "What do you think?"

"Kid's adamant, followed us out and repeated his statement, even made a threat, but I put the fear of God into him, I think."

"What's this guy's address? Any prior arrests?"

It was only a handful of doors down from the restaurant run by Ahmsted and his sons. Kelso knew the neighborhood fairly well.

"I've got Dwight looking into priors. Anything else, Chief?"

"Leave word with your a.m. replacements not to approach this guy—"

"Not to?"

"I'll check this one out myself."

"Then you think there's something—"

"Also leave word to canvass the neighborhood for others living there who have noticed anything unusual either at the butcher shop, or in the way this guy Malinowski's been conducting himself. Any changes of habit, anything out of the ordinary for the man, you know."

Thirteen

The following morning Inspector Kenneth Kelso was out early, driving toward the Fullerton/Pulaski area where the Ahmsted restaurant—a place called The Delightful Deli—and Louis Malinowski's butcher shop shared the same block. Kelso radioed headquarters, got in touch with two of his special unit members, informed them of his whereabouts, and asked if any priors were on the books for Louis Malinowski.

"Nothing officially on record."

"What the hell's that supposed to mean?"

"Well, nothing on Louis Malinowski *Jr.*, the guy you're talking about, but Ahmsted's kid . . . well, he kinda threw a flag down on the play. Seems Malinowski's father committed a pretty nasty crime when our man was just a kid."

"Mac, what's pretty nasty?"

"Murder."

"Are you shittin' me? Really?"

"Killed his wife in a rage."

"How?"

"Knife, or *knives* from the sound of it. He was a butcher, too."

"When and where?"

"1958. Same location you're heading for."

"Christ, this is shaping up, Mac."

"Agreed, you maybe want backup?"

"No, too soon for that, but it's not too soon to start knockin' on doors, say within a block or two of the shop."

"Got it. And Chief? be careful. This guy saw his old man do it to his old lady. He could be psycho, reenacting—"

Kelso laughed into the radio, "Hey, Mac, when'd you turn into a shrink?"

"Been readin' up."

"Keep up the good work. Meet you and Bob at Ahmsted's, say about noon."

"Got it."

"Out." Kelso clicked off, glad that he had let someone know his intentions. The car moved into the area slowly, a jam up ahead, some problem evolving into much cursing between a cabbie and a guy in a Ford Torino, decked out in frills, including window shades. It was an old neighborhood that'd become a conglomerate of ethnic groups, where family-run establishments were operated within the same space zoned as residential, the storefronts on the street level, apartments above. Despite all the efforts of city planners and zoning board commissions, developers and bulldozers, some of Chicago's ethnic neighborhoods had miraculously survived the onslaught of the years, and this was one of them. For

Kelso, a lifer, it was like driving back into the past, as if time, if not quite held still here, was at least held in a kind of quasi-cease-fire.

The block was lined on either side with picture windows filled with hardware, liquor, furniture, musical instruments, books, electrical appliances. There were toy and novelty shops, a pawnshop, the requisite corner bar with broken neon sign, a sad little grocery store with crates of vegetables heaved into the window, Ahmsted's deli, and further down a Chinese take-out. Still further down a red and white candy-cane pole indicated the location of the friendly neighborhood barbershop. Amid it all, hiding away in the urban forest, was Malinowski's sign—or more appropriately, his father's sign. It'd gone untouched for so long the letters were peeled and faded, proclaiming: Lou's Butcher Shoppe.

Something about the place made his skin itch. He wondered as he cruised by, if there could be a haunted butcher shop in the middle of Chicago in 1989. Could be, if this place used see-through, four-foot-long bags with custom thick seams and loops for hooking up meats neatly in the freezer. He wondered if he could possibly be close to an answer to the series of crimes facing him. His mind ticked off the victims, the clues the dead had grudgingly given up, the facts that had led him to this busy neighborhood where mothers hung out windows shouting for their kids; where customers still dickered over prices; where men like Ahmsted and Malinowski were street characters as well as businessmen.

They should have no trouble learning about Malinowski's outward appearance, his temperment, and proclivities. Many a neighbor would fill in such gaps. The cautious thing to do would be to follow the course he was taking now, cruise on by and remain out of sight. The butcher suddenly showed himself, putting a sign on the door. But then he was gone as quickly as he came, disappearing from Kelso's sideview mirror as the car moved down the street. Malinowski had hung a sign on the front door, probably a price slash or an increase of some sort. The suspect was wearing a bloody apron.

Kelso went around the block, picking up speed, readying to go around again, to give the whole thing a re-think. As he did so, he wondered about the wisdom of backing a bit away from his prey. Give him time to hang himself. Just enough rope to do himself in. The other alternative, the one he'd originally believed necessary—before he had the facts about Malinowski's childhood trauma—was to burst in on Malinowski in his shop with a hatful of questions and quasi-allegations.

If he slowed down, got the goods on the man beforehand, and it was adding up to something odorous, that would give him grounds to swear out a warrant for search and seizure. He could confiscate anything on the premises, some of which could seal a case against Malinowski, if he was, indeed, a mass murderer. Kelso imagined hauling every goddamned plastic bag and container the man owned downtown for Dean and Sybil to inspect for trace elements of blood and mucous and body fluids. He might find a cache of steaks laced with drugs. There was no telling what evidence this guy could destroy if he knew they were onto him, or even if he suspected it. If there was evidence that could nail a ghoul like this killer, who slowly suffocated his victims inside this shop, or in Malinowski's private quarters above the store, Kelso wanted possession of it. He'd seen too damned many felons and killers walk away for lack of physical evidence.

On passing the store again, he saw the sign that'd been put out, squinting to make it out. Be Back Soon, it read.

Damn! He was gone!

Kelso cut into an alley that took him around back, but there was no sign of the man. He cursed his luck and stared at a pair of tire tracks that were wide and spaced well apart, likely those of a van. He recalled the rail man's advice when they cut him loose, "Look for a white van with writing on its side, like a milk truck."

A powerful desire filled Kelso, a desire to walk over to the shop, take the stairs to the back of the man's flat, and break the door down. He had to fight back the desire. Anything discovered in such a way would be useless to them. Still, it would tell them they had indeed the right man targeted.

He toyed with the notion a moment longer, but instead got on the radio, alerting any units in the area to his need. "Be on the lookout for a white van with lettering, something like Malinowski's Butcher Shoppe with two *p*'s and an *e* in shop. If you spot suspect van, do not approach, but keep in sight and please report." Several units responded, one asking how to spell Malinowski. Mac came on also. He and Bob were only blocks away.

"You want us to proceed as planned or go looking

for the van?"

"As planned."

A few minutes later, while Kelso was locating a parking place on the street, his radio crackled back to life. "P-102, this is Unit 72, we have your van in sight."

"This is Kelso. Where are you?"

"Lincoln National, it's parked in the lot. Presume driver is inside. Early hour bank."

Cash-flow problems? Kelso wondered. "Thank you, 72."

"Anything further, 102?"

"Don't allow him to see you. Keep tabs on him at the same time."

"Can do. Over and out."

"Out."

Then Kelso saw a short, stocky old woman in a sweater and scarf, what Kelso's mother called a babushka, at the door to the butcher shop, stomping up a whirling dervish of the street dirt that had accumulated in the doorway. She looked an obvious regular to the shop. Kelso knew he wanted to buy the woman a cup of coffee over at Ahmsted's and chat with her, if she was not frightened off by him.

He got out of his unmarked unit and sauntered over to the shop, and as he got within earshot of the woman, said, "What a nuisance! I need to get in the butcher shop and it's closed! Damn, oh, pardon me ma'am. Sorry."

"Damn is right!" she repeated the curse. "This is not the first time, you know!"

"Oh, really? I thought Mr. Malinowski was quite reliable."

208

"Ha! This is getting *reliable*, waiting out in the cold!" It was a balmy seventy, a bit windy.

"Look, why don't we wait over at the deli for him to open and while we're there, I could buy you a cup of coffee? And—"

"I don't drink the stuff."

"Oh?" She was gray-haired, nearly toothless, her face sunken, but the eyes bright with energy.

"I'll take tea, though."

"Tea it is then."

"But I don't know you? Do I know you?"

"I'm Ken, Ken Kelso of—"

"Kelso, oh, yeah, you been away for awhile, but I remember."

She couldn't possibly remember. Kelso had never met her in his life before.

"I'm with the Chicago Police Department, ma'am."

"Oh, really? My, you've come far."

"Miss, ahhh—"

"Mrs., Mrs. Morris Kunkel."

He led her to Ahmsted's where no one knew him. The place was short-handed, the old man still in the hospital. The atmosphere was subdued, the clatter of dishes ringing.

Over tea and coffee and pastries, Kelso began asking Mrs. Kunkel about previous times she'd found the shop closed to her. She was loud and sure, but also vague about just what day it was.

"It's very important, Mrs. Kunkel. Was it two days ago?"

She thought on it hard, scorn and frail teeth showing with her scrunched brow. "Yes, yes, because

209

I went down to Field's that same day on the bus."

"Do you have any idea when the shop opened that morning?"

"Very late, almost nine-thirty."

"Now, Mrs. Kunkel, are you certain of all this?" He'd jotted down the essentials of her "testimony." She'd watched him do so in awe of the fact.

"Yes, as sure as rain. Something's wrong in here," she said, looking around the restaurant. "Where's the old man? Where's Ahmsted?" she shouted.

"Hospital," replied one of the waitresses. "Heart attack."

"Oh, my lord."

Kelso didn't want her getting completely upset. He said nothing about the dead boy. Apparently some of the help at the restaurant hadn't been informed either.

"Now, tell me, Mrs. Kunkel, have you noticed anything else lately about Mr. Malinowski, anything unusual, out of the ordinary, anything you thought peculiar to his usual habits or customs?"

"Drinks a lot."

"Oh? And he didn't before?"

"Well, I haven't seen him falling over, but he has headaches in the morning and his eyes are all bloodshot so bad he cut himself the other day, bled right on my calve's liver and the paper it come in."

Kelso's heart skipped a beat, realizing instantly what this meant. He took in a deep breath of air, ran a hand across his own excited features and looked about before asking, "Mrs. Kunkel, do you think you could find that calves' liver? I'll pay you twice as much as you paid for it."

She giggled like a schoolchild. "Oh, really, Mr. Kels, I . . . I couldn't."

"Twenty dollars. Twenty-five."

"But it's ate," she said, giggling more.

"The wrapper it came in, do you have it?"

"I'm not in the habit of—"

"Is it in your trash bin yet?"

"Possibly . . . I think, maybe . . ."

"Mrs. Kunkel, it could prove invaluable. It could even save a life."

She frowned at this as if she were staring at a naughty boy who'd just told a whopper. "Young man, you may have it if you like, but I'm not at all in the habit of having men up to my apartment."

"I'll stand outside," he countered. "Just place your trash bin out in the hall."

She pursed her lips. "For twenty-five dollars," she reminded him.

"All right."

She downed her tea and donned her babushka, saying, "Come along then."

When they exited the restaurant, she said, "He's back. Look, I don't want to make another trip back. I'm going over to get my needs."

Kelso knew there was no arguing with her. "All right, look, I'm your nephew—"

"What?"

"If Mr. Malinowski should ask. I'm just helping you shop."

"Malinowski knows I don't have any nephews, that is if he ever listens to me."

"All right, you don't know me. We go in separately, and exit separately . . . say nothing to me."

She frowned but nodded and went on her way. He gave her leeway, uncertain if he should go in and meet this malcontent Malinowski himself or not. Part of him said yes, part of him said be patient and stretch out the caution. Cops the world over were still looking for that creep, Emil Schletter. Should Malinowski bolt, it could go just as badly. Another little voice, as irrational as it was, told him he couldn't let Mrs. Kunkel go into that shop alone, although she'd obviously been doing so now for years and years.

He went in behind her and found the shop busy with two others. Mrs. Kunkel was loudly protesting that she should be allowed to go ahead of the line, as she'd been the first to the store. The big man behind the white porcelain and stainless steel and glass— Malinowski—looked rather plain and ordinary. The grimace about the mouth and the indent at the top of the nose, directly between the eyes, gave him an angry, John Ireland sneer, but otherwise, he looked as normal as anyone in the room. Kelso, pretending interest in the meats displayed, watched Malinowski's reaction when the shoppers began talking about the fact that Ahmsted had been looking desperately for his youngest boy, and that he was now in the hospital. Malinowski evinced complete and total shock and disquiet.

Kelso noticed how large the butcher's hands were and how they folded the paper over the meat; he saw a small scar just above the little finger on his left hand, a slit as might be made by a knife. Malinowski asked one man how his wife was doing, if she'd gotten over the flu. The customer tried to joke about his wife's

212

condition, saying it'd come on in 1979 and hadn't left her since. But the tone of affection told everyone he was truly worried about her. Malinowski said, "Here, take some soup meat. Make a broth from this, you'll amaze her."

The man tried to pay, but his butcher refused, "My little contribution to getting her well."

Mrs. Kunkel butted ahead of the rest and got her order. "You've put me off long enough, Louie!"

"Yes, Mrs. Kunkel," he said, and looked into the eyes of his other customer, begging patience with a slight shrug. Mrs. Kunkel tried to bargain for a better price per pound on the ground beef she ordered. Malinowski was firm with her, not budging an inch, giving tit for tat. She stormed out without a word more. Malinowski served his next customer, apologizing profusely.

Then Malinowski looked up at Kelso over the scale. "And how may I help you, sir? New to the neighborhood?"

"I'm in the market to buy a store like this one."

"Oh? Are you a butcher?"

"No, no! Real estate, and believe it or not, I've had two people this week looking for freezer storage and equipment like you've got here. Ever think of selling?"

Malinowski studied him closely before saying, "No, I have not."

"Could get you a handsome deal."

"Not interested."

"I see . . . well, for the record, except for the condition of the outside, you've got a nice shop here."

"Thank you."

Another customer came in, jingling the bell. Kelso studied his opponent a moment longer, sizing him up. Malinowski smiled and waved at the woman who entered.

"Got any good tenderloin today, Louis?" she asked.

"Midway on your left."

"You mind if I have a look at your freezer space and conditions back there?" asked Kelso, pointing at the large walk-in freezer door.

"Public don't go back there."

"Hey, I'm talking a big deal, lots of cash, friend. Got a buyer on the hook right now, and if you were to—"

"How much?" he asked. "How much cash?"

"Depends on the condition of the freezer and what you've got back there in the way of equipment."

"All right, let me take care of Mrs. Porani and—"

"All right. Now you're talking, Mac."

Malinowski frowned, "Ahhh, what the heck, go on back and look around all you like. Just don't touch nothing."

This sudden change took Kelso by surprise. Louis was cool, acting like a man who had nothing to hide. He stepped behind the counter and walked back into the freezer. It wasn't completely startling to see that Malinowski had his sides of beef and larger cuts hanging in sanitary, thick vinyl bags on hooks. He'd seen the same arrangement at meat-packing firms downtown. The enormous, body-lengths of beef in particular strained against the system where they were hung, not by a hook through the meat, but a loop in the enormously strong bag. All were connected to a grooved track overhead, and it could all be hydraulically moved to a stainless steel work table, frigid to the touch.

Kelso stepped further inside, part of his mind telling him that if Malinowski suspected he was the heat, all he'd have to do was to shove the freezer door closed. Still, he was drawn in by something both puzzling him and escaping him at once, something eerie about the place in its tidiness. No meat cleavers left out, not a single thing to mar the shining stainless steel tabletop against one wall. The floor was quite clean, and yet the man did much of his butchering back here where difficult cuts had to be made with power saws. Kelso stared closely at the dangling carcasses, feeling as if any moment he'd be looking into the face of some poor teenage runaway staring out at him. The thick bags and smoke film of hoary frost over them distorted the features of the things inside each bag. But his tour turned up nothing.

Maybe Malinowski was clean after all, despite the mounting coincidences and Mrs. Kunkel.

One way to be sure. He exited the freezer, chilled to the bone. "What do you think?" asked Malinowski. "Fine improvements inside, hey?"

"Yes, very impressive."

"And clean! I run a clean establishment."

"Yeah, it's spotless," said Kelso, realizing that it had been extremely clean, as if ice could not be dirtied, soiled, or stained, not even by blood. "Can I bring someone to see it later, or perhaps tomorrow?"

"I'm still not interested," he replied, "but if you

want to show someone else around, fine."

Kelso laughed. "Very good, Mr. Malinowski, you didn't back off your ground beef prices, and I don't expect you to part with your shop for less than it's worth."

"Which you didn't say."

"Estimating . . . hmmmm . . . at or about one-twenty."

He shook his head, "One-twenty? One-twenty what?"

"With the equipment, that is, one hundred and twenty thousand."

Malinowski's poker face twitched at the sum. "You bring this man around tomorrow . . . and we talk for sure."

"Good, good!" Kelso took his hand in his and shook it.

"You have a card, a number to reach you?"

Kelso made a show of searching for his card. "Bless it, I left without any. But here's a number." He gave him his home number. "Just a one-man show, my office, but it ain't long before I'll get back. Just leave a message on the phone if I'm not handy."

They parted, Kelso taking a deep breath in front of the place, still unsure about Malinowski. If he was a mass murderer, he was cool, perhaps a sociopath, or the type of killer who saw nothing truly wrong in fulfilling his need to kill. On the other hand, he didn't balk at opening his freezer to him. But the Mr. Clean aspect of the freezer disturbed him also. So did the sudden turnaround regarding selling the place, as if it struck him as a good notion. Of course, the mention of one hundred and twenty thousand bucks might turn anyone's head. He felt the man's eyes on his back, watching him leave. Without a card and no insignia on the car he got into, Kelso knew that he'd blown it if the man was in the least apprehensive. Still, the butcher waved good-naturedly out his window, so Ken returned the wave and drove down the street where he doubled back and relocated Mrs. Kunkel's place.

He parked and entered the old woman's building, searching for her box. When he found it, he rang and announced himself. After this, he spent an awkward ten minutes outside her door looking like the proverbial odd duck, going through her trash. Peeking out, watching, Mrs. Kunkel said, "I do hope you understand. I couldn't possibly put myself behind a closed door with a man, not ever."

"Neighbors'd give you a hard time about it," he replied. "Sure, I understand."

"Oh, no, it's not that, be damned what *they* think of me. It's just that, well, Mr. Kels—"

"Kelso."

"—you see, I was raised proper. Women today," she grimaced and almost whispered, "no upbringing."

Kelso found it, the paper that had covered Mrs. Kunkel's calves' liver. It had a large bloodstain where the liver had defrosted. There were wide rivulets off this stain as it fused with water, most of it blotting out a smaller stain in one corner, a stain he prayed was made by Louis Malinowski's blood. "Is this it, Mrs. Kunkel?"

"As I live and breathe, it is."

"You're sure? You're very sure?"

"Well, didn't I say so?"

"Can you offer me a plastic baggie to place it in?"

"I'm so sorry," she said sincerely, "I might've offered. They are an expense, though."

Kelso dug into his wallet for the twenty-five he owed her and kicked in another buck for the baggie.

When she handed out the baggie, she said, "My trash now, Mr. Kels."

"Thank you," he began to say, but she closed the door on him. He had purposefully not talked to her about giving official testimony at this time on anything they'd discussed. She was as unreliable a witness as he had ever encountered. She couldn't even keep his name straight. But she seemed adamant about the paper. Malinowski's blood must now be the witness against him. Kelso rushed away with it, anxious to find Sybil Shanley who could compare it to the minute sample take off the Ahmsted boy's mouth.

Louis Malinowski knew now he had done the right thing by taking the safety deposit box which no one but he could touch, placing his records there along with the master chart. He also breathed easier in regard to the condition of the freezer. He'd been right to sit up into the wee hours of the night in the cold room scraping blood droppings and splatters from the ice-bound walls and floor, scrubbing the table and the bags that had been spoiled by the likes of Robbie Ahmsted. In fact, he'd wisely placed any bags he'd used in that way out in the van. A good thing, too, because he wasn't sure if the real estate man was what he said he was, or if he was a cop. The latter seemed more likely. Who in his right mind would be willing to pay a hundred and twenty thousand for this dump?

As the day wore on, Louis's resolve to stand his ground wore thinner. Mrs. Kunkel called him on the phone with a witchy and disturbing warning: "You will be marked by your blood, Louie, *marked*. I hear the talk around about that baby of Ahmsted's, and now I know." She rung off, leaving him feeling exposed and thinking up a way to get Mrs. Kunkel into one of the bags in the van.

Then he saw stirrings about the neighborhood, a patrol car or two too many, men in neat suits talking to his neighbors. Others seemed to be watching his place.

He began a cool sweat watching from inside the air-conditioned shop. More and more the real estate guy seemed a phony. Then he racked his brain, recalling vaguely that Mrs. Kunkel had been in at the same time as this stranger to the neighborhood. Had the police put her up to calling him, to frighten him into a stupid move?

Near one in the afternoon, he took steps, calling a friend and setting up the appointment he ought to have made long before. At nightfall, he would make his move. Timing would be very important, but they mustn't catch him with the van. He'd have to take a beating on the price, but there was no helping it.

All day, each time the bell on the door jingled, he caught himself up, expecting someone with handcuffs and a Miranda card. Someone had seen Robbie come to him that night. Somebody knew. The bastard kid had either told someone or had let himself be seen. The cops asking the questions all over the street were getting closer and closer.

He knew he could not live in prison. He knew he could not live without Solomon, without the ritual killing and sacrifices to him, without being in touch.

Being in touch . . . it meant all to him. Being in touch and being touched by the ethereal, eternal hand of his savior, the spirit that lifted him from death when he was a child, the one who taught him to retain his breath and thus freeze inner needs during those long hours his father had trapped him and deprived him of all but frozen air.

And now, after all this time, after learning the true teachings of Solomon, the idea of being cut off from practicing his *religion*—for that was what it'd become—was unthinkable.

His only chance seemed to be in fleeing, to dissolve into the flow of life in another metropolis, or a quiet, rural area where lost motorists might fill his needs. He'd find something, somewhere, and once settled he'd contact Solomon again and plead for his help, plead for him to take him with him this time.

At nightfall, he'd make his move. Too bad there wasn't time to visit Mrs. Kunkel, that bitch.

Fourteen

Kelso radioed the moment he returned to his car, trying desperately to get in touch with Sybil Shanley. He felt he owed her first crack at the suspect bloodstain inside the clear plastic bag on the seat beside him. She wasn't available.

He asked for Dean's extension and Grant came on, sounding annoyed, saying into the phone, "Medical Examiner's Office. What is it now?"

"Dino, it's me."

"Oh, Ken, what's up?"

"You a bit under the weather?"

"Backed up, and Sybil called in. Seems she's got a touch of flu, or something."

"Maybe I've got just the thing to get her in this morning."

"And what might that be?"

"A sheaf of butcher's paper with a bloodstain on it."

"Ken, what's so great about this stain?"

"It's a long shot, but it could match the blood she

221

got off the Ahmsted kid."

"How . . . where'd you get it?"

"A little field work. Look, I'm going to round my boys up, give them a pep talk and a word of caution, and then I'm on my way. Think you can entice Sybil in for this?"

"I'll threaten to do it myself. That ought to get her here quick."

"See you in about an hour or so."

Kelso buzzed about in search of Mac and Bob, his two "running footmen" this morning. They'd be inside buildings and talking door to door about Ahmsted's son, declaring him, for the time being, missing, a ploy Kelso had suggested. No one wanted to get involved in a murder case; it was a lot easier to speak of an MP than a corpse.

Kelso now had the problem of locating his men who were away from their radio car, while at the same time avoiding the butcher's eyes. It might take more than an hour or two.

It was not easy, but Kelso finally located Dr. Sybil Shanley, feeling, as did Dean, that she deserved first crack at the microscopic analysis of the butcher's blood. Meanwhile Kelso and Dean had an early lunch, Kelso laying it all out for Dean, everything that had pointed to the butcher Malinowski.

"Shit, Dean, at the moment we're investigating two veterinarians—"

"Vets?"

"They use similar types of these bags for disposal. And we're serious about this mannequin maker—an artist of the human form he calls himself. We've also got a gay furrier."

"Furrier? Oh, the bags. I get it."

"Thing that did it for me was the list Sybil jotted down. What she figured out from the lab work."

"Strong instincts and a long gab with Dr. Taylor."

"Then I learned this guy's old man was a weirdo. I did some checking. Our suspect was a little kid when it happened. Seems he was maladjusted, mal-fed, mistreated, sometimes locked away for days, *sometimes* in the goddamned freezer according to case records going back to—"

"So you decided to pay a little visit?"

"Saw the freezer, same one, with modern improvements."

"Admittedly, it seems strange he should follow in his father's line of work after what happened, but maybe he's working out his problem."

"Precisely, working it out on others. Shrinks got a name for that, don't they?"

"Transference of aggression, I think."

"Close enough. What I don't understand is the lack of fingerprints on the bag we got."

"Gloves?"

"Wore none, at least that I saw."

"Water was all over the bag. Frost before that. Prints formed in the frost and melted with it."

Kelso told him about how he had learned of the blood on the paper he brought in, why he felt it could be Malinowski's. He chuckled over Mrs. Kunkel a few times, when he mentioned the calves' liver.

Dean kindly informed him that the blood on the

paper would be easier to raise and study than any he might've found on the liver, and a print might be raised from the paper, too.

"Even if Mrs. Kunkel hadn't eaten the liver?"

"Even if."

Dean realized that this could be the big break they'd all been praying for. He had telephoned Sybil with the news before they left the office. She, too, realized the implications of the butcher's blood, and although feeling ill, she was on her way. When they returned to the lab they found her already at it. She'd put all else aside.

She first snipped a paper circle of the blood believed to be Malinowski's. This she placed into a metal chamber that bombarded it with a chemical spray that dissolved the entire thing into liquid. The liquid was then placed into a gyrating chamber and the various elements were separated. Besides the pulp, there was animal blood and water, and Sybil's heart stopped at the sight of the indicator on the paper graph noting human blood. The small amount of human blood was taken at the bottom of a tube to a slide. There was only enough to form one decent slide. She did the work with Kelso watching over her until she could stand it no more and banished him to the coffee room. She promised to tell him the moment she had any results.

Sybil was irrationally certain she had the killer's blood. But the only way to prove it was with a complete battery of tests comparing it to their earlier sample. One test was a one-shot opportunity that would destroy the sample. This method called for the sophisticated use of an electron microscope keyed into the computer and equipped with a micro-photo camera. An electron photo of the two samples, side by side, would irrefutably tell the tale, corroborated by a computer model of the sample. It was foolproof and admissable in court, but risky if the electron bombardment wasn't precise. If all went as planned, it would show that it was or was not the same man's blood.

The earlier sample had only been subjected to the test for genetic makeup, a more precise identifier than the electron photos and even fingerprints, but one the courts were still haggling over as admissable and reliable. She must choose the more acceptable because, reliable or not, she couldn't take a chance on a DNA identification being thrown out of court, as mad as that irrational fact was. A high-powered attorney with the right moves could get a judge and a jury to see DNA testing as modern day mumbo jumbo or witchcraft.

She still had two blood samples which she felt would line up under the ordinary comparison microscope. Blood could be matched some dozen ways, each point might drive another nail into the killer's coffin, if she could make those matchups.

She decided to do so under the ordinary approach first, logging each. It would take time. Afterwards, with both samples intact, she'd be free to destroy them in the electron microscope, keeping detailed records of the process so that defense attorneys and other forensics experts called in to testify against the validity of her work would have nothing to chip away at. This was an area of forensics that Dean had drilled into her over and over again. She had seen mistakes and sloppy work in the lab come back to haunt Dean and reflect badly on the lab. It was just the sort of thing a creep like Dr. Fowler was waiting in the wings for.

Then she went for the earlier sample in the tray filled with samples of fluids, scrapings, skin, fibers, hairs, and blood taken from Robbie Ahmsted's body and labeled as such. She began flitting her fingers across the vials, slides, packets, when a disturbing fear rose in her, a feeling that the sample was not here. On closer inspection, she found that indeed, it was not.

She tried to remain calm, getting on the intercom and asking Dean where it was. No doubt he had it for safekeeping since Kelso's initial call had gone to him.

"Are you sure it's not there, Sybil?"

"Then you don't have it?"

"No, I haven't."

"Dean!"

"Take it easy, think this through. Ahmsted's work was being done the same time as the Jane Doe previous to him. It may've just gotten placed in with hers?"

"And if it's not there?"

"One step at a time. I'm on my way."

She'd already searched through for it before he got to the lab. "Nothing, damn it. Dean, how could this happen?"

"Where's Remmer?"

She got on the intercom and p.a. and ran him

226

down. He showed up almost immediately.

"How long a lunch does he think he has?" Sybil was bitching by the time he came off the elevator.

"Here he comes."

"You think he did it? You think he dropped it and thought he'd just sweep it under?"

"Don't jump to conclusions."

Remmer was as confused as they, claiming he knew nothing of the disappearance.

"You've made mistakes before, Remmer," shouted Sybil, "so how're we supposed to believe you now?"

"I swear!"

"You're careless, and you don't give a shit for—"

"Sybil!" Dean shouted her down. "That's enough."

Dean put his hand on Jim Remmer's shoulder, moved him off a foot or so, and stared into his red face. "Jim, if there was an accident, anything at all, we've got to know."

"I'm telling the truth."

"Jim, I want you to retrace your steps yesterday during the autopsy and thereafter."

"Retrace steps," Remmer said, looking around, making the motions, shaken and unsure about his own certainty now.

"Think of every contingency."

"Carr," said Sybil, suddenly. "That sonofabitch took it."

"Why on Earth—"

"To foul us up, don't you see? For his pal Fowler!"

"That's a half-baked notion at best, Sybil. I don't think you're thinking too straight at the moment."

She rushed to a phone and began dialing. "We'll

227

just see about that." She barked at someone at the other end, "Where's Dr. Carr?" She waited for a response. "On a case . . . well, you tell him to get in touch with the M.E.'s Office, Dr. Shanley, the moment he contacts you."

She slammed down the phone. Kelso entered, wanting to know what the problem was, seeing that they all looked stricken. Sybil looked to Dean for help, "You want to explain it to him?"

As Dean began to do so, Kelso's face dropped, too. "Why now—with this Malinowski guy of all people—does there have to be a blunder," said Kelso.

"It was no blunder. It was Carr," said Sybil with anger and certainty.

"Carr? What's he got to do with it."

"He was in and out of the office all day yesterday, and—"

"Sybil, we can't accuse the man without evidence."

"And I let myself believe he was all right," she finished.

When the phone rang, Dean picked it up. It was Carr. He'd been contacted about some urgent matter there. Dean held him in check a moment before saying, "Carr, we've mislaid or misplaced a blood sample taken off the Ahmsted boy. Have you *any* idea of its whereabouts?"

"None, Dr. Grant."

Grant said to the others, "He hasn't any knowledge of it."

"Give me the phone," shouted Sybil.

"No, not in your present state, Sybil!" Dean hung up when she grabbed for it.

Exhausted, she then slumped into a chair. "The

other sample's useless without the first."

"What a setback!" said Kelso, leaning now against a desk.

Remmer shrugged and said, "But we don't know for certain if it was a match anyway. And—wait a minute! Dr. Grant, you had another team working on the Schletter stuff, and they were sharing equipment and space."

"You're right," said Dean. "Let's have a look."

"Won't do you any good," shouted Sybil as they rushed into another lab area where the Schletter evidence was being kept. Dean ran his eyes over the tray of materials, three times the amount they had on the Ahmsted boy, some of it gruesome to the eye. He scanned for slides and vials, staring at the labels. Then he saw it, one labeled Blood Sample #4, Robbie Ahmsted deceased. It was mishandled from the start, with Ahmsted's name on it, it could be mistaken for the victim's blood. Dean knew for a fact that Sybil had done the labeling on this one, as it was in her handwriting. It was then placed somehow in the wrong tray.

When he held it up, Dean gave her a victory signal. She didn't need her face rubbed in it, not now, and not in front of all the others. "We got it!"

Sybil rushed to him and instantly saw her mistake. She cursed herself for the time lost, the aggravation, stress, and false accusations she'd made.

"What happens now?" asked Kelso.

"We proceed with the tests," said Dean. "We'll call you, Ken."

Sybil stopped Kelso at the door by saying, "Everybody, I'm . . . I'm sorry for the way I behaved.

Jim . . . forgive me."

Remmer frowned, "Ahh, it's all right."

"We're all under a lot of stress, and it was an honest mistake."

"And what I said about Dr. Carr!"

The three men assured her that Carr would never hear it repeated, and Dean reassured her that Don couldn't possibly have gotten much via the aborted phone call.

But when Don got off the elevator, he looked pretty tightly wound.

"Damn it," said Kelso, "I'll talk to him."

"No, I'd better. Dean, maybe you and Jim can get the tests begun."

"Sure, Dr. Shanley, no problem," said Dean.

She went out and met Carr halfway, taking him off to a quiet corner of the building, Dean's museum of murder weaponry upstairs.

"What's going on? I don't understand," he said all the way up.

She told him in detail what had happened, and about her terribly wrong suspicions, and just as they disembarked from the elevator and into the museum of knives, pistols, blunt instruments, ropes, and railroad spikes, she added, "Now choose your weapon, and do with me what you will."

He stared for some time before breaking into a laugh, his eyes beaming. "I think I should put your head on the guillotine, Madame."

She apologized again. "I had it coming, and I understand. I'm just glad that slide showed up."

* * *

Kelso had informed his people to keep an eye on the big butcher and his shop, and they'd done so all day. They ate greasy french fries and sandwiches for lunch, snacked on bagged corn chips, talked to people in the area, and now it was nightfall, or close to it. Nothing unusual to report.

Then something happened. Someone going by the butcher shop started away at a sprint after looking inside. The man raced down the street, shouting, "Fire! Fire!"

The detectives in the car half a block down made out the faint wisps of smoke curling from the shop and they suddenly realized the red darts at the window were flames.

"Place is on fire!" shouted Mac. "Call for help!"

Mac was Lawrence McEachern, a twenty-year man with a good twenty-five pounds too much about his middle that made him useless in a street chase. He was a shooter, though, and could bring a man down without injury to any vital organs, when he chose to be discreet. He'd been picked for this duty because he had worked many serial murder cases in the past, and because Ken Kelso and he went a long way back. He'd agreed with Kelso at the outset that the suspect looked and felt right, but after a day-long interrogation of his neighbors, he wasn't so sure anymore. He'd favored another suspect before, a pimply sonofabitch who got off on mannequins, made them for a living and quite likely slept with the damned things draped about him. His apartment had been something else.

Mac got to the door, his partner now rushing after. Mac rammed in the door after two lunges. Somewhere inside there was a weird noise like sizzling bacon.

"Get outa' here, Mac! It's going to blow!" shouted his partner when the place exploded in their faces, sending Mac's dead body over the top of his partner's.

Bob Stoddard was alive long enough to feel the excruciating weight of Mac's fiery form atop him, the flames bleeding into Stoddard below. In a moment, he, too was dead, and the fire truck's siren was silenced for him. The firemen first on the scene were halted before the sight of a black, burning human heap in the gutter, alongside a faded sign with missing letters.

Fifteen

The news went from Sybil to Dean to Kelso and Carr that the blood typing was a perfect match in every respect; that the electron microphotos without a doubt aligned perfectly. This meant that the foul blood scraped from Robbie Ahmsted's bruised mouth and separated out from the boy's own, was in fact the very same blood brought to the lab on the butcher's wrapping paper ferreted out of Mrs. Kunkel's trash. The blood that had allegedly originated with Louis Malinowski.

"That's great! That does it! I can call my guys and they can move in and put the arm on this creep right now." Kelso was beside himself with excitement.

"And we owe it all to Sybil's persistence," said Carr.

"A real terrier, this one," said Dean, hugging her to him. "Once she sinks her teeth in—"

"Is that your kindly way of calling me a bitch, Dean?" she asked, making them all laugh.

"We can move in on probable cause now, search

the entire place for more evidence, confiscate his whole damned freezer if need be. Great!" Ken was ecstatic, on an adrenalin high, when the phone rang.

"I'll get it," said Dean, who lifted the receiver and listened for a moment to someone at the other end. "Ken, it's for you. Urgent."

"Yo, Chief Kelso, here. What's up?"

Carr and Sybil were talking about celebrating. Then everyone turned to stare at Kelso as he shouted, "What? How long ago? I'm on my way!"

"Chief?" asked Carr. "You okay?"

Kelso's face had gone white and he stared at the assembled people around him.

"What is it?" begged Dean.

"He's escaped, hasn't he?" asked Sybil.

Kelso shook his head, his face a mask of despondency, the opposite of a moment before. "Two of my detectives . . . one an old friend . . ."

"MacEachern?" asked Dean.

"An old friend . . . and another of my detectives . . . they're both dead."

"They were monitoring Malinowski, weren't they?" asked Dean, recalling an earlier conversation with Kelso about the situation.

"How'd it happen?" asked Carr.

"What happened?" Sybil asked at the same instant.

"Wish I knew. Some sort of an explosion at Malinowski's shop. Guys must've gotten too anxious, but that wouldn't be Mac's way. Don't know what happened. Got to get down there."

"What about Malinowski?"

"Right now fire's out of control. Could be he was trapped inside. They don't know if anyone's inside

234

the building."

Sybil began speculating aloud, saying, "He must've known we were closing in. Could be he did himself in."

Kelso nodded. "Taking Mac and Stoddard with him. Damn!"

"Oh, God," moaned Sybil, "if only we'd gotten the evidence sooner."

"No one's shouldering the blame for this," said Dean to her sternly.

"I don't know, partner," Kelso said to him. "Maybe I could've done something different."

"Bullshit, Ken!" But Kelso was rushing off. "I'd better stick with him," Carr told the others.

"We'd better get over there, too," suggested Dean, "if you're up to it."

"Just try to keep me away. I hope Malinowski did kill himself. I pray they find him in the rubble."

"That, my dear, is what we're all praying for."

Louis Malinowski's meat-wagon van shot from the rear of his shop the moment a pedestrian obliged him by shouting fire. His last and final good-bye to the old place was with an axe which he took to the cooling pipes, sending out a spray of volatile freon that would in a short time ignite with the fire to send the entire building up in a conflagration. It would buy him the time he needed.

He tore away from the neighborhood and heard the explosion behind him. He'd packed only the essentials required should he manage to again acquire a victim. The truck he must unload, however, and this was pre-planned.

He turned down a dark street where the lights had been knocked out by street kids, past a mile of chain link fence, a graveyard, a park, and onto another side street that brought him face to face with two rows of run-down factories. Amid these was a garage, the lights on, welding sparks flying. He drove in with the van. The owner of the shop, a friend whom he had supplied good cuts to, turned over another truck to him at a fair price. They had cut the deal over the phone, and Malinowski couldn't be too choosy if he wanted to get a refrigerated van on short notice. The other part of the deal was that the old van be dismantled and the parts used as spares.

His friend argued the stripping but Malinowski won. Without its being done, there was no deal. It was only then that his friend realized Malinowski was hot, but he had handled hot cars and hot people before. He simply raised the ante. Malinowski meant to raise the ante, too, from a pay phone and from a distance, and in the end the deal would be equitable to them both.

Once his friend was halfway into dismantling the older van, Malinowski would give him a call and inform him about his culpability in a series of murders; Malinowski'd warn that if anyone should ever locate the van and catch up to one Louis Malinowski, he'd tell the authorities that all the deaths had been the work of two men, and not one. This should keep his *friend* at bay.

The garage was a dump, a filthy pen at the back of an alley in the shadow of buildings on either side, and its owner was a black man who lived hand-to-mouth, with one foot in the financial grave. The deal was good for him, and it'd go well for him if he played dumb about the van. But Malinowski couldn't trust Hinsen to break down a perfectly good van. He'd want to leave it intact, paint it for resale. That alone would make sense to the man, unless he had a better reason not to. Malinowski got out of his van, and in plain sight of Hinsen removed the vinyl sacks, his see-through body bags, and then placed them in the back of the newer van, piling them into a neat square. Malinowski planned to take his act on the road. The notion had a sort of madhatter's appeal to him, and he sensed that Solomon, too, would approve, or at least understand why he had had to destroy the shop.

More and more today he felt the urge to give rise to Solomon, needing desperately his council in all this, knowing the depth of Solomon's wisdom was eternal. Later, when things calmed down a bit, he'd find help to conjure Solomon. Reunited, the old power would return and he'd know what to do.

Hinsen exchanged the key and papers for the cash that Malinowski had brought as down payment. Hinsen asked no questions, just eyed the old van like a vulture. He smacked his lips, happy over the cash, talking about how his wife would eat her words tonight.

Malinowski waved good-bye and tore from the garage. He'd make his call to Hinsen tomorrow, allowing him a brief time to revel in his good fortune.

Malinowski wondered where he might go next. He was shed of the shop, a free man, free to move about now, his cover as an ordinary, neighborhood Joe shattered. He might try a dash across state lines, or to Canada, but an insistent, urgent need must first be satisfied. He must have counsel with Solomon.

He cruised toward the near northside of Chicago, a strip called Broadway where prostitutes were easily had. "Why not," he told himself, feeling safe for the first time all day.

Fire fighters were replaced by fire investigators, among them Kristie Howlett and her canine companion, the German Shepherd, Pete. The exact cause of the explosion had to be determined. Also still to be determined was whether Malinowski had or had not died in the fire. Kelso already had his doubts. By now he had come to think of the man as more than just an ordinary man, but rather a demon of sorts, able to withstand flames. He also saw no sign of the evil man's van.

The whole scene recalled to mind the madness of an earlier killer who used fire for kicks. In this case Kelso was sure the fire had been set up as a smokescreen—literally—and was convinced they would not find Malinowski's body inside.

It was three in the morning before the blaze was under control and the site safe enough to ferret through the bodies. Despite the explosion in the shop, fire deaths were minimal, due in great part to the building having been buttressed by neighboring buildings on both sides. Fire fighters went to the upper floors of surrounding buildings and helped the people living above Malinowski's shop and flat out that way. Aside from Mac and Stoddard, there was one other fatality and two injured firemen. For an explosion and fire of its size, Kristie Howlett told Kelso and the others, the fire had been well managed. It might have caused a great deal more damage.

There had been no secondary explosions; nor were there any gas fumes or a hint of gas leakage from within. This led the more knowledgeable fire fighters to wonder at the cause of the explosion.

Pete, Kristie's bomb-sniffing dog, could also sniff out bodies. While nothing would make him happier than to gaze down on Louis Malinowski's lifeless, scorched form, something deep inside Kelso told him that wasn't in the cards, not tonight.

The forensics team of Grant and Shanley, along with Carr, entered the building far to the rear of Kristie Howlett and other fire and arson investigators. Kelso was with Kristie, disregarding the risk to his own safety. The blazing fire and shocking explosion had gutted the shop and torn out great chunks of the ceiling on the second floor. Much of the debris had crashed through, adding fuel to the fire. The arson team informed the civilians, including Ken, that it was dangerous to enter the building. They all went ahead anyway, poking about the eerie, dark remains where the smell of charred wood mixed with other odors to stifle the breath.

Kelso was the only one in the team who'd been in the shop before. He signaled where shelves, counters, and displays had been, and the door to the freezer area and a back door that opened on a petite, fenced yard, a path going out to a garage, a dumpster, and an alley. He also noted, atop a debris pile, a large, floor-model freezer on end that hadn't been there before. The hole above indicated that it had fallen through when the fire had weakened the structure. Dean went to the freezer, snooping about it. Kelso went along with Kristie who followed her dog. The dog made a beeline for the walk-in freezer. Inside they found a watery floor, parts from blown apart meat and an axe handle. They also found what Pete was sniffing at, the ripped-open pipe that Malinowski had used as a bomb.

"Freon escaping into the flames," said Kristie, "highly volatile."

"Freon?"

"A propellent under pressure. Door was left wide open."

"Look around for the bastard's body," said Carr.

Sybil and Dean were standing about the toppled freezer. It had been thrown open only *after* the fire was put out, its contents intact. Now Dean held up a handful of wrapped packages.

"Very likely your typical, *sedative* cuts," he said.

"Hey, I saw some of the guys with chops and steaks under their coats," said Kristie.

"Better get the word around," said Sybil. "I wouldn't even trust this guy's cold cuts."

They fanned out, searching for any sign of Malinowski's body, while Kelso walked out the back door and went to the garage, snooping around in the dark there with his flashlight. The light made a gloomy glow in the plain-looking garage filled with what one might expect a garage to be filled with, except that it contained no vehicle. He'd give it a thorough search by daylight. For now, he wanted to talk Kristie into getting him access to the flat upstairs, or what remained of it. He knew he was in for an argument. But this guy was still alive. At large. He knew it in his soul.

He returned to Dean and said, "Dino, he's not here. He got clean away, I can feel it."

"There's several feet of rubble here. We don't know that he didn't blow himself away."

"He had a van, and it's gone, and it didn't fly away. My guys made a mistake, and they paid for it with their lives. Whatever it takes, I want this guy."

"What do you propose?"

"Kristie, I want your support on this. Get me help if need be, but get me to the second story. That room up there's got to be searched."

"Ken, it'll be safer by daylight, a couple of hours."

"We don't have a couple of hours with this freak."

"I'll see what I can do, but the Fire Chief's not about to give us his blessings."

"Then let's go see him together. As I recall, he owes us, doesn't he, Dean?"

Dean shrugged, "For what, doing our jobs? You sure you want to pull on that thread?"

Kelso turned to Dean and came eyeball to eyeball with him. "I'll pull and push anything and anybody to get this bastard. Now, are you going with me?"

It rubbed Dean the wrong way to throw his weight around and that's what Kelso was proposing.

"I'll do it," said Sybil. "It's still my case."

"No, it's our case, and we'll do it together or not at all."

Carr stood nearby, saying abjectly, "I can't believe it. I thought it was over."

"He wants it to be over, too," said Sybil, her arms wrapped about herself as if she'd caught a sudden chill. "He does, but on his terms, and not before."

Dean and the others stared at her, Dean recognizing the symptoms of obsession in her. She, like Kelso, had become both enraged and obsessed by the murderer, to the point of believing she could know what was in his gnarled and pathetic mind.

"Then what's our next move?" asked Dean.

"Get an APB out on Malinowski and his van, for now," replied Kelso. "Till something comes of it, we search his place." There was something else Kelso was trying desperately to recall, but for the moment it escaped him.

The bag was laid flat and opened of its own accord, making a crackle, like a snake unfurling. Malinowski purposefully selected the shortest, weakest-looking streetwalker he could find, enticing her with payment for her services. When he told her he wanted it done in the back of his refrigerated van, she giggled and called him kinky. She didn't actually balk until he threw open the door and the frigid air ballooned out at them.

"This . . . this is weird, mister . . . I never—"

"There's always a first time," he said.

"I don't know, man. It's got to be freezing in there."

"No, not quite. I wouldn't want you to get too cold."

"Shhhhhhit," she moaned, "I don't know, mister."

242

"Louis, call me Louis."

"Louis, I thought maybe you had some ice cream or whip cream back here, but this, this is solid ice."

"Double the money."

"Cold in there."

He grew impatient and raised the gun he'd purchased to her eyes. "Ever seen one of these?"

She started and attempted to pull away from his grasp.

"Inside, inside or I splatter your brains."

"What're you going to do to me?"

"Just want to love you, that's all."

"Please, mister—"

"Inside now!"

She moved with a jump and he pulled the door closed. He had parked in a deserted alley behind a closed shoe factory. The place was isolated.

Inside the van he turned on a light and pointed to the body-length bag. "Undress and get into the bag."

"What?"

"It'll warm you up, I swear. I've seen it happen. You'll be sweatin'."

"It's freezing," she said, touching the stiff bag.

"Do it! Do it or else!" He jammed the barrel of the gun into her teeth and held it there, hurting her, blood trickling from her mouth.

"All right," she mumbled, shaken and shivering.

He watched her undress, his excitement building. "Into the bag, now . . . *now!*"

She was blue under the light, her arms folded tightly around her scrawny body. She was whimpering and repeating the single word Please over and over.

243

"You'll see. Inside the bag, you'll warm up."

"You gee-t o-f-f on *th-is?*" Her teeth chattered now.

"Lay down in the bag!"

She moved too slowly for him and he slapped her hard in the face. She got into the bag in a near-fetal position, and he immediately went to his knees and brought home the zipper, up up *up!* And it was done. She was collected and she was his now—his and Solomon's.

Her eyes widened as she stared out through the bag at him, a carbon dioxide film already beginning to color over her imperfections. He undressed and readied the necessary items for the ritual, calling out Solomon's name as he did so. She began shouting from inside the bag, pleading. He looked down at her in a daze that left her only when he jotted down notes on the clipboard he held. She seemed, by comparison, relatively at peace and calm, accepting of her fate, obliging. Resigned? He wondered and put the notation down. She'd called herself Diane and joked about being Lady Di. Lady Die would be more apt. "Di," he cooed softly to her now, "Die for me, Di. Die for me and Solomon."

Her pleading intensified along with her kicking and scratching. Like a butterfly in a net, he thought, and jotted this down.

Perhaps with her, he could reach Solomon and find the true path that would take Louis Malinowski home for good and forever.

It might take all night. It might take more than all night. In the back of the van, his new temporal home as it were, he could take his time.

Sixteen

The case was God-given copy to the newspapers who were claiming that the police had fouled up the investigation and allowed the killer time to escape. That was Mac's epitaph. That was what Stoddard's family had to read in the morning edition. That their lives were lost due to blunders. As dawn approached, Kelso had to be restrained from breaking heads. It was no surprise that wherever a fire and Chief Inspector Kenneth Kelso showed up these days, reporters were sure to go. They'd pieced together enough of the tenuous pieces of the puzzle in the aftermath of the explosion at Malinowski's to believe they had the inside story. With deadline approaching within the hour, they rushed to press with what they had. Police had been given a description of the maniac and this was an easy matter for the press to get hold of and print in the morning edition. Alongside the story, a sidebar was run totaling up the killer's known victims with as many pictures.

Unfortunately, no photograph of Mr. Malinowski existed, and so a nearly blank police sketch must do for now. The newsmen had fulfilled their duty to the public trust. Meanwhile, publicity surrounding the case was fast becoming the variety Kelso hated. It fed on fears, for one thing, but even more important, it was of the variety that could get a psycho case tossed out on technicalities if they ever got Malinowski before a judge and jury. God forbid the psychotic killer's rights should be trampled, and that his name appear in print without the preamble of alleged, or that he be called sane or insane, capable or incapable, or referred to as *crazy* or *evil*. Shrewd maniacs before Malinowski had used the system to escape full punishment; some had even walked as a result of blunders made by police and/or prosecutors, blunders whose origins might often be traced back to the press.

One story on Malinowski ended with an abrupt edict to public officials to do their jobs, and to put an end to Chicago's worst nightmare: the Meat Man. Another was calling the killer the Bloody Butcher. It was just such epitaphs that irked judges, and which defense attorneys hit the prosecution with, claiming no one, given such handles, could get a fair trial. All that Kelso could do was issue his own internal edicts that any policeman using such terms would be promptly suspended, for all the good it'd do.

The search through Malinowski's charred flat uncovered some items which might help to hammer home the prosecution's case, however: some clothing and several pairs of shoes which had escaped flames. The clothes would provide fibers for the forensic team. Dean was particularly interested in a torn

246

jacket, the pocket ripped away. He'd found a jagged patch of cloth no larger than a thumbnail on the Ahmsted body. Carr had taken a plaster cast of a particularly good shoe print at the site along the river where the girl had been found dumped and bobbing on the surface. He'd done the shoe print at the same time he had taken casts of the tire impressions left at this location. Now the shoes from Malinowski's closet would be matched to the cast. If fourteen match points could be found on either of the shoes, the man's guilt would be substantiated.

All of this must wait for tests and microscopic probes. Meanwhile the sun rose again and Chicago awoke and traffic moved like one immutable animal from place to place. Another day, Kelso thought. Louis Malinowski remained at large. There was not a single sighting of the fiend from any unit in the city. This invisibility troubled Kelso greatly, but he was drained, both physically and emotionally. He had returned from the fire bomb scene to his apartment where he slept fitfully. His answering machine would have to do for him for a time. As Ken Kelso slept, his mind lazily played over all the various facts. Something was eluding his fatigued brain. When he awoke he did so in a tired and frustrated state, but then it popped into his mind. Two things actually.

Malinowski had driven his van to the bank that morning. He had transacted some business in the bank. His van was easily spotted once the description had been given, but not anymore. It had been seen nowhere in fact. These facts led him to two conclusions. One, there might be something at

247

Lincoln National worth looking into, and two, the van had been stashed out of sight, perhaps in some nearby garage, a garage where the man might rent space, perhaps.

It was coming on dusk when Kelso got up, showered, and shaved, and after a bite, went to his answering machine to collect his messages. As he ate, he listened to Kristie's spritely voice, asking after him, a worried edge there. Then he listened to Carr who told him what he already knew, that the cast taken at the riverbank that day matched one of Malinowski's shoes down to the minutest detail. Another forensic nail in the bastard's coffin, if he lived to see a courtroom, Kelso thought. Then Dean came on with another update for him. It was confirmed that Mac and Stoddard had died of the explosion. An eyewitness had come forward and said that the two men rushed at the shop while others were frantically rushing away. Some took it as a noble attempt on the part of the two officers to help anyone trapped in the building, going forth to warn them. Kelso saw it as what it was: falling into Malinowski's viciously laid trap. Dean also had more news, more about shoes. Dean's lab had found excessive amounts of coal dust and tar on the killer's shoes, ground into the soles. Embedded in the tar were grains of wheat.

"This tell you anything?" Dean asked before time was up on the message and he was cut off.

Kelso considered the strange combination. Tar, coal, and wheat. What did that suggest? It suggested ships and foundries, cargoes and storage and steam powered by coal. It suggested the Chicago shipyards, of which there were quite a number. It also recalled to mind, as he was sure it did to Sybil's, that a young victim very early on—ruled an anorexic suicide by Carr as the attending M.E.—was found floating in the Chicago Ship Canal. It had been before Sybil Shanley's one-woman crusade to uncover the list of asphyxiated victims. Carr's suicide might have been one of them.

He got on the phone and immediately dispatched units to all shipyard ports where the big ships docked to take on or unload large cargoes. He told his detectives to hit the larger ones, and he told one and all to do some snooping for a van with the words Malinowski or meat on it, tan to white. They were also to forage about for Malinowski himself, considered dangerous, possibly armed.

"Also forage about your respective areas for," he hesitated sending the message to dispatch, but then went ahead, "for any bodies that might turn up. And put two men on a detail to shake down garages in Malinowski's neighborhood, five mile radius for now."

Kelso then went to see a banker.

Malinowski had sucked into his nostrils the last of the CO_2 the whore was able to give up. Three times with her, long and strong and good sessions that brought him closer and closer to Solomon, so close in fact he had thrown down his clipboard, so taken away was he. The last ended in Solomon's reaching straight out of the emptiness and placing his otherworldly hand on Malinowski's heart. Solomon gave him a directive, a directive that would lead to a complete and whole reunion. Within a twenty-four-hour period he must take the breath of three victims to become at one with Solomon, and bring peace to his soul.

Two more before the early hours of the next morning, only two more, he told himself, counting Diane as number one. The girl might be missed in this area, and someone might've seen her get into the van. With her stiff form lolling from side to side in the back, Malinowski searched for greener pastures and a place to hide until nightfall.

He drove. Around the city, past police cars, up and down quiet little communities with cottagelike homes, past the rotting neighborhoods overtaken by time and decay, past the Gold Coast area along the Magnificent Mile, he drove. As he drove, he did a great deal of thinking and calculating. He was meant for better things. He was a man, after all, and man was linked with the upper spheres.

He played a symphony of strings as he went about the city, and he thought some more. Man was the microcosm of the cosmos, and in his mind the universal essence of the soul resided. Malinowski was comprised of all the energies and substances out of which the universe was fashioned. His body and breath held all the levels of etheric matter, the elements, the potencies. The workings of his very own lungs and other organs were in harmony with the mechanism of nature. Earth was present in his flesh, the cosmic waters in his bodily fluids, fire in his essence, and the very atmosphere in his vital airs. He comprised all the elements of which the universe was fashioned.

Solomon had said as much, but Malinowski was only now learning the full lesson—that he could transform himself into a different and higher order of being; that he could be like Solomon.

It all seemed so simple and correct and ordered now.

He lifted out the container of Valium capsules from the dash box and fondled and tossed them about. He wanted to mix the remaining Valium into a liquid mixture with water, set up a hypodermic to put his next two victims out quickly and efficiently. Using a gun was foolish, amounting to a mere bluff on his part. The victim would do him no good if she were shot dead or injured, the breathing stymied. It would serve no purpose whatsoever in the world to have shot Diane. Without the capacity for respiration, unable to breathe in and out inside the bag, her lifeless form could do him no good whatever.

The lungs were remarkable organs. They cooled the feverish mind and the fiery heart. The pulmonary functions were opposite of the cardiac functions, and in this sense formed a triumvirate with the heart and the brain. All actions were then reciprocally related. But the lungs were the seat of power and righteousness, for, like the stomach, the lungs absorbed part of the ethereal "emptiness." Although seemingly empty, the lungs were full and whole and complete, making them the executives of the heart and mind. For it was the energy inhaled with each breath that was the vitalizing charge giving strength to the human organism. Therefore, it was also the vitalizing charge giving rise to the soul.

251

Empty, yet full and whole. It seemed the perfect symbol of his lifetime relationship with Solomon.

He'd spend the remainder of the day preparing the sedative and needle. Then when he was ready to strike, he'd do so with ease and efficiency to fulfill Solomon's directive. He must find a completely remote area of the city where he wouldn't be observed or interrupted in his important preparations.

Ken Kelso had spent the better part of the day getting a court order. Finally, with it in his hands, he took two uniformed officers with him to Lincoln National on Lincoln Avenue at Addison. Inside he located the bank's vice president, and when he couldn't get satisfaction from him, he located the president. A locksmith was called in and by three o'clock he had Louis Malinowski's safety deposit box and its contents impounded, pending full investigation.

While he was there, he learned that Malinowski had closed both his business and personal accounts at the bank. It amounted to a little over seventeen thousand dollars.

Returning to headquarters, Kelso covered his desk with the spread sheets Malinowski had folded into tight squares and forced into the box. The papers were a bizarre record of the man's murder spree, a surefire conviction awaited Kelso on this evidence alone. But it floored the big police Chief, making him sit down, his head dizzy.

In cold and analytical detail here was a record of each person murdered, and precisely how long it took for them to die, some lasting for hours. The "accounting" made Kelso ill, so ill he could not bear to be alone in the room with it.

He telephoned for Dean, asking if he could drop everything and come over. At the moment, Dean seemed the logical choice and the only one he could share the grotesque facts with. He'd let Dean pass it along to the others.

In the time it took for Dean to appear at his door, Kelso had gotten some good news, and he told Dean this now.

"Oh, what's that?"

"Schletter, Emil Schletter, caught in Rio. He's on a plane now with his hands cuffed. End of his career."

"Great! That wraps up one horror show."

"Brace yourself, Dino, and look at what's cluttering my credenza."

Dean stared at the papers that covered the tabletop, each seemingly a purchasing form. But under the category of what type of meat was requested, the line was filled in with the name of a man or woman, one of them reading Robert Ahmsted, another Jory Bemis. Dean realized the others were names that identified the various John and Jane Does that had been victims of the Suffocator.

"Christ," he moaned, "where'd you find *these?*"

"Malinowski's lock box at the local bank that did business with him."

"Jesus, Ken, did you read this stuff?"

"Yeah, pretty gruesome."

"Gruesome's an understatement." Dean's eyes scanned the list with its boxes and manufactured categories: age, size, weight, time of endurance. Like

253

Kelso, he could not take it in all at once. It must be digested very slowly, if at all. "This man's inhuman, anybody who would do this . . . it's worse than . . . worse than drowning someone. Then to do it repeatedly! Letting up just enough for the victims to regain consciousness, so he could have another go at them! Turns my stomach."

"If I ever get my hands on this guy, they'll be putting *me* away for murder, Dean," Kelso said quietly and calmly. "Meantime, let's see if we can make any statistical correlations between the victims, anything readily apparent. Why men on some occasion, women on others? Women predominate, but is this necessarily important? What do you think?"

"What do I think?" Dean's pent-up anger exploded. "I think the guy's a mental, a psychotic, and nothing he does makes sense to me, or you, or to his victims, and trying to draw little diagrams for your detectives isn't getting us any goddamned closer to putting an end to this freaky bastard!"

Kelso absorbed the anger of his friend. He reached into a lower desk drawer and brought out a bottle of Johnny Walker Red Label. "Sure, I know how you feel." He snatched up two shining shot glasses. He poured himself and Dean each one. "Drink up, we deserve it."

Dean frowned, accepted the drink, and downed it in one neat clip, gasping at how good it tasted. "Thanks," he said simply. "Sorry."

"No need. Dean, I know this guy's not gone anywhere. He's lying low, like a goddamned wolf, waiting for nightfall, waiting to strike again, somewhere in all that—" he indicated the wall-sized map of Chicago's hundreds and thousands of arteries. "We got all that to cover, and not enough men to do the job. But hell or high water, we're going to bust this sonofabitch's chops, and if I'm in on it, God help him, I swear."

Dean couldn't for a moment blame Kelso. Something about a killer who toyed with his prey, made young, helpless women suffer and beg, and this— hang on by a thread of air so he could repeatedly seal them off. It was enough to make any man go off in a fit of rage. "Any leads, any ideas?"

Kelso told him about the units having been sent out to scour every shipyard in the city on Dean's tenuous evidence. "As fair a place to start as any."

The phone rang, and in a moment Dean could make out enough of the conversation to know that one of Kelso's detectives had located Malinowski's truck. Kelso was excited once more, jotting down the address. "I'm out of here," he told Dean.

"Where'd they find the truck?"

"Little hole-in-the-wall garage called Hinsen's Car Repair, some ten blocks from Malinowski's shop. Damned thing's been cut down, parts sold off already, but we've got somebody to shake down, and that's what matters. We'll make this guy sing, or lose his nuts."

"Hey, Ken, go easy."

"Not anymore, Dino. Now's time to kick butt and take no prisoners."

"Good luck!" Dean shouted and put away the booze Ken had left out before he returned to his lab. He wondered the entire way back if he should share the information about the macabre survey of death Kelso had found in the murderer's possession. He wondered if it would serve any purpose to do so, and he wondered if Kelso hadn't wanted it kept between the two of them for the time being. He decided nothing could be accomplished at this stage by sharing the grotesque details with Sybil. She'd had enough to assault her senses in the last few days.

Leroy Hinsen was no match for the detectives who bounced him around his own place, much less Chief Kenneth Kelso. Kelso bulldogged his way through the outer garage, shoving things over as he came toward Hinsen whose eyes enlarged with each step Kelso took toward him.

"Has he coughed up what he knows?" Kelso asked his man.

"He's holding back. Says he hooked the truck when it was in a loading zone, brought it here and since it's gone unclaimed, he broke it down for parts."

"That's bullshit. This truck was on the street less than two days ago!" countered Kelso. "So, Hinsen is it? Want to try the truth? If not, you're looking at a long stretch for grand theft auto and anything else we can dig up on you!"

"It ain't my doing!"

"What ain't your doing?"

"Malinowski did all that killing himself. I never killed nobody, not ever."

"Malinowski tell you about killing anyone?"

"He killed a lot of someones! But I swear, I never

knew, not until earlier today when he called me."

"He called you? Called from where?"

"I swear I don't know."

"Your ass is going downtown. You want to shut your place down, send that mechanic out there home?"

"I can't afford no shutdown."

"You can't afford not to! Two of my men were killed last evening by your pal, Malinowski!"

Hinsen kept shaking his head, "Ain't no pal of mine!"

"Not if he lets you hang for his dirt, no! So, you and me, we're going to be pals, we're going to be the best of buddies, aren't we? Aren't we?" shouted Kelso, and then to his men, he said, "See that this trash gets packed up and sent downtown. Let me know when it's delivered. Meanwhile, this place is closed until further notice. No telling what forensics can do with the back of that cab. See if we can free up a wagon to dump it into and get it to our yards. If not, well then, we'll get Carr down here, maybe Shanley."

"Right, Chief." And they watched Kelso storm out as quickly as he had come, a big man who carried his weight well. He seemed confident for the first time in a long while. They were onto something here, and Kelso had the look on his face of a hunter closing in on his prey.

Born in Texas and reared in Arizona, young Kyle Thomas was a long way from home. Even after two years on the Chicago Police Department and six months at the academy, he wondered if Chicago

257

would ever feel homey. A stint in the Navy had left him in Chicago without much money and no foreseeable future. Following the advice of a friend who happened to be a cop, he tried the academy and found it to his liking. Just military enough to give him a push, and just civilian enough that he could stomach it. His Navy days hadn't been nearly so much fun.

But no one warned him about nights like tonight.

Kyle Thomas was rangy at six-foot-four, and his size had earned him the nickname Munster from the old TV sitcom. His riding partner joked that he made a good shield. Dennis Hummings was a normal-sized human being at five nine, and had seven years on the force. Hummings had patience and smarts, while Thomas had quickness and muscle. Most of the time this made for good teamwork. Hummings was the first black man that Kyle Thomas had ever had a close relationship with. Kyle had saved his ass once. Hummings had returned the favor twice. They kept to a strange ritual that Hummings had had with earlier partners, notches in the paint at the tip of the hood of the squad car; one side was Hummings's notices, the other Kyle's. They weren't the number of kills, but the number of times each man had saved a life.

Hummings had taught Kyle a great deal, and as cocky as Kyle was, he knew the man had a lot more to teach him. Each man had great respect for the talents of the other, even an envy. Hummings longed to be a better marksman, and when no one else was on the range, he allowed himself a lesson or two from his white bread partner. Kyle was a master shot, raised with a gun in his hand, a marksman even with the unsteady .38 police special, which most cops never expertly mastered. Hummings was the expert at talk—any kind of talk that was needed in any given situation. His mouth was a potent weapon against anger and potential violence. Kyle had seen him diffuse a potentially riotous gang confrontation with a smoothness Eddie Murphy might envy.

They'd done good work together, having made more collars in the past two months than any uniforms in their South Side precinct.

"Whatchu lookin' so grim for?" asked Hummings when they'd gotten out of the car earlier. They had been sent to the shipyard on the canal in search of anything suspicious.

"Some duty we got! We should be keeping an eye on Zoraster and those punks of his in Stony Park, man. They see we're not cruising, and no telling what hell's going to break."

"Guys like Kuwandi Zoraster we can see coming, like you see a bug coming across the floor at you. He'll get stepped on hard one of these times. But this creep butcher, hell, man, he killed two cops."

The two men flashed their lights into every black corner, checked about aimlessly. The yards rambled on for several miles and the ships tied to were real buckets. Nothing to look at and no one about. Several of the warehouses stood open, access to them easily gained. The outer gates that would be locked much later served as a generic deterrent to crime and theft here. Most of the warehoused goods were inaccessible, locked within the larger, more rambling structures. The outer hulls with tin roofs were temporary shelters that offered protection from the rain and sun to large shipments of anything from grain and minerals to sticky widgets and recycled pipe, coming and going along the great international waterway of which Lake Michigan and the Chicago River system were just a part. Materials and goods went from here to overseas after making the trip up the great St. Lawrence Seaway.

One warehouse smelled of mildew, rats, and grain. The grain smells Kyle recognized as both barley and rye. "Had time, we could brew us up something good," he joked.

They came on a warehouse that smelled of coal, a thick, oily odor that choked them. It made Hummings think of hot tar, the predecessor of asphalt blacktop, that pinched the nose for days after the street workers laid it down the path of an alley alongside his childhood bedroom.

"You hear what they're saying at headquarters?" asked Kyle *Munster* Thomas.

"About what?"

"'Bout those two cops that blew sky-high at that butcher's."

Hummings's light picked up the tailings of an enormous coal pile ahead of them inside the warehouse, and in the dark, it seemed like the tail of a dragon. He flit the light over the top of the coal pile, saying, "No, what?"

"Said they'd been boxed up as neat as pork chops by the coroners and were going for a buck ninety a pound."

"Shit, I hate that," replied Hummings, stopping cold and flashing his light into Kyle's face.

260

"What?"

"Sick, man, all those damned exploding-meat jokes we're getting over the radio. What kind of respect is that?"

"Hey, man, just telling you what I heard."

They began to move around the mountain of coal in the darkness. Something about the place made Hummings's skin crawl. Goose bumps. He felt them popping up all over, and he felt as if someone, or some animal—something—was nearby and watching them.

"Suppose you think this kind of duty's below you, huh, boy?" Hummings said to Kyle, just to make some noise, not really interested in what Kyle thought.

"Tell ya' what I think about this butcher creep. Instead of us beating about places like this, we ought to corner every mother's son who ever knew the guy and put the squeeze on 'em."

"Detectives are doing that."

"Not hard and fast enough."

"I smell something bad." Hummings's light moved about jerkily.

"Rats, this damned coal," suggested his young partner.

"Sewage more like it; you get that?" He sniffed at the bad air.

"Detectives aren't doing enough. Newspapers said as much in the last edition."

"Whataya' working for the *Times* now? You ever hear about the time a reporter cornered Chief Kelso in the john?"

"No, what?"

261

This time it was Hummings's joke. "Asked the Chief why it took him so much time to get things done."

"What'd Kelso say?"

"Said, 'You oughta' try crappin' with a gun in *your* pants.'"

Munster laughed, and Hummings joined him, but as he laughed Hummings's nostrils filled with the revolting odor once more and he began choking. So did the big kid.

"You smell it now?"

"Hell yes! Like . . . like something dead."

Their lights went ahead of them as their steps were suddenly small. Kyle looked up, shrugging his shoulders on seeing a smokestack firing out a billowy, black cloud of soot and cinder from a foundry some distance off. "Damned shame what they're puttin' in the air night and day."

Hummings didn't hear him. Hummings had frozen in his tracks just behind him, the flash illuminating something white and ugly beneath the stone floor, beneath a metal grate, wiggling on the surface of six inches of water.

"What is it?" asked Kyle, turning, sensing that Dennis was scared. Hummings let out with a sizzling, fretful sound like air escaping through his navel. Kyle's eyes followed the beacon to what it illuminated below the grate.

"What is it?"

"It's what stinks."

"But what the hell is it?"

"It ain't Jello gelatin. Call for backup. Hurry!"
The more experienced cop had already whipped out

his gun.

Kyle just argued. "Hey, could be raw sewage or fish. Yeah, fish from one of the goddamned boats. A health hazard maybe, but sludge is—"

"Goddamnit, kid, it's bones you're lookin' at, bones and decayed skin. Get somebody the hell out here!"

"All right! All right!"

As Kyle turned toward the car, his partner said between clenched teeth, "Get it on the box! That crazy bastard's been here!"

"Gonna' make us look like fools when they pull that crap outa' there! I don't know what that is, but it ain't human, look at it!" Kyle stared again at it.

In his ear, Hummings said, "Rats man, rats got at it." Then he nearly whispered, "Now go at it, boy! Double quick!" Hummings then gave the bigger man a powerful shove that sent him staggering away with the ugly thought hammering at him. Hummings held his stomach, his head feeling like a top, woozy and disoriented, as he watched his partner run for the squad car. He envied the distance Kyle had put between himself and the thing behind him in the grate, the something that had earlier given him goose bumps even before he smelled it.

Then Hummings located a corner the other side of the great coal dragon, his stomach going into an uncontrollable spasm. In an instant his stomach relieved itself of all that he'd had for dinner.

sheer frustration.

She went down the hill later when her mind felt

Seventeen

Most of Louis Malinowski's meat wagon was in one piece and was removed from Hinsen's garage intact, and hauled to the corner of the police garage reserved for forensics investigation of vehicles. Most vehicles were being checked for chipped paint, hair embedded in grillwork, anything that might place a certain vehicle at a certain intersection at a time when a crime was committed, often hit and run or robbery. Donald Carr had just cracked a case involving a bank robbery in which the getaway vehicle—a battered, old FTD with faded baby blue paint over an earlier, dealer paint job of jade—had proven to be the same car that careened into a parked car while racing around a corner. While leaving traces of the two paints that identified it behind, the car also left minute samples of the second car's paint job on it. Particles of paint had jagged edges, invisible to the naked eye, but below a microscope they were like jigsaw pieces. Identifying them was child's play.

Donald Carr had spent an hour on Malinowski's

truck, scouring it for prints, fibers, hairs, dirt embedded in the once ice-covered floor, stains that might prove to be blood. He picked up microscopic dust particles and flakes that might add to the horror story of Mr. Malinowski. At this point, every shred of evidence they could compile would force another nail in Malinowski's medico-legal coffin.

It had been out of a sense of determination to help Sybil Shanley, more than anything else, which now prompted him to do his level best. He still felt a great sense of guilt at having betrayed her confidence, and almost losing her as a result. He'd since told Dr. Mortimer Fowler where he could go. That might at some future time come back to haunt him, but he didn't care. What mattered most right now was Sybil, and putting an end to the career of a mass murderer.

Carr had telephoned Sybil when the truck was hauled in, letting her know that all the samples they had gotten from the truck would be—if possible— duplicated for her. All tests would be open to her department, he had told her. She and Dean had left the scouring of Malinowski's truck to Carr, and he now felt he must repay their confidence in him.

One of the more interesting finds since then had been soil in the back of the van. He'd matched it to a sample he'd had a technician take of the soil along the riverbank where the one victim had been dumped while still inside the body bag. Another infinitesimal sample picked up certain signs of coal dust, soot, cinders, looking suspiciously like the sample Dean Grant had taken from one set of shoes found in Malinowski's possession.

Carr believed that Malinowski's days were numbered. For the first time in a long time, he felt good about the case. Although the man remained at large, he knew it had to be only a matter of time before he was apprehended. Already a full description of the new vehicle Malinowski was driving was going out to all units in the city. What Carr, Dean, and Sybil in particular had managed to amass in the meantime would bury the SOB.

"Dr. Carr!" someone shouted across the garage at him. He looked out of the back of the van.

"Call from Chief Kelso!" shouted the police mechanic. "You're to pack up and meet him in two minutes at the gate."

"But I'm not finished here!" He looked from the mechanic to his tech assistant who shrugged.

"Hey, I just deliver messages," said the mechanic.

Carr took off the white lab coat he wore over his clothes and folded it into his valise, preparing to leave, grumbling.

Carr left the final gathering of evidence from the van to his assistant. He rushed out to meet Kelso and slid into the passenger side of the car, his case in his lap. "What's up, Chief?"

"Nothing definite, but sounds like we could have another body on our hands." Kelso raced for the expressway.

"Suffocator victim?"

"Why do we always give these creeps handles like that? Shit . . . yeah, maybe."

"So what makes you think—"

"Found body parts in a shipyard."

"Body parts? Hacked up? That's not Malinowski's style, is it?"

"Did I say hacked up?"

"You said parts, so I assumed—"

"Dr. Carr, what gives with Malinowski's truck? Anything?"

Carr brought him up to date.

"This body we're going to see was found in a shipyard where there's lots of coal."

"And the condition's bad."

"Been there for some time, stuffed in a drainage ditch or something."

"Oh, Christ." Carr breathed deeply, perhaps the last deep breath he'd be taking for a time. It promised to be a long night. "You get in touch with Grant and Sybil Shanley?"

"My office will. They'll follow us, I'm sure."

"They're going to want a look-see. Make some tests, including the soil, the coal, match it to what they've got."

Kelso nodded through it all. "'Spect so."

Carr hoped to have most of the forensics done before the two other doctors arrived. Between them, Grant and Shanley had had very little breathing space and very little time to sleep or to relax. He'd do what he could to take up the slack, and to curry the favor again of the M.E.'s Office and Dr. Sybil Shanley.

He secretly looked forward to seeing her again tonight, despite the circumstances under which they'd be brought together.

Malinowski had to rid himself of the body that was still thumping around in back of the van. Every time

268

he took a sharp turn, there it was, the telltale thump, thump, *thump!* It was driving him crazy. Besides, he needed the space. He had made the necessary call to Hinsen, and the man was freaked, he could tell, even through the phone, knowing he had the hot meat wagon, and knowing his pal, Louis, meant to implicate him if he was caught. Malinowski felt comfortable about Hinsen's now breaking the van down, selling it for parts. No one was looking for a dark blue van without lettering on it. No one looking at the van from the outside would know it was refrigerated unless they happened too close and felt the chill, or saw the curl of icy air that inevitably seaped through the cracks where the seals had seen better days.

Malinowski drove to a shipyard where he'd dumped bodies before. It was nearly eight and dusk was descending. As Malinowski approached, he saw flashing lights in the distance, perhaps an ambulance.

He was already dockside when he realized the lights were those of cops. Someone had either had an accident, or someone had jumped ship and defected, so large was the crowd. Or, someone had discovered a body that he'd left here on an earlier occasion.

He stopped the vehicle and stared straight ahead. Darkness was falling fast and he was fairly certain, no one had seen him, thus far. He wheeled the vehicle in behind an enormous piling of lumber and held his ground. Should he be seen driving off, it could go badly. He killed the motor and went to the rear of the vehicle. From the looks of the lumber stacked all around him here, rows beyond this, it would sit here for some time. He yanked open the back door to the van, cooled air engulfing and refreshing him in a cloud that seemed to cling to him in the night air. He hefted out the inert form of the dead girl, opened the zipper, brought it down the length of the bag, and removed her from her plastic womb. He carried the rigid body to a crevice found between the lumber piles and dumped the carcass unceremoniously here.

He returned to the van and sat on the hood where he could peer out between the sheets of lumber at the doings of the authorities about two hundred yards distant.

"Two more," he told himself quietly, "just two more and I'm home free. No more *needs* to fulfill, no more pain to endure, just put my faith in Solomon."

A thin Chicago policeman in a wet suit was prepared to go down into the drainage sewer after the bloated and jagged flesh pile below the grate. The killer had covered the grate with the nearby coal, and there was going to be great difficulty in determining just how long the body'd been here. Sybil's estimate matched Dean's own, a little less than five weeks, maybe four. Carr concurred after taking a bit more time to view the remains from on high, using a powerful police flash.

The grate over the decayed body of the victim was hauled up. It was heavy and two men did the work, but it wasn't so heavy that one man could not have raised it. Already, the police standing about were stuffing their noses with Vick's Vapor Rub to cut the stench to their nostrils. The frog man waddled through the opening with a stricken look on his face, which had taken on a pallor close to that of the victim's own. The condition of the body was far worse than the exhumed Jory Bemis's had been. Water lapped at it and curled open wounded flesh where animals had gotten at it. Great chunks of flesh were completely gone, consumed by the rats.

The Chicago yards were filled with them. Larger than many breeds of cat, capable in numbers of bringing down a dog, they roamed almost at will about the shipyards at night; roamed all day below, in the drainage system where the partially mutilated body lay. The sight was worse, Dean told Sybil, than the bits and pieces they'd found in the pipes about the Schletter home, for here was the recognizable whole shorn into a puzzle of parts, some sections of which were picked clean. When they tried to pull the corpse up, it fell apart.

There was a collective groan and a moment of doing nothing. Then once more they began the work of scooping out the remains. Early on it was determined to be the body of a male, between the ages of eighteen and thirty, difficult to be exact. It would also be virtually impossible to know for certain that he was a victim of the Suffocator. There was nothing left of the larynx area or the first to go tissues: eyeballs, epidermis. Perhaps the lungs would tell the story, but decomposition might erase the signature of suffocation there.

They labored over the body for almost an hour. Carr held up, along with Dean and Sybil. Kelso, unable to watch after the body literally fell apart in their hands, had spent much of the time nearby in his

271

unmarked unit, head in hands.

The other units began disappearing when Dean told them they were just about finished. An ambulance awaited the body, or what was left of it, to take it downtown to the M.E.'s for further examination. The others had gone, Dean was ready to call it quits as soon as Sybil and Carr finished the sample-taking they wished to make.

Then a radio dispatch directed at Kelso came over the wire. Kelso shouted to Dean and the remaining cops to follow him.

"What's up?" asked Dean.

"Another body's been located."

"Jesus, where?"

"Stony Island, Lake Calumet, Port of Chicago Harbor Facilities."

"This bastard's been busy for a long time from the looks of that poor devil we just dredged up."

"We've got to get over there, Dean. Pronto."

Kelso yanked the remaining police units. No need to leave anybody else but the ambulance attendants and the two coroners, he reasoned. The crime scene had been marked and cordoned off, the ET was Carr, and he had about completed his work. All that remained was to somehow get the body's various pieces into the ambulance, and this was being done via a large, black body bag. If the hospitals were using see-through vinyl bags, you wouldn't know it here. The waiting ambulance attendants had seen a lot, but the two veterans had given wide berth to this one, smoking and going off for a walk by the river's edge.

Kelso, with an entourage of flashing cars and Dean

in the seat beside him, tore from the area for the distant Calument River and the shipyard at Stony Island. Sybil gave a wave to the waiting ambulance attendants, and while they zipped up the bag and were putting the bouncing and rolling parts into the ambulance, began giving them orders.

"Hey, we're union, Doc, and it's almost supper time!" said one.

Sybil exploded. "You eat after this man's remains are deposited at the City Morgue, and not before, damn it!"

"Hey, hey, okay . . . okay."

Carr came alongside her and tentatively put an arm around her. She leaned into him.

"You sure you want to follow Dean and Kelso anymore this night?" he asked.

"No, I'm not sure, but I don't have a choice. Oh, Don, how much are we going to have to take? How much before this maniac is stopped?"

He shook his head, guiding her toward the water's edge. "According to the Chief, he's tried no big escape maneuvers, taken no trains, planes, or buses. He thinks the man's still in the city, still lurking near here, most likely in hiding."

They could hear the less than medlodious sound of the ambulance siren as it coughed into life and died away like a wounded animal. At the last of its whimper Sybil, holding tightly to Don Carr, began to feel silly and angry at the hot tears that were coursing down her face.

"Damn it, I swore I wouldn't let this case get to me," she said, looking up at him.

He reached for a handkerchief and began dabbing

at her eyes and cheeks. Suddenly he leaned forward and kissed her. She returned his kiss passionately, wanting to blot out the horror of the night.

As she kissed him there, her breath going into his, comingling, she thought of the meaning of the kiss and how it was viewed in times past as literally breath-taking. That once another human had stolen your breath, they had a strange power over you.

With this thought before her, she felt a sudden, powerful little dart strike her between the shoulder blades. She thought for a split second she'd been shot, or stabbed, so painful was the plunge, and her eyes met Don's. He was staring straight back at her, his face showing anguish. As he stumbled away from her with a silly expression on his features, she felt something hanging between her shoulder blades. She reached back until she touched it and plucked it out. It was a plastic tube. She stared in confusion at the hypodermic needle emptied of its contents. She heard herself as if from far away as she asked, "Don, what did you do to me?"

Then she realized she was on her knees, faint and weak, and that Don was struggling with someone in the dark. She saw Don fall hard against the concrete. She watched as in a kind of slow motion his head bruised, the skin breaking, the blood seeping into the dirt. From her kneeling position, she looked up into the face and eyes of the maniac, Malinowski, recognizing him from the police sketch being circulated. In his eyes was the whole story. She was to be his next victim.

Eighteen

Sybil Shanley didn't know what was causing her discomfort, or where she was, or what prompted the hallucinogenic images bombarding her mind. She was in a foreign place, an alien world delicately balanced on a hair's breath, on her last breath. She felt trapped and cornered and helpless. She felt a disorder in the universe and recalled an ancient Latin phrase, *axis mundi*, the fulcrum of the world. It meant that a disorder in the microcosm disturbed the entire universe at once, that an impact on Earth reacts on all spheres. It was a belief held by Dean that mankind's evil infected nature.

She had never given it full thought, the life of man pulsating to the hidden rhythms of the cosmos, and yet man was patterned after that macrocosm. In man all states of heaven and hell resided, beauty and decay; every shape and geometric form could be seen during an autopsy, every sign and symbol with all their inner meanings, potent and significant. In man's system resided every possible means of locomotion and mechanical principle. In him resided the universal numbers, colors, rays, elements; the cosmos in all its dimensions and durations, time from immeasurable aeons to incalculable micro moments; the disposition of the constellations, the traits of the zodiac. In man and woman were all changes of season and temperatures, all times of coming and going, existence and becoming, of being, of not being. In her was reflected the solstices, the equinoxes, all the moving, living panorama of the universe. All except the eternal flux . . . air.

She needed air . . . more air.

Sybil's delirium continued. Her head was round, and so was the sky; like the earth, her feet were heavy with gravity. Her organs within the abdominal and thoracic cavities corresponded with the five elements; her vertebra to the fortnights making up the seasons; and her 365 bones to the days in a year.

She saw herself on the autopsy slab, beneath the lights, Dean and others picking her apart.

She wanted to shout. Didn't they know that she was a world in miniature, that within her was the sun, the moon, and the stars? That it was all delicately balanced?

She felt a sudden spasm when she envisioned a cold scalpel placed into her depths. This affected a change in the speed and depth of her breathing. Her heart rate shot up along with her blood pressure, altering the oxygen, carbon dioxide, acid, alkali, lactate, and calcium content in the blood, and it was affecting her brain. She heard a persistent, loud buzzing coming from inside her head. She felt sweaty and unable to fend off the doctors working over her exposed organs.

Her vision deteriorated, making them mere shadows that gelled into one, large, ominous shadow. She felt disorientated, on the verge of blacking out.

She felt her muscles become rigid and sensed she was on the verge of complete stupor, or a cataleptic state. Something deep within told her she must reduce her breathing rate, slow it down consciously, or she would die. She knew that slow breathing increased the CO_2 content of the lungs and blood, despite the fact it would reduce the amount of oxygen reaching the brain. But if she reached the point where the brain autonomously accelerated to gather in more oxygen, she'd reach a safer trance state, wherein the brain would produce the faster alpha rhythms associated with transcendental meditation.

She could not long endure, however, for prolonged suspension of breath would lead to a high concentration of carbon dioxide in the blood and to CO_2 intoxication. Little wonder she was hallucinating her own autopsy.

Where was she? Why couldn't she breathe? How had she become so cold? What was the strange, amorphous shape over her, and where was the light coming from? Should she go toward the light? Was she dying? Or was she already dead?

Before she again blacked out, she heard a peculiar sucking noise, not unlike an animal at its dish, and she imagined a giant gar fish with an elongated body covered with scaly, bony plates, its snout tucked against her face. What the sickening sound might be, and whatever the sinister meaning of the final, awful image, she could only guess at before a blizzard of falling snow and ice began to rain down over her mind, silencing it, giving it peace and reassurance.

Louis Malinowski had prepared two hypodermic needles with the Valium. The concentration was potent enough to send a man right down, and it had. He didn't know why he decided to carry both syringes with him when he left the relative safety of the truck behind the lumber, but it'd been fortunate that he had. *Luck? Or the hand of Solomon at work?*

Louis Malinowski knew now that Solomon would stand by his word. He knew without reservation that Solomon had in some wholly mysterious way sent him here at just the moment he might strike out at the two unsuspecting people embracing at the water's edge. Solomon could see into the future, and he wisely guided Malinowski toward his future. Louis had left his van and proceeded on foot toward the direction of the authorities, once he saw that they were thinning out. He had remained well hidden as he did so. Some unconscious force moved him closer and closer, and at the exact right moment, he found himself within a short distance of his prey. How very neat to end it all here, two for the price of one, as it were.

As the lovers embraced, Malinowski brought the syringes home, one in each back at the precise same moment, promptly incapacitating the woman, and, without much difficulty, the man as well.

He then returned to his van where he'd already prepared the body bags, his clipboard, forms, pencil, and a suitable temperature. He didn't want the temperature to detract from their breathing.

He had then pulled the van into the coal warehouse not far from where the man and woman lay unconscious. He knew his time was limited, and that these two could be missed. He rushed the man's form into the back of the van with some difficulty. He hadn't looked nearly as heavy as he was. As the butcher worked, he had stepped on the man's glasses, crushing them.

While he positioned the man into the bag and placed him prostrate in the back of the refrigerated car, he heard moans come from the woman. He rushed back to her without having completely stripped the man. No matter, he tore out any keys or sharp pens that could conceivably punch a hole in the vinyl bag. He told himself again that he must work quickly. He then did the same for the woman, he had stripped her to the waist when he thought he heard something, a shuffling of feet. It was distracting enough that he stopped in his frisking of the woman and cocked an ear. He imagned the worst, that it was more police with guns. Some had been hiding out in the surrounding darkness. Or they had doubled back to close in on him, knowing he'd been behind the stacks of lumber all along. Irrational? Perhaps, perhaps not. Should he take the measure of the man, or men? Could it be at all possible that one or more of the cops had held back? That it was a setup, some sort of decoy operation? He grew increasingly worried over this notion. He picked up the gun he'd kept nearby should he require it. He took a few steps away from the woman before he was satisfied they were alone. In another moment, he heard it again, a faint scuttling noise that he now recognized as rats.

They'd obviously come to inspect the damage done by the humans, searching for that which had been taken from them.

"Not to worry," he said to them aloud. "You'll have more in due time."

Malinowski had then said to hell with the woman's skirt, leaving it, rushing the job of getting her encased, zipping it up tightly. He was anxious to get on with it, anxious to see the ritual through to its natural end; to finally and truly unite with Solomon; to pass from this world *himself* on to Solomon's plane. Solomon had told him it could be done if he could gather in the breath of three victims within a twenty-four-hour period. Given the amount of hallucinating brought on by the CO_2 high, time was wasting. Louis wanted done with it by morning.

He imagined a life without threat, without pain of memories, old injuries; a life on the wind, a life as free and innocent as the breath that the woman captive breathed out of her lungs at this moment.

Once she was ensconced in a bag, zipped and ready, he returned his attention to the man. He'd begin with him, then go to the woman, and back and forth between them.

His plan was to do them together as much as possible. He felt this would please Solomon.

He'd never done two at once, however, and he had to take some time to determine the logistics of doing so. He'd have to move quickly. He wanted to dispense with his scientific record for this purpose, but some deep-seated voice told him he must continue his record, record the fact he'd taken the breaths of three victims, within a twenty-four-hour period. Should he actually be taken up by Solomon and freed from this miserable existence into Solomon's world, he must leave an accounting, an explanation and a door . . . a door that might open for others like himself who were tormented in this life.

Without further fear of second-guessing, without any further adieu, Louis Malinowski stripped himself down and pulled the freezer doors closed on himself and the two soon-to-be corpses. He sat over their heads, concentrating on the man first, recording his reactions, then those of the woman. He was growing impatient and frantic for that first breath of the changed air inside the first bag when he heard faint moaning and then coughing coming from inside the woman's bag. He watched her for a time, found her pretty, far prettier than anyone else he'd done. She'd please Solomon, no doubt of it.

Then he turned his full attention back to the man who was at near-starvation level already, his chest heaving. He'd not even fully recovered from the knockout drug yet, and Malinowski worried he'd given them both too much of the stuff. It would delay the vital process.

Upset with himself, Malinowski brought the zipper down on the man's bag, allowing in more oxygen. He then did the same for the woman. He must get it right. There'd be no second chances.

Cold and sweaty, like a chill and fever, is what she felt first, coming to gently, serenely, as if in a safe place all sectioned off. Her in her place, everybody else in theirs. She sensed things around her long before all her senses were properly functioning. She sensed the encasement, like a coffin or a cocoon. Her hands felt along its perimeter, finding it very cold, refrigerator cold, to the touch. It seemed like a recurrent bad dream she'd been having:

Something is swirling around her, just outside the encasement. Movement seems amplified along with sound. She can hear a ringing in her ears, the swirling of blood in the spirals of her ears, even her most private parts, and every nerve and fiber feel exposed and short-circuited. Her breath's labored and irregular.

But it was only a bad dream, a nightmare, she told herself, one from which she'd escape, if she could just shake off sleep. Funny, though, the last thing she remembered was standing alongside the canal with Don Carr, feeling that awful pain in her back and seeing Don fall, struggling with a dark form that hovered over them in the end.

As it did now.

Her hand touches a portion of the seemingly safe encasement that tells her it is ribbed, that it is a *zipper!*

Her mind fights the illusion, denying what her fingertips have just told her: *It's no dream, it's real!*

She fears terribly what her eyes might reveal should she open them. Pulling on her deepest inner strength to mount an offensive against the nightmare that denies its own existence, she forces open her eyes.

She wants desperately to scream and scream again, but instead, she manages her fear, knowing where she

282

is and that her fate is being dictated by a madman.

Still only half conscious, she recalled the deadly venom he'd injected into her. She recalled having somehow gotten to her feet, only to tople into *his* arms. She feared for Don Carr's life. Was he left to bleed to death outside somewhere? She sensed she was inside a closed space that was refrigerated. She tried to shake off the effects of the drug. As she managed this, bits and pieces like snapshots in her mind returned. She recalled a feeling of sheer weightlessness that was replaced by a harsh, plasticky thing being placed over her. Half-dazed and unable to see, due to the drug and the opaqueness of the bag, she looked up at a naked little light. The interior of the bag was covered with the remnants of her own breath, and it made her feel dead already, just a visiting spirit.

The perspiration increased, dripping down her forehead to her ears, tickling her, telling her that she was indeed still alive. Over her lumbered the dark shadow. It made her wince and turn her head and gaze to her left where there was nothing but a dark wall. She turned and gazed to her right, feeling helpless on her back this way. When her eyes went right, she had to focus on this strange wall which was not a wall at all, but another bag with another person in it, perhaps a long-dead person. She fought for courage when she closed her eyes to the horror. Opening them again, she tried desperately to make out the features of the occupant of this bag, and to try to determine if the other victim was dead or alive.

The lumbering form over her seemed to be hovering far more over this other bag than her own.

She found breathing difficult. She coughed and her body began a spasm which she managed to get control of. Once more, she focused all her mind on the second victim and what Malinowski was doing to him! It was a male, but the contour of the profile told her worse. It was Donald Carr!

"They were packing up when we left," said Officer Hummings to Dean, who'd asked him if Doctors Shanley and Carr hadn't been behind him.

The body at Calumet Harbor turned out not to be a victim of the Suffocator, but a victim of other foul play, a gunshot in the small of the back. The man was left with ID and was easy to pinpoint as a drug dealer. It looked like a deal had gone suddenly sour, a connection severed. Kelso forwarded the opinion it might be the work of some sort of vigilante, given the caliber of the weapon used, a Saturday-night-special version of a twenty-two pistol, or so his experience told him.

Consequently, Kelso had put it on the radio, and most likely Sybil and Carr had gotten the word, had decided Dean could handle it, and had gone home for the night. Whether they did so together or separately, he guessed was none of his business. Still, when he telephoned the office and Sybil had not touched base with the people there, he began to feel a little discomforting disquiet trickle into his brain.

Since he had the office on the line, he asked if the ambulance men who had towed in the last body were anywhere in the building. They were located and one came on. "Did Dr. Shanley give you orders with respect to the remains?"

"Yeah, tagged and placed, no problem."

"Mr. Cigliosi," Dean stopped him. "Did Dr. Shanley or Dr. Carr indicate they would follow you back?"

"You kidding? They were making out when we left."

Dean clicked off the radio and found Kelso staring in at him. "Everything all right?"

"I suppose it is. Seems funny of Sybil not to have checked in either with me or downtown after sending a body in. Not like her."

"Hey, love does strange things to people."

Dean put on a lopsided grin and nodded, "So, you noticed, Mr. Detective."

"Have to be blind not to. Come on, no need to worry about those two. I think it's a good match."

"Just not like the new Dr. Sybil Shanley. I could see her disappearing like this a year ago, maybe . . . but *now?* Doesn't fit."

"Dino, you'll see her tomorrow."

"I know that. Just the same, if they were going to her place, they'd have had time to get there by now." He rang and rang and rang but got no answer.

Now Kelso said, "Try Carr's number."

"What is it?"

Kelso thought a moment then said, "555-1948."

Dean asked dispatch to put it through and they did, without result.

"Give me that," said Kelso, calling into headquarters, asking if Carr had reported in, or if he was in the building. "This could take some time," he told Dean.

285

Nineteen

Donald Carr was nude, so far as she could tell. She, too, was nude, at least to the navel, for she felt her skirt about her legs. Then she remembered something important, something that could save her life, and she prayed silently that God had not allowed Malinowski time to search her, as he appeared to have rushed through the stripping process. She wondered how long she'd been out. She prayed Carr was still alive. She wondered how soon Malinowski would get to her, when suddenly she felt a wave of nausea and faintness come over her, threatening to put her back under. No air. He had the zipper closed tight.

Gasping, another spasm cutting through her, she fought for air when suddenly she heared the metallic *urr* of a zipper as it was slowly opened. Her eyes focused just enough to see Malinowski's mouth and nose, like a giant, misshapen pig's snout filling the hole where the only air might enter. She tried to locate the scalpel in her skirt pocket, the one Dean had given her with her name engraved on it, the one she carried everywhere. She needed to feel the solidity of it. Her fingers reached for it and slowly found it and she felt a surge of relief and power filter through her mind and body. There was a way out, but did she have the strength?

Certainly not at the moment, part of her said, while the other part screamed to get from Malinowski's mad clutches at once. Still, her arms felt numb and useless. Could she even wield the damned scalpel in her dehydrated condition? As a child her father had once captured a small bat that had wreaked havoc in the attic of their Iowa farm. After hours encased in the airtight jar, the mouse-sized animal was, when she had finally opened the container to release it, amazingly alive. It had sunken and shriveled into itself and was completely soaked with perspiration. It couldn't walk let alone fly, yet it remained alive.

Now she was the bat, and she meant to survive. Malinowski was taking in great whiffs of the spoiled air inside the bag, sucking in her exhalations, and she was too weak to stop him.

His ugly mouth and nostrils flared one last time and he was gone, leaving the zipper cracked for barely a moment longer. She gasped and held tight to the scalpel. Doing the wall side of the vinyl bag, she began to etch a hole in it. The scalpel was razor sharp but it still took several swipes in her weakened condition to make the all but invisible incision. Still, it was made, and she began to feed herself on the precious oxygen, regaining her senses with each breath.

But what about Carr? How could she help him? It would take time, and time was something he had very little of. Then again, staring back at him, she fearfully wondered if it was not too late for Carr.

Outside and over her, she heard Malinowski chanting some odd words over and over. A scattered laugh or gleeful chortle escaped the maniac from time to time as well. He'd come back for more soon, she thought, and when he did, she'd be ready. She prayed she had the strength.

There were two worlds now, two dimensions. That on the inside of the bag and that on the outside. Malinowski wanted to be inside with his victims, she realized. Malinowski's ritual had to do with a death wish. He wanted what his victims received.

She wished that she could oblige him. She wondered if she could use the information against him. Then she thought she heard herself coughing, only to realize it was Carr. He was still alive! But for how long?

The lumbering shadow that blocked out what little light there was in the small enclosure suddenly retreated. She knew it was a risk, but she must take it. She slit through her bag on the right. Carr's was buttressed against hers. She continued to cut until she slit a hole into his bag as well, when suddenly the light was gone again. Malinowski was hovering over them.

She was certain he had seen her activity, and yet the haze and film over the breadth and length of the interior of the bag made seeing in or out nearly impossible.

When nothing further happened, Malinowski

went into another chant, perhaps tripping out or trancing on the carbon dioxide he'd inhaled. Sybil bided her time and gained strength, praying Don would be all right.

Grimacing with both excitement and anxiety, Louis Malinowski, in a state of semi-trance, called out again to his god Solomon for help.

He knelt over the woman. He knew her as Dr. Sybil Shanley now, and her boyfriend was Dr. Donald Carr, a policeman. He'd gotten that much from her bag and his wallet, for the purpose of filling in the blanks on his final forms.

Malinowski sank deeper, opening the zipper just a tad and placing his eyeball there. He stared carefully down at the lady doctor, confused to see that while she was breathing shallowly, it was too easy, too regular for the amount of time she'd been starved of oxygen. It didn't figure, unless she was one of those rare people capable of breath retention for long durations. Yet, earlier, she'd looked in worse condition. Now this. It didn't figure. He couldn't make head or tail of it, wondering if it was a sign from Solomon.

He placed his mouth over the hole he'd created, sucked in the exhalations of the good doctor Sybil Shanley. He filled his lungs with her air, stealing it and her essence for himself and for Solomon. He told her as much, speaking through the small perforation he'd made, when he thought he heard her respond in a near inaudible whisper. But that was impossible, unless . . . unless Solomon had come and was trying to speak through her near-lifeless form. It might account for the return of color to her skin.

"Solomon? Solomon? Speak, speak to me," Malinowski cried, bringing the zipper down the length of the bag and placing his hands on her shoulders, shaking her and calling out, "Solomon, take me! Take me tonight."

"V-v-e-r-y," her lips parted and her eyes opened, as she finished, "w-e-l-l." At the same instant she brought the scalpel up, the blade slicing a jagged path across his abdomen, but not deep enough to suit her. She was weaker than she'd thought. But it was enough of a wound to startle him into a surprised scream and to an awkward sitting position across from her. In the dark of the van he examined his wound like an animal.

Strange noises escaped him—gasps and a stunned, "Ahhh, ahhh, ahhh." He packed ice around the wound and held himself, nursing it.

She got up slowly, her naked breasts splattered with his blood. She never took her eyes off him. Malinowski moaned like a child and his eyes grew wider and wider. He kept repeating the name, "Solomon, Solomon.' It became a cadence.

Despite her overwhelming horror and fear, Sybil suddenly realized she had the upper hand with Malinowski. He seemed to have gone into a mild state of shock, brought on by the combination of the wound and the hallucinations he'd strived to achieve with her and Carr's dying breaths. For the moment, holding his wound, sitting upright on the icy floor, he was subdued. Sybil knew she hadn't a moment to lose, however. Holding firmly to the scalpel, she ripped a larger hole into the bag restraining Donn Carr. At the moment, Carr looked as lifeless as a space traveler in a state of suspended animation. She feared it was too late for Don. She grabbed up a black metal bar which lay alongside Don's form, and with it she began pounding away at the lever on the back door that held them captive.

Malinowski's enormous, bloody hands took hold of her from behind, pulling her down, dragging her back. She felt the cold floor and the stiff, tearing plastic of the bag once more enclosing her. Terror of being returned to the bag blotted out everything else and she began swinging the metal bar at him. The bar connected with his temple, sending him reeling back, only semiconscious at first, and then out from the combined loss of blood and the blow to the head. Somewhere in the struggle, as he snatched her back by the hair, she'd lost the scalpel.

She felt a rush of warm air and realized that the van door had come open. She was inches from safety, and Malinowski was. unconscious. Breathing a little easier, she looked around and located her blouse. She rushed to cover her shivering limbs, and then to pull Don from the van. She must revive him before Malinowski came to.

She got down from the van, and from this vantage point, she took firm hold of Don's cold legs. With all the energy she could muster, she pulled him out a few inches at a time. Her face was smeared with a mix of Malinowski's blood and her tears. Don was like a rug, heavy and inert and unwieldy.

Her own hands were frozen blue, filled with stinging pain, the nails jagged and torn, clutching the metal bar in one hand and snatching at the bag that held Don Carr with the other. She yelled at Carr, trying to get through to him, and she pounded at his legs in an attempt to revive some feeling in him. She pulled and pulled until he and the bag fell from the back of the van and lay on the ground.

He remained unconscious, or dead. Putting aside the metal pipe, she started tearing away at the zipper that confined Don when suddenly she heard a maniacal scream. Sybil looked up and saw Malinowski's form fly straight at her. She dived for the underside of the van, clawing her way along the filthy boards of the old warehouse he had brought her to. Scuttling crews of rats seemed to taunt her, as if they were in conspiratorial contact with the madman at her heels.

She dared look back, hearing noise behind her. Malinowski had lifted Carr's body and returned it to the back of the van. From the timbre of the sound, from Carr's stillness earlier, she deduced that he'd succumbed before there was a chance to help him.

"One more! Damn, I just need one more!" Malinowski was roaring and suddenly on his stomach searching for her, but she'd already scurried out the side and was racing for the cover of darkness toward the deep interior of the chasm of the enormous storage house.

Malinowski raced after her, stomping over the boards, shouting like an angry child. "Bitch! You're ruining everything!"

She nose-dived behind some stacks of boxes, holding her breath like an expert now. She could sense him, sense the danger as he rounded the boxes.

She looked for a way out, but he was too close. Then, knowing it was her only chance, she shoved wildly at the boxes and they spilled over his head. They were heavy boxes, filled with nuts and bolts that spewed forth like a shower of stones over Malinowski, skidding on forever across the accordian of boards that made a rough wood floor.

Sybil raced deeper into the dark, going behind rows and rows of lumber. When she stopped, she was panting, and the panting made it difficult to hear his footsteps, although she knew he was close at hand. She remained here, crouched like an animal, her heart pumping so hard she could scarcely breathe. She knew she couldn't remain where she was. She moved down the stacks and rows of lumber, found a hole, and darted down another way and another until she came to a crevice which she squeezed into. She couldn't see the end of it in the darkness, but then, neither could he, she reasoned. Going deep into the crevice as quietly as possible, she blanketed herself in darkness.

For a moment she relaxed, catching her breath, slowing her heartrate, willing herself to be calm, calmer, calmest. Quietly she sucked air into her lungs. lovingly and thoughtfully she did this, enjoying the taste of the air and the smell of the wood. Then she saw him at the end of the row, staring straight down into the black hole where she hid. He could not possibly see her, she reasoned, and yet he continued to stare as if he did. She moved in slow motion, silently inching further and further back, never taking her eyes off the demon who pursued her so relentlessly. Another few yards and she'd be on the other side, able to move on to a new and better hiding place. She backed up another few inches when she lost her footing, falling over something suddenly in her way, making a terrible noise as she did so. She crawled hand over hand to get away from the obstacle. When she suddenly realized it was a dead woman, no doubt dumped here by Malinowski, she gasped and stumbled away, knocking over some loose boards. This brought Malinowski racing at her thorough the crevice, his mad eyes glowing in the night.

Sybil only now realized she'd dropped the scalpel when she fell, and her hands scurried about the corpse in an effort to relocate it. He was coming at her. She searched and searched. He was getting too close. She gave up the search, turned, and got from the crevice and ran and ran without daring to look back.

"I'll get you, bitch! Bitch!" she heard him ranting behind, close and closing in.

She stumbled and hurt her leg, ripped her knee and bloodied her shin, and kept going to the tune of his laughter. She was in the open now in the center of the huge storage shelter. She guessed that the enormous complex wasn't very far from the coal storage, and if so, there'd be grates and the drainage system. She ran into the darkness in search of a hole to crawl into.

Then behind her she saw him come into and out of what little light filtered in from the lamps outside. He had a gun, and he'd been close enough to fire more than once, but he hadn't. He wanted to save her for the bag. But time was running out, running out for him as well as for her. He might use the gun out of sheer frustration.

She went down on all fours when her naked feet touched a grate. She began working it loose, looser, and then pulled it away. It took more strength than she thought she possessed, but she managed to lift and push the grate away, a grinding noise accompanying the action, giving him her location. She looked down into the empty, gaping hole and heard movement down there. And she remembered the rat-eaten body of the man they'd pulled out of such a place tonight.

She shivered and gasped and made her move.

Louis Malinowski was frantic. She'd escaped him, escaped Solomon, too. But not for long, he promised himself. Then he heard a metallic sound and the grinding of stone. He knew instantly her plan and followed the sounds she made in her pitiful attempt.

He came up on the open hole with a ferocious leap, his arm going the full distance up to grab her, but his fingers touched only empty space. She wasn't there. Before he could raise himself up, the heavy metal grate came crashing down on him, striking him in the back of the neck and shoulders. Two or three inches higher, it might've knocked him unconscious, or killed him. As it was, it shook him badly, yet he managed to hold tight to the pistol, his finger pulling off a round in a kind of reflex action, frightening her off.

Malinowski heaved himself up and lay against some bundles, listening to the grain inside them seep downward to seek their level. That was all he wished to do, seek his level, to find Solomon, and now one woman, one bitching woman, stood in his way. He was outraged at the thought, and pain or no pain, he pushed on in pursuit of her, tracking her through the spirals of darkness and the labyrinth of the warehouse.

Just then Louis saw a light at the very end of the big facility, and running toward the swinging light, he saw the woman named Shanley. He braced himself, cocked the gun, aimed for the lantern, found the silhouette of the night man who was holding it and fired.

Sybil had gasped when she saw the light coming out of nowhere, believing at first it was Malinowski. But her mind kept telling her that Malinowski was only human, after all, and handn't the capability of spirits or demons, and so the light must be brought by someone else. It represented help.

She had raced toward it, crying, gasping, pleading for the help she needed, stumbling just as a shot was fired and the man with the lantern hit the ground with a powerful thud, inches from her a hissing sound escaped him. He was dead.

"Don't move!" Malinowski shouted. "Stay right where you are, or you're next."

She called his bluff, off at a trot, kicking the lantern and causing its light to spiral about the interior of the building in a strobe effect until he crouched and picked it up. Paying no heed to the man he'd killed, Malinowski just kept coming.

"Dean, Kelso, somebody," she whimpered, "help me!"

She found the door where the watchman had

entered and ran in the direction where she thought her car might still be. But she was turned around, and soon knew this as she came up on the other side of yet another warehouse. Malinowski had obviously driven her and Carr some distance from the original location, but where *was* she and how far was her automobile? And how long could she run and hide from him?

She knew now that he didn't want to use the gun on her, that he wanted her alive, to return her to the hellish death suffered by Donald Carr. She'd as soon die in a hundred other ways. And she might before dawn arrived.

She heard his pounding footsteps as the man was now trotting toward her. She ran along the perimeter of the building and found an entryway and a stairwell that went down into the depths, a foul smell rising up out of them. She heard the rumble of living things here and realized the stalls here were filled with livestock, no doubt the purpose of the watchman. The place was filled with hay bales and watering troughs, cows, pigs, sheep, and horses. She ran the gauntlet, straddling a sewage ditch, until she made it to the end of the room.

Down the stairs she had been on, he came, and for the first time since the van, they stared across at one another.

"Leave me alone," she demanded.

He shook his head. "Solomon wants you."

"We know all about you, Malinowski."

The use of his name seemed to cut through to him, at least a little bit.

She continued, seeing him stop. "Louis Malinow-

298

ski. Saw your mother murdered before your eyes when you were just—"

"Shut up! It's a lie!"

"—just a boy."

"Lies! It wasn't my father!"

"He locked you up, beat you, didn't he?"

"No!"

"Beat you and locked you in his damned freezer, didn't he?"

"You bloody bitch! Shut up! Shut up!"

He slowly began to raise the gun as if to fire.

There were stairs to her left, out of his line of vision. She allowed him to come a step nearer before darting up, taking them two at a time, racing once more for street level. A shot ricocheted off the wall where she'd been standing. The animals responded with all manner of noise and bustle. But above it all somehow, she could still hear his feet pounding toward her in response, as if keeping in sync with her frightened heart. There was no reasoning with him. There was no *reason* in him.

The check at headquarters did not turn up Carr, and as far as Dean was concerned, something didn't smell right. Kelso, tired and frustrated by this long night, did not react positively to Dean's suggestion they return to the site of the other body to check on Carr and Sybil.

"They mighta' went to have a bite to eat."

"Not after what we just dug out of that grate. No way."

"They may've gone to a movie."

299

"Not Sybil."

"They may've checked into a motel."

Dean frowned and shook his head, "No, I'm telling you, I've got a bad feeling about this."

"Bad feeling, huh? So, we're back to hunches and bad feelings. What happened to all your scientific know-how?"

"Ken, I'm seriously worried about her. Call it what you like but—"

"All right, all right . . . I give. So, Dr. Grant, what do you propose we do about it? Go all the way back to the other boat docks on the canal where we left them? Or what?"

"That might put my mind at ease, to see that they haven't been stranded there."

"Stranded, hell, Carr's got a radio—"

"But he came over with you, remember? They've got Sybil's car, and it's not equipped."

"Well, why the hell don't you get her equipped?"

"I'm working on it."

"*Working* on it? Hell, you're always working on it, Grant. When the hell you going to stop working long enough to *do* something about it!"

Dean knew Kelso was agitated and upset over the poor prospect of locating Malinowski and ending the butcher's career as a serial killer tonight. He allowed for this in his response to his friend. "We only spent a million plus on the new facilities already this year."

"Taxpayers' dollars, going to combat crime," said Kelso. "Sad state of affairs. Money that might go into education, feeding the homeless, has to support crime labs instead. Shit." Kelso sighed heavily, took off his hat and rubbed his brow with the sleeve of his sweat-smeared shirt. "Dean, I'll take you back over there, but do you know that I've got a guy downtown needs interrogating very badly, and another fruitcake laying waste to people every ten square miles, so . . ."

"So?"

"So, come on, let's get over there and have done with this nonsense."

Along the way, to break the boredom and silence as Kelso sped past signs that were now so familiar as to induce a feeling of déjà vu in Dean, he talked quietly about Malinowski. "Very weird fixation this butcher has. Not on knives slicing flesh, or on meat cleavers cleaving bone, like you might expect—"

"Yeah, I've tussled with that a bit myself, and all those wild death certificates or charts he created on his victims! What an oddball."

"Strange all right, a fixation on watching people—trapped people—slowly succumb to a state of un-feeling and un-breathing."

"Shrinks'll have a field day with this guy. Who knows," replied Kelso with an unhappy laugh, "maybe somebody'll even write a book, or fashion a Nintendo game around Louis Malinowski and his butcher shop. Little Pac Man figures bagging you up, huh?"

"Then there's the fascination with ice, the freezer. It would naturally slow the breathing down, lengthen the suffering, and this guy seems very much into watching others suffer."

"I'd like to see that he suffers before this is over."

Dean stared across at his old friend, understanding his hatred completely.

"A bullet's not going to do that, nor will the courts."

301

Twenty

He seemed to find her in each black corner, as if he had eyes that could penetrate the vast darkness of this place. He came on her heels each time, until she was ready to fall at his feet with exhaustion, tormented into giving herself over to him. But each time that she allowed herself the thought, she recalled the horror of having awakened on the inside of that body bag.

She found a stairwell that took her up to a second story in yet another warehouse that shared the common link of the canal alongside. A window looked out over the deserted shipyard. There was no one to help her, nothing to do, and no way out. She'd come to the end, for he stood below, shouting obscenities up at her, and there was no other way down.

Did he know she was here, or was he merely guessing? She was unsure, until she heard his footsteps on the ladderlike, wooden stairs. He took each slowly, allowing the play of the squeaks to get to her, calling out the epitaph, "Dead bitch, dead bitch, dead bitch.''

She looked in every direction, above and below. To jump back to ground level might break her leg. Above her was some sort of grain elevator that stuck its long snout out the window she'd peered through, more like a hayloft window than anything else. Just below this were some freight cars standing idle on the tracks outside. Nothing, no where to turn, until her eyes focused on a ladder hanging on the wall, almost blending in with the wall.

The next stair squeaked.

"Coming for you, bitch . . . bitch . . . bitch."

She yanked down the heavy ladder, banging about as she did so, sending down sheaves of hay over the side, telling him he was right to come this way. With a ropelike sound the ladder cascaded out the window, scraping the sill raw and landing with a resounding thud in the empty boxcar below.

The squeaks on the stairs increased proportionately and he was on the loft, his eyes trying desperately to penetrate to every corner and crevice. He slowly took it all in and moved to the loft window. With a final look in the dark corners all about him, he opted to look out the window. He studied the stillness in the well of the black bottomed box car, an ugly, rusted metal thing with an enormous empty belly.

Taking careful aim, Sybil leaped from above him where she'd climbed, out onto and around behind the grain shute that was the nose of the grain elevator. Her body sent him crashing down into the boxcar where she heard the terrible impact that echoed out of the empty chamber.

Sybil lie on the soft hay shaken, holding onto herself and her sanity and crying softly, safe at last. Exhausted, she only wanted a moment to rest before making her way back to Donald and the van, get her bearings, and make her way back to civilization. Only wanted a moment to regain her strength, lick her wounds—the leg stinging like madness—and to catch her breath.

Dean and Kelso found the shipyard gates locked against them at this hour, and no watchman about. It was dark and very late, and Kelso yawned for a solid thirty seconds before saying, "Dino, the place is empty."

But Dean was staring into the thick, fog-bound distance. "There's Sybil's sedan. Hasn't moved an inch. See it down there?"

Kelso had to get out, go to the chainlink fence, and stare for a moment before concurring there was indeed a car some distance down, at about the location they had all been earlier. "Could be someone else's car."

"Could be Sybil's! Damn it, Kelso, we've got to make sure."

He sighed heavily. "Take too long to get the owners. Got something in the trunk might help." He went to the back of his unmarked squad car and popped the trunk. Beside an enormous book, *The Illinois Criminal Code*, was every imaginable tool. "Rules change so damned much, and there've gotten to be so damned many of them," he said, tapping the book with his index finger, "got to carry them with me." Now, from the pile of tools, he selected an enormous bolt cutter. With this Ken returned to the fence and snapped off the lock as if it were a turtle's head. He and Dean shared honors in getting the gates opened wide.

They returned to the car, put away the cutters, and drove through, headlights doused because Kelso didn't relish the idea of having a head-to-head with any watchman they might run into. As they advanced on the dark blue car each grew certain that it was indeed Sybil Shanley's automobile.

"What do you think?" asked Dean.

"Car trouble?"

They got out of the squad car and circled the sedan. Keys were in the ignition.

"Turn it over," suggested Ken.

Dean did so and the motor purred into life. He cut the engine and said, "Odd . . . very odd."

"Let's explore aways on foot. I have a flash," said Kelso who'd dug it from beneath his dash. A few feet along, they heard the scratching noises of rats.

"Damned rats," said Dean, recalling what they'd done to the body in the grate. "I hate them."

"They own the place, Dean. We're just visitin'."

"What about Malinowski? When he dumped that body here? Was he just visitin', Ken? Or did he come here often because the place appealed to him?"

"Who knows . . . Maybe he used rat meat in his butcher business, selling it as some exotic dish—kangaroo, maybe."

They were each talking to relieve the eerie silence of the place. The yards and warehouses went back as far as the eye could see, looking, in the fog, like a

Hollywood backdrop. To Dean, it looked somewhat like a view of another world on another planet.

Kelso suddenly knelt, his flash picking up fresh tire marks. One had left a tire burn where the vehicle had peeled off.

"What is it?"

"Look for yourself."

"Large vehicle . . ."

"Pretty good axle spread, maybe a van?"

"Lots of vans must come and go here."

"Yeah, yeah, right." Ken said, "Let's go in a little deeper."

Dean recognized that Kelso's internal antennae as up and buzzing now. They returned to Kelso's car and drove forward, headlights out. They passed several silent warehouses before they saw a door flung wide, and inside it sat the squat outline of a dark van.

Dean stared into the soupy fog ahead, it seemed to be growing thicker as he looked into it, swirls of it taunting him. Somewhere in the distance the sound of a boat whistle, but nothing more. Trying desperately to penetrate the depths of the cloud fashioned from the river, he felt something solid and heavy pressed into his hand.

"Here, take this," Kelso told him, pushing a .38 Police Special into his hands. Ken flipped open the glove box and snatched out a second, even larger revolver. Quietly, they got out of the car and approached the silent van.

A kind of blue light and blue steam rose spiritlike from the back of the van. It filtered out the open door, mating with the curling fog in a ghostly dance.

Another few steps and they could make out two twisted body bags at the foot of the van, one twisted in a particularly grotesque fashion. Inching ahead, they saw a third body bag unfurled and lying flat deep inside the van, but this one seemed inflated.

"Careful," Kelso cautioned Dean.

For Dean it was like being watched from somewhere high above, as if he and Kelso had become specimens under glass, and when they stepped into a spot of light coming down from a pole, it only added to the illusion. Another few steps and they were standing at the portal of the van where they dared look into the frosted interior.

She nearly fell asleep there, and she might have, if he hadn't made the mistake of dropping the gun from his damaged hand.

Sybil awoke to find him on the ladder, a few rungs from the top, reaching out desperately for the sill. When he saw that she was alerted, he began moving with vigor, tearing at the next rung, crying out, "I'll kill you! You're my *dead meat*, mine and Solomon's!"

She leapt to her feet, backing away, kicking out at the ladder, but his weight against it was too much to cause it to topple, no matter what she did. Malinowski lashed out at her kicking feet, trying to topple her, and he succeeded. He pulled her toward himself.

She screamed, feeling herself giving way, going over the edge. She lashed out repeatedly with blows to his face, kicking with all her strength, pulling hard on the wood siding, trying desperately to regain her feet. She'd have to run back the way she came, through the maze that had so horrified her, back to his van and his ugly handiwork. "God, help me!" she pleaded and found herself loose from his grasp. He'd had to grab onto the ladder, losing his balance there.

She scrambled to her feet, her arms flailing until they hit a heavy chain dangling in the dark. He was coming over the edge when she realized what the chain was for and with a mighty pull she threw open the grain elevator door. Malinowski didn't know what hit him when the tons of grain cascaded down like an avalanche, sending him backwards into the hole from which he'd just crawled. Sybil ran, leaving the elevator door chain wrapped tightly about a beam, allowing it full force. Without a moment's hesitation, she regained the main floor and ran in the direction of the van, her heart pounding. She ran and was suddenly caught up in a man's arms, making her scream in the dark until she heard *his* voice and realized the fact that it was Donald Carr.

Together they slumped to the dirty floor, holding one another tightly. In the distance, but rushing toward them with flashlights, were Dean Grant and Ken Kelso.

Epilogue

"Dr. Sybil Shanley," she derided her reflection in the mirror. Her eyes were sunken and weeping from lack of sleep. She'd lost an extreme amount of weight at too rapid a pace. Unable to eat, with sleep more elusive now than the killer had been, she found that whenever she did doze off, it was into a series of never ending, horrid images. All this even with Donald Carr beside her in bed. She felt like a shadow of her former self. No more controlled and easy life. For the first time, she knew what it must be like to be the victim of a rape, for the brutal attack on her life had been a kind of rape. Louis Malinowski wished to rape her of her life. For the first time ever now, she truly understood and empathized with Grant's wife, Jackie, who had undergone a similar attack the year before. How smart she'd thought herself all along; how stupid and naive all her platitudes and education now seemed. Nothing could withstand the kind of physical torment she had gone through and that still lingered. How long would it linger in her every conscious and unconscious thought? Had Malinowski succeeded in turning her into an emotional cripple?

The story seemed to be summed up within the frame of her apartment mirror, staring back at her. Who was this beaten, terrified person looking her in the eyes?

She feared the long day with nothing to do with her hands. But she feared going out, even stepping onto the street for a newspaper. She feared others might see her and see through her. She feared the night's coming, and feared closing her eyes again, her mind racing for countermeasures to fend off sleep. For sleep was not sleep anymore. Sleep was a creep show in which she must endure again and again the torture of suffocation, locked within the plastic shell, with Malinowski staring down at her nude body.

The phone rang. She let it ring on until whoever it was got the message. Everyone knew she was here. Everyone knew she didn't want to talk to anyone, including a shrink. She ferreted about the apartment, cleaning and picking up and re-ordering things, changing the furniture. All things she would not normally do.

Later the phone rang again. She guessed it was Jackie Grant again, hounding her. Jackie wanted to tell her again that if she didn't seek professional help, she might never again take charge of her life, her career, her emotions, her thoughts, her fears; that she'd never be the same Sybil Shanley, or the kind of doctor that she had been before her near-fatal encounter with that maniac.

From the grave he was coming at her still.

The maniac reached a hand out to her, dragging her down with him.

He claimed large portions of her life, claimed larger portions of her mind.

What was she to do?

One part of her mind was like a clear crystal ball and saw everything occurring in a clinical, detached, and even professional light. This part of her knew that Jackie and her other friends, including Dean and Kelso, were correct: she must get counseling, and quickly if she wished to survive. That her personality would not necessarily survive intact without help. That the incident had changed her forever.

Another part of her hid from all of it, including that rational side of herself. This part feared the first step; feared it so strongly, it was physically painful.

"You fought the bastard that night!" her rational side shouted at her. "You can fight and win now!"

But she shriveled back from the mirror and the shout. From the other room, she could hear the reflected person in the mirror shout again: "You can't let him beat you now!"

But that was crazy. Mirrors can't talk. Reflections in mirrors couldn't shout at you from across an apartment. It was impossible, as impossible as Malinowski coming back to haunt her.

She awoke again this morning with a start. She'd been running and running through a dark tunnel, the sides closing in around her. Then the front and back closed on her, and she was left in total darkness. She clawed her way along the sides of the tunnel, only to slide back, and each time she slid back, she felt

Malinowski's grip on her ankle. Then she'd begin to choke, her air cut off, and the coughing spasm would wake her.

She found herself alone in the room, light filtering in. Donald had already gone, leaving a note beside the bed which told her he'd call her later. She'd planned to remain home, away from work another day or two. She looked again at the card with the psychiatrist's name printed on it, Dr. Marilee Taylor.

"What're you waiting for?" she asked herself.

For two days Jackie Grant had either telephoned or visited, and each time Jackie told her that Dr. Taylor was her best hope.

She took a deep breath, lifted the phone, and dialed the number. The sound of the phone in her ear reminded her of the labored breathing inside the bag. Lately, all sounds reminded her of something to do with breath and breathing and people's death rattles. Of dying breath. It threatened to make a madwoman of her. Jackie was right. She needed professional, long-term help. She couldn't make it on her own.

She got Dr. Taylor's answering service and left a harried message for her, leaving her number. She got up and showered, finding that even the refreshing, cleansing water made a breathing sound. The steam filling the room reminded her of the frosty air of the refrigerated van. Looking into the mirror through the steam, was like seeing herself inside that bag.

She heard the phone ringing and ran naked for it, desperate to talk to someone, anyone.

"Hello, Dr. Taylor?"

"No, it's ahhh, me."

314

"Who is this?" she didn't recognize the voice.

"Remmer, down at the lab."

"Oh, Jim. What is it?"

"Just thought I'd say so long."

"So long?"

"Hangin' it up. This corpse trade, it's just not for me. After that last thing they brought in, I just don't have the stomach for it."

"Sorry to hear it, Jim."

"Are you?" His tone was accusatory.

She took a deep breath, "Hey, Jim, if I was hard on you, it was for the lab and the best possible—"

"Save it, Dr. Shanley, for the next schmoe. Besides, I know it's the truth. I'm just a square peg in a round hole here. Just wanted to say good-bye, properlike. And to tell you, congratulations."

"Congratulations?" It seemed an awkward word for the circumstances, even from awkward Jim Remmer.

"Never thought I'd see that bastard on the cutting table."

"What? Who?"

"Autopsy's this morning."

"Autopsy?"

"On the creep?"

"Creep?"

"The suffocator guy."

"What?"

"You didn't know?"

She hung up the phone, her mind racing: *autopsy?* On Malinowski? Why? What purpose would it serve? What did Dean hope to get from an autopsy? And

315

why'd she have to hear about it this way?

She got dressed immediately, feeling glad to have somewhere to go, a mission to complete.

Dr. Sybil Shanley burst into the autopsy theater, demanding to know what the hell was going on. On the table was the body of a man she had never known, but a man who had attempted to destroy her—Louis Malinowski.

Behind surgical masks, Dean Grant and Donald Carr stared back at her, unable to at first reply. Dean took down his mask and said, "To be certain."

"Certain? Certain that he's dead, or certain that he was ever human? Goddamnit, certain of *what?* That his brain is made of the same thing yours and mine's made of? Or is it you want to bury his parts in separate graves?"

Kelso stood nearby, obviously part of this little conspiracy, and he spoke up. "I insisted—"

"No," said Dean, "we both wanted this."

She shook with disbelief. "Why're doing this, Dean? We know what killed the man. What's the point?"

"The fall might've killed him."

"So, so what's the difference? Either way, he died."

"We wanted to know," began Carr slowly, "if he suffocated."

She gulped and nodded, understanding now, hearing it in the timbre of Carr's voice. Carr hadn't had a decent night's sleep since the incident, and like herself woke up in cold sweats, fighting for breath, nightmaring over the horrifying experience they had both endured. The night bouts with the fear may be the only thing that had kept them together. She wondered about this, wondered about it often. Nothing seemed able to allay the recurrent horror.

"So, you think by knowing for certain that Malinowski died from lack of air beneath a ton or more of grain, then maybe you can sleep better at night, huh, Don? And what about you, Kelso, is it revenge that motivates you, too? Knowing the man slowly drowned in a sea of grain? Will it make you any more of a man to know he got his just desserts? That an eye for an eye had been served him?"

Neither Carr nor Kelso answered, but their silence was enough.

She turned on Dean. "You might've told me your plans, Dean."

"We thought it best," he began, but she cut him off.

"Still trying to protect me, after all this time, huh, Dean? Well, open your eyes, all of you, because there's no protecting me any further, and as for your reasons for autopsying Malinowski, I find them professionally reprehensible and morally wrong."

"You didn't see your name on his death certificate," said Carr, gritting his teeth.

"What?"

Kelso was shaking his head. Dean was staring at the floor.

"What's he talking about, Dean? Ken? Answer me."

Dean moved away from the corpse and took her aside in his fatherly fashion. "You didn't ask me my reasons, Sybil, why?"

317

"I assumed yours might be better. Are they?"

"No, not really. I want to know beyond any doubt that this man who inflicted so much prolonged suffering on others, died an agonizing death. Call that unprofessional if you like, call it immoral and unethical," he said, dropping his gaze, "but it's also the truth."

"Do you really think for a moment it will provide any of you with the remotest satisfaction?"

"Perhaps men need revenge more than women," said Carr.

"That's bull, Don, and you know it."

"All right, Sybil," said Dean. "Go with Ken here to his office. He has some records Mr. Malinowski kept—"

"Records?"

"On his victims, and the method with which he dispatched them. You want to undertand my rationale? You cannot, until you see *his* rationale." Dean pointed with his scalpel at the dead man. "Now, if you'll excuse us, Dr. Shanley, we have work here to do."

She stormed out. Kelso placed a hand on Dean's forearm, staying the next cut. "You sure about this, Dean?"

"Yes, she has a right to the truth, to full disclosure. perhaps then she'll understand our combined need for today's . . . autopsy."

Kelso frowned, unsure.

"Look, we've tried mollycoddling her, right, Carr?"

Carr frowned now, but nodded.

"And we've tried to get her to start seeing Marilee

Taylor. And Jackie's been after her. Maybe this is just the jolt she needs."

Kelso heard Dean continuing on with the autopsy as he left. He located Sybil in the hallway and took her down to his car and to his office.

An hour later, after seeing Malinowski's insanity as it translated to paper, in the dead man's shaky handwriting, her mood changed. She became quiet, and to Kelso's way of thinking, too calm. Then one of Kelso's sergeants stuck his head in the door and said that a Dr. Taylor was outside, wishing to see Dr. Shanley.

Sybil looked up to see Marilee Taylor standing in the doorway. "Let's talk, Dr. Shanley," she said quite simply. "I got your message, and I learned about your ordeal from Jackie Grant."

"How did you track me down?" Sybil asked.

"I telephoned your place but you were out. I tried Grant. He told me you were here. I cancelled my morning's appointments. I hope you won't disappoint me."

"No, I won't. I need your help. Just look at me, I'm a wreck, can't sleep or eat."

"You look just fine, but we'll talk. Inspector Kelso, is there somewhere we can be alone?"

"Sure, use my conference room. This way," he said and just before he closed the door on doctor and patient, Sybil said, "Ken," stopping him.

"Yes, Sybil?"

"Tell Dean and Donald I . . . that I understand now . . . about the autopsy."

Kelso nodded, "A very normal reaction, Dr. Shanley."

"He's right, you know," said Dr. Taylor, placing a hand over Sybil's.

Kelso closed the door on them, feeling that Sybil Shanley was going to be all right, and that Dean, once again, had done the right thing.

Later in the day, Kelso got the word: Malinowski had died from ingesting and inhaling grain, so much inside his lungs, larynx, throat, and nostrils as to prove he was quite alive when the suffocating began.

Had Louis Malinowski been killed by the fall, he'd have been wholly unable to have inhaled so much of the grain.

"It doesn't bring any of the victims back," said Dean, summing up. "It doesn't change the hideousness of the crimes committed by the man. But I admit to an old Puritanical need that's been satisfied."

"Revenge?" Kelso asked.

"Let the punishment fit the crime."